Comfort Me With Apples

By Peter De Vries

NO BUT I SAW THE MOVIE

THE TUNNEL OF LOVE

COMFORT ME WITH APPLES

Comfort Me With Apples

by PETER DE VRIES

Little, Brown and Company
Boston · Toronto

Fifth Printing

Parts of a few chapters of this book appeared
in a somewhat different form in THE NEW YORKER

Published simultaneously in Canada
by Little, Brown & Company (Canada) Limited

PRINTED IN THE UNITED STATES OF AMERICA

For Katinka

Stay me with flagons,
comfort me with apples:
for I am sick of love.

THE SONG OF SONGS

Comfort Me With Apples

One

IF AN ORACLE told you you would be a shirtsleeve philosopher by the time you were thirty, that you would be caught in bed with a woman named Mrs. Thicknesse, have your letters used for blackmail and your wife threaten to bring suit for sixty-five dollars because that was all you were worth, you would tell him he was out of his mind. Yet that is what happened to me, and not because I was out of mine. We know the human brain is a device to keep the ears from grating on one another, and mine played that role well in the rational and moral pinches I will try to recreate. What we do in the pinches depends on other equipment and on all that has gone before to make us what we are. The past is prologue. Right, and Man is not a donkey lured along by a carrot dangled in front of his nose, but a jet plane propelled by his exhaust. So perhaps a brief glance at my background is in order.

My sharpest early memory is of a summer-night storm during which we were sought out by lightning. Our family of four (I have a younger sister) were all in the parlor at the time, and saw something nibble the golden fringe of a scatter rug, run over my mother's shoe buckle, lap at wall plugs (not looking for an outlet, just foraging for metal), rummage in an open sewing kit, and browse along a shelf of books, leaving the gilt in some of the titles illegible. I remember thinking that in its career across the living room it seemed to resemble some whimsical and very wicked marmalade. I'm not defending this comparison, merely reporting a childhood association itself lightning-swift. Anyway, it bounced off a pair of pinking shears on a table and shot out through the front door into the yard where it ended its call by splitting up a cord of wet kindling.

That was only preliminary to a hurricane, Clara, which howled out of the Atlantic and cut a wide swath which included our city of Decency, Connecticut. Several ships sank, millions of dollars' worth of property lay strewn along the Eastern Seaboard, and the salt had to be humored. The wind and rain got almost everything along our municipal beach except a bronze statue of a Minute Man, which had however been battered into neurasthenia by a thousand predecessor storms and now wore a look of Byronic fatigue. "Now we know," my father said unclearly. Suggesting that the current may have passed through other matter than I have enumerated.

Those meteorological twenty-four hours have always been to me symbolically like the Mrs. Thicknesse business which struck in later life, and not because *her* name was Clara, too. Near-calamity is never completely digested; that is, we keep thrilling ourselves with thoughts of what *might* have happened. The fascination of the narrow escape. Now I can never hear of an amorist being shot in the tabloids, or anywhere for that matter, without evoking, with a delicious shiver, that charged name by which my own and my children's was so nearly riven. Just as I can never, at breakfast, put a knife to marmalade without spreading coagulated lightning on my toast. All connections are fused.

But to get back to my background.

I think I can say my childhood was as unhappy as the

4

next braggart's. I was read to sleep with the classics and spanked with obscure quarterlies. My father was anxious to have me follow in his footsteps — if that is a good metaphor for a man whose own imprints were largely sedentary — and he watched me closely for echoes of himself that were more felicitous than most. He advised people to have intellect, and to look beneath what he called "the epithelium of things," though he did discourage scrutiny of his own motives.

Living on a little money my grandmother had left him, he spent his time exercising a talent which was more or less in his own mind. He wrote essays of a philosophical nature which he sent to those periodicals off which he tried to rub some of the bloom on me. They were all returned. This gave him a feeling of rejection (rather than one of submission) and he developed internal troubles. He went to a hospital for observation but they found nothing worse than what they called a sensitive colon, which is I suppose an apt enough ailment for a man as meticulous about punctuation as he was.

The hospital library was nothing to brighten his stay, and he rather truculently offered to "send over something decent" as soon as he could, a promise he set about fulfilling the minute he got home.

He drove back to the hospital two days after he was discharged, with a few cartons of selections from his own shelves. I rode along and helped carry them in, through the emergency ward, from which the basement room where the ladies' auxiliary handled books was most conveniently accessible. It was an icy day in late winter, and I picked my way carefully behind my father with a small boxful — he toting a rather large packet on his shoulder, like a grocery boy with an order. The walk we traversed sloped upward across a short courtyard, and at a turn in it my father's foot shot out from under him and, loudly exclaiming "Damnation!", he went down, spilling culture in every direction and breaking a leg.

The bone was set free by the hospital, which also gave him a room without cost ("No it is not handsome of them to do this — it would be outrageous if they did not!"), and soon he was propped up in the same bed again dipping into his old copy of Plutarch, available to him from a trundled cart of books now noticeably enriched as to contents.

What displeased him constitute a history of our time. He could not abide typewritten correspondence or most people's handwriting. He hated radio and couldn't wait for television to be perfected so he could hate that too. The very word "psychosomatic" was enough to send him into symptoms for which no organic cause could be found; the decline of human teeth he laid to the door of toothpaste, "surely chief among the sweets properly arraigned as villains," as he asserted through dentures which clacked corroboratively. He hated everything brewed in the vats of modernity. He hated music without melody, paintings without pictures, and novels without plots. In other words, a rich, well-rounded life.

The house on the outskirts of Decency we lived in was built around a silo, which became my father's library. Swiss cheese, except for the silo, comprised the principal masonry, as the dank airs which continually stirred the draperies attested; the wiring was, to put it no lower, shocking; the fireplace drew briskly but in the wrong direction, sending out ashes which settled like a light snow on our family and on the strangers within our gates, for in those years my parents loved to entertain. They had lived originally in a dinette apartment in town but had begun to drift apart and needed

6

more room. The capacious new house did in fact ease their relations, getting them out of one another's pockets I suppose, and I can still hear my mother wailing over some new kitchen crisis, "Oh, God," and my father answering cozily from the silo, "Were you calling me, dear?"

He believed that the art of conversation was dead. His own small talk, at any rate, was bigger than most people's large. "I believe it was Hegel who defined love as the ideality of the relativity of the reality of an infinitesimal portion of the absolute totality of the Infinite Being" he would chat at dinner.

It was my father's example which, more than any other single factor in my life, inspired in me my own conversational preference: the light aphorism.

I belonged in adolescence to a clique of pimpled *boulevardiers* who met at a place called the Samothrace, a restaurant and ice-cream parlor run by a Greek who let us pull tables out on the sidewalk and talk funny. The Greek's name was Andropoulos but he had Americanized it to Nachtgeborn, which blended in better with the heavy German population that dominated that end of town, and which he therefore thought better for business reasons. He was a prickly sort who was always complaining that this country was commercial, especially when trade was slack and he was more irritable than usual. We expatriates, be that as it may, could be seen there every evening loitering over coffee and pastry, or maybe toying with a little of what the Greek called fruit compost. I often wore my topcoat with the sleeves hanging loose, so that the effect was like an Inverness cape, when it was not like that of two broken arms. An earnest youth on the high-school debating squad, who got in with our set by mistake one *soir*, tried to interest me in politics by

7

speaking of the alarming layoffs then occurring in the Department of Agriculture.

"I had thought," I said, smiling round at my disciples as I tapped a Melachrino on the lid of its box, "that the Department of Agriculture slaughtered its surplus employees."

This attitude grew into a *fin-de-siècle* one of cultivated fatigue and bored estheticism, marked by amusement with the colloquial mainstream. I would lie full-length around the house and with a limp hand wave life away. My mother took this as an indication that I had "no pep," and urged a good tonic to fix me up.

"No, no, no!" my Father said. "This is what they call Decadence. It's an attitude toward life." He turned and looked down at the horizontal product of their union, disposed on the sofa with a cigarette. "He'll come to his senses."

"Instead of coming to one's senses," I airily returned, "how much more delightful to let one's senses come to one."

My mother, a thin, sentimental woman who often broke up funerals with her weeping, tried to get me interested in "healthy" books like the jumbo three-generation novels she herself couldn't put down.

"The books Mother cannot put down," I said, "are the ones I cannot pick up."

"He *is* run-down. Now I don't care."

Seventeen. Slightly above medium height, slender, with clothes either too casual or too studied — it makes no difference now. I had a pinched-in, pendulous underlip, like the pouring lip on a pitcher, which must have conferred an air of jocularity somewhat at odds with my intention to be "dry." Anyhow, to sit and say "Thomas Wolfe is a genius without talent" was a lot less trouble than was gone to by

8

my contemporaries, who got their effects by riding around in old Fords on the sides of which were painted SEVEN DAYS IN THIS MAKE ONE WEAK.

My best friend was a schoolmate named Nickie Sherman, and he needed a good tonic too. Between the two of us we wrote a junior college class play that realized far more fully than anything Oscar Wilde ever did the Wilde ideal for a perfect act as one in which there was no action whatever. Ours was laid in the drawing room of an English country house known as Wise Acres, where fabulous wits foregathered and paradox was so far the order of the day that the cook complained the upside-down cakes came out right-side-up. Often seen at Wise Acres, which gave the play its name, was a celebrated detective named Inspector Vermouth. Our one concession to occurrence was in the form of a murder which, however, Vermouth forewent solving because he admired the malefaction so.

A man at the piano entertaining the week-end guests was shot by a pistol secreted within the instrument and wired to go off when a certain chord was struck, a combination of notes so avant-garde as to be likely to appear only in the music of Villa-Lobos, which the murderer knew only that guest was likely to perform. Inspector Vermouth declined to seek out the perpetrator on the ground that he might find him. "And it would be a shame to send him to the gallows," he said. "It was a capital crime."

That our pursuit of nuance was causing even greater strain under Nickie's roof than under my own was brought home to me when his father phoned me, one morning when Nickie was in New York, and asked me to come over — he wanted to talk to me. Mr. Sherman owned a tailor shop a mile from our place where he pressed people's pants while they waited. It being a slow morning with no customers, he

9

was pressing his own pants, while he waited. He stood at the steam iron in his shirttails and shook his head as he told me how Nickie had been worrying him lately.

"Ecks all the time tired and listless — *and* talks odd," he added through a cloud of steam as he bore down on the press. With his foot on the pedal he regarded me over a pair of half-specs, like those worn by the man on the Old Grand Dad whisky label.

"How, odd?" I asked, drawing up a chair. "Can you give me some examples?"

Mr. Sherman turned a pants-leg over and ruminated. "Oh, he's loving life far too much to take part in it, there's too much nature obscurink the billboards . . . I don't know. He's always been a bright boy, but now that he's educated, half of what he says sounds fibble-minded."

I explained perversity and paradox to him — without recourse to *Wise Acres*, which Mr. Sherman hadn't seen. Fortunately the illness of his wife, a woman of Spanish-Irish extraction, had kept them both home the night of the production.

"Paradoxes are where everything sounds the opposite of what it should," I discoursed. "You're not supposed to take them too seriously. That business about loving life far too well to participate in it — Nickie means that he wants to be an observer of the passing scene so he can enjoy it more. They call that esthetic. Nickie's precious."

"He's dollink. Always was dollink boy. But what's going to hepp'm should he stay in the anesthetic? I want he should snap out of it."

"He will, Mr. Sherman."

"I hope so." Drawing on his now crisp trousers, Mr. Sherman ran a critical eye over mine. "Take off your pants and

I'll press them so it shouldn't be a total loss you came down here."

I demurred but he insisted. And while he gave my trousers the hot sandwich, I strolled about in shirttails elucidating further what I could of the attitude he had encountered in his son. "It's what they call *fin-de-siècle*. That means the end of the century," I said.

"Dot's how menkind will talk in de future?" he asked, peering at me over the half-glasses.

"No, no, the end of the *last* century, not this one. But it *is* modern in the sense of the *way* he says things. That's known as 'understatement.'"

"He shouldn't lay it on so thick."

As Mr. Sherman overturned my trousers on the iron he seemed also, in his mind, to be revolving the phenomenon just touched on, as the symptom of a larger and more far-reaching decay in human sensibility.

"Poems got no rhyme, books got no stories," he mused in a sudden uncanny echo of my own father's pet peeves, "and now jokes got no point. I was riddink in a magazine about the latest, those hairy-dog stories. Dot's high-class? *Phooey!*" He gestured at my trousers on the iron. " 'When they saw how tight his pants were they thought they'd split.' That's by me humor. I think jokes and stories used to be funnier in my time," he finished with a considered terseness.

"Can you remember some others?" I asked, sitting down again.

Mr. Sherman accepted the challenge. He lit himself a cigar and then immediately set it down in an ashtray nearby.

"There was this fellow from the old country. Immigrant," he began. "He did his best to learn the customs here. But

11

he says to his friend one day, says, 'I don't know. One minute they tell you do one thing and the next something else.' Friend says, 'How do you mean?' Fellow says, 'Well, the other day I'm sitting in church and they all sing, 'Stand up, stand up for Jesus.' The next day I go to the ball park and behind me everybody is yellink as loud as they can, 'For Christ's sake, sit down!' "

I ran all the way home as from a revelation still bursting volcanically behind me, and for days was shaken by the glimpse of a humor more visceral than any I had dreamed had existed since the cave-man days. At the same time my father cracked down on the offbeat as represented in my nuances, on the ground that they were disrespectful to my mother who could never possibly hope to understand them. I was finally punished for epigrams and paradoxes by being sent to my room. Here is the way that worked.

One evening at dinner, my younger sister Lila and my mother were teasing me about a girl named Crystal Chickering whom I had been dating. My mother remarked she'd have guessed I'd have preferred Jessie Smithers because "Jessie laughs at absolutely everything a person says."

"That is because she has no sense of humor," I said, buttering a roll.

My father stiffened in his chair. "I'll ask you to apologize to your mother for that."

I think that behind this, more than a chivalrous regard for her capacities, was a sense of compunction he himself felt over having neglected her all these years, leaving her to what he eruditely called her "needlepwah" while he sat with his nose in Goethe or went off on vacations by himself.

"If I'd made a fool of the mother who bore me, my father would have given me short shrift. Explain to your mother what that last so-called paradox means. I think I'll insist on that."

The fact was that he didn't understand it himself, and so, while pretending to be indifferently worrying a fishbone out of his mouth, he listened alertly to the exegesis I was glad to give.

"I simply meant that a sense of humor implies discrimination, selection," I said. "So laughing at everything, as Jessie Smithers does, isn't the same as having a sense of humor."

"That clear it up for you, dear?" On receiving an affirmative nod, my father returned to his food.

But my mother went on:

"You mustn't think I *mind* not understanding what the boy says, Roebuck. Goodness gracious, let him talk over my head the same as I talked over my mother's. That's progress."

Feeling perfidy in the form of aphorisms to be uncoiling everywhere about him, my father came to dinner in a Norfolk jacket. We had a dog, Pavlov, who lived for our table scraps: I mean those mealtime squabbles to which he listened with soft thuds of his tail and a look of seeming comprehension. One evening as we sipped our coffee in the living room, I crossed my legs and remarked in regard to poise: "There are only three women in Decency who know how to enter a restaurant."

My father made a truncheon of his *Yale Review*. "Is your mother one?"

"I don't know, Popper, I've never seen her enter a restaurant. I'm always the one who's with her when she does."

"That does it — upstairs. For myself I don't care — paradox away. But I will not have you insulting your mother with language fit for nothing but a Mayfair drawing room.

Upstairs!" he repeated with a flourish of his billy. That allusion to his neglect of my mother had gone home! I rose and, kissing her good night, went up to my room, glad to get away from the hurly-burly.

That Sunday evening at supper my mother remarked on the very trait in me that was unstringing my father, though touching on it obliquely in a reference to Nickie Sherman, whom we'd had to dinner the day before.

"He should learn that when you get *too* smart and clever, it isn't much better than being what you boys call corny," she said.

I nodded. "Excessive subtlety does negate itself. It is like being winked at with both eyes."

"You'll apologize to your mother for that last remark," my father said, his face red from bad claret and a lifetime of plain damn exasperation.

"But I'm agreeing with her!" I protested.

"Yes, but she doesn't know that. That poor woman doesn't understand a word you're saying. Agreeing with her is no excuse for talking over her head, sending her own words back over her head. I've warned you about this matter for the last time. Grieving her mother heart with words so elliptical — "

"What does elliptical mean?" my mother asked him.

" — so in excess of what she can comprehend — "

"Now who's running her down?"

"Upstairs!"

"But I've got a date," I objected.

"You should have thought of that sooner."

Rather than waste precious time arguing, I went up and started serving my "sentence" without delay. It was usually about an hour for epigrams; somewhat longer for a paradox. It wasn't till nine o'clock that I was let out tonight, after apologizing for the obscurity of my rejoinder, and promising never to do it again. By that time, of course, I was dressed. I was now half an hour late for my date with Crystal Chickering, toward whose house I legged it, as a consequence, with commendable pep.

TWO

CRYSTAL CHICKERING was a girl of my own age who lived on the other side of town. She was one of the milk-white daughters of the moon, but her father — and now we come to the last of the elements ranged against me — was a cracker-barrel philosopher. He dispensed homespun wisdom to readers of the *Picayune Blade,* our local evening paper, who wrote in asking for help on their everyday problems. He ran their letters together with his advice, usually packaged in maxims, of which he had volumes all (in notebooks of his own) cross-indexed under types of trouble. "I like to hit the nail on the head with a saw," Chickering, who signed his column "The Lamplighter," was fond of stating. He finished each column with an inspirational thought for the day which he called a Pepigram. That he was my favorite character went without saying, and I took care not to say it either to him or to his daughter. One had a lot of work to do on her yet before she would understand *why* her father was one's favorite character. A lot of work. He was like those Currier and Ives prints which, having outgrown them, one then laps the field of Sensibility to approach again from behind and see as "wonderful." She was often, not to make any bones about it, pretty wonderful herself. It was borne in on me, one evening when I was

16

dropping allusions to Baudelaire, that she was under the impression it was the name of a refrigerator.

But I had jammed *The Flowers of Evil* through her by reading the bulk of it aloud, and tonight I brought over a new album of *Boris Godunov*.

Setting the records on the family phonograph, for we had the parlor to ourselves, I said, "Do you like *Boris Godunov?*"

"Oh, yes," she answered from the sofa where she was settling herself. "Which composition of his is it?"

I heard the great ships baying at the harbor's mouth, and chuckled, already aboard — clean out of this, escaped. I had that exhilarating sense of being a misfit that I could taste almost anywhere in Decency and that was, in a sense, my birthright.

Crystal closed her eyes and listened to the music. I stood over her, taking in the soft thighs and breasts, which together with the snowy arms and floral purity of the throat more than offset the normally discouraging upstate returns. She was wearing a shawl with a lunatic fringe, which I discreetly drew off her shoulders and spread across the grand piano where it belonged.

The music over, she expressed her pleasure in it. Then after a pause she said: "What is the purpose of marriage?"

"What?"

"That was our subject for discussion in Girls' Club this afternoon."

Crystal had, together with other girls at Biddle Junior College, been given a course in the social graces by a woman named Miss Bourdillon who told them that men liked women who could keep the conversational ball rolling. She was also faculty sponsor of the discussion club. The girls emerged from her tutelage using expressions like "not excluding" and "in which event," which may have explained Miss Bourdillon's own single status. The conversational ball here, at any rate, rolled briskly forward.

"What did you decide about marriage?" I asked.

"Its main purpose is the procreation and rearing of children. Everybody wants those. It would be terrible to go through life without them, don't you agree?"

"Yes. There is only one thing worse than not having children, and that is having them."

"Would you venture to say there are people who don't know what they think about something until they've heard what they had to say?"

"I'd venture to say you can make anything dismal by finding reasons for it."

"Just what does that mean?"

"Nothing. I don't want to get married. *I just — don't — want to get married.*"

"We're having our first quarrel," she said thoughtfully, as though noting a milestone in our progress.

To kiss into silence the lips from which such bromides fell, and turn them to the laughter and sighs for which they were intended, seemed precisely that formula for tinkling pleasures, for caught felicities, for which we are so sumptuously cued by nature. Especially charming, I thought, was Crystal's habit of getting clichés just wrong. The first inkling I'd had of this amusing grace note in her was when she'd said, "I was mad as a March hare at you for not phoning." Another time I'd been cool as a cucumber toward some proposal or other of hers. Sauces were rich as Crœsus. And so on. When I fell down the cellar stairs and broke my arm, and damn near my neck, she said, "It couldn't happen to a better guy." I folded her in my arms, arm rather, and was the soul of forbearance while she told me that I had the most magnetic personality of any fellow she'd ever met.

One evening in midsummer I was early for a date we were to spend with nobody home at all, even upstairs. Her folks were at a testimonial dinner for the editor of the *Pick*, as her father the Lamplighter called the *Picayune Blade*. There was no answer when I rang the doorbell as George Jean Nathan, and, following the strains of the Love Duet from *Tristan* which seemed to be coming from somewhere in back, I walked through the empty house and found Crystal in the yard, with a portable phonograph spinning away on an inverted apple-crate. She herself was stretched out on a hammock with her eyes closed and one hand out-flung above her head. I had a feeling she had seen me coming, quickly set the record going and hurried back to the hammock in time for me to see her lying on it in a trance of appreciation.

She was wearing yellow shorts and a red halter, the evening being warm. Her hair was gathered into a ponytail knotted with a red silk ribbon. On the grass beneath her was an empty Coke bottle with a bent straw in it. She appeared at length to become aware of me standing there and she rolled her head toward me, her eyes fluttering open. "Oh, hello, Chick."

I snapped a burning cigarette into the grass and walked up to her. She extended a white hand which I took in both mine and ate like cake. She rolled her head away again with a sigh.

"This music. Lawrence Melchior."

On persuasions from myself, she rolled out of the ham-mock and onto a blanket lying on the ground nearby. She pulled the grass and, as one who knew good music, my hair. "This night." It was darkening, the air wreathed with musks of summer, as if crushed from the grape of Dusk. A moon hung like a gong above the regiment of birches behind the house. We turned on one another deep, drowned gazes, and exchanged a kiss that reduced my bones to rubber and my brain to gruel. It all happened more quickly than it takes to tell. Now I have only a few minutes of freedom . . . I thought in my throes . . . now a few seconds, now none.

I lay back like a clinker thinking, Oh, my God. Crystal moaned, "What have we done?"

I spent the next days scorching myself with the question, *What if . . . ?* The sight of perambulators sent galvanic shocks through me. I would wheel one through an eternity of ridicule because I had succumbed to a single folly and that to the music of a composer whose work I had termed mucilaginous. Oh, my God. The great ships bayed at the harbor's mouth — nevermore for me. For me nevermore those storied seas, those ports whose names toll in the heart like bells. I heard instead voices, local in origin and of an almost hallucinatory force: "Shotgun wedding, you know." "You mean *Chick Swallow?* The one who was always . . . ?" "Yes, the old *flaneur* himself." (*Flaneur:* One who strolls aimlessly; hence, an intellectual trifler.) Think of a *boulevardier* pushing a baby carriage!

I hid in my room with the door locked most of the time. Once I stood at my dresser mirror and looked at myself. My face was tortured on one side, like a good actor's. I contorted it into deliberately gruesome expressions of woe so as to give everything an exaggerated and theatrical cast, and, by this means, make what I was worrying about seem to have no basis in fact. My plowed hair, rolling eyes and dying-fish mouth did create an atmosphere of relative absurdity, and I

20

smiled: of course all this would blow over. Six months from now I would be laughing at it. I had just about convinced myself of that when the idea of tallied months struck me with fresh horror and I was back where I started.

There were the voices again. I tried at first to drown them out with a phonograph I had in my own room, but there were no compositions which could not, by deplorable associations, return me to my *crise*. And the voices continued: "You mean that guy who was always knocking conventions?" The same. "He seemed to be that type that they call the carriage trade. Well, I guess *now* . . ." No! Never! I would go to Lethe first, I would twist wolfsbane. Oh, I would pay the last farthing, but I would go hence. I would slip into the hospitable earth, and among her dumb roots and unscandalizing boulders make my bed.

All this distraction threw into illumination again what I had felt that other evening earlier in the year: that Crystal Chickering was not for me. *I must under no condition marry this girl.*

I was walking down the street one afternoon during the cooling-off period when I saw a sight that gave the winch of agony an extra turn. Nickie Sherman was approaching. He had our *Zeitgeist* well at heel, for, one hand in his trouser-pocket and the other swinging a blackthorn stick he was affecting those days, he drifted up and said in his most somnambulistic manner, "Hi."

Stark, staring mad, I answered, "Hi."

"What cooketh?"

Suddenly, instead of regretting the encounter, I saw a way of turning it to advantage. I would remove the sting from having to get married (if such was the pass things would come to) by taking the line that that was what I wanted. This would need a little groundwork, and to lay it I sug-

21

gested we drop in at the Greek's, which was a block from there, for some coffee. We did. The tables at which it was our wont to dally in the cool of the evening were in their accustomed places outside, but this was the heat of the day and we went in. Several women gabbled at a table about a movie they had been to. "Matinee idle," I murmured to Nickie as we drew our chairs to sit down at ours.

We ordered coffee. Then Nickie, who had laid the black-thorn across an empty chair, asked again, "Was ist los?"

"I've been having an affair," I said, glancing matter-of-factly around.

"And?"

I shrugged. "It gets to be rather a nuisance. We pay for security with boredom, for adventure with bother. It's six of one and a half dozen of the other, really." I shifted some condiments about on the tabletop. "Shaw makes matrimony sound rather attractive with that Puritanical description he has of it somewhere. I'm sure you remember it."

Nickie watched the Greek shamble up with our coffee. When Nachtgeborn had set the cups down and waddled off on his duck feet, Nickie said, "Shaw is great up to a point, and then one thinks, 'Oh, Pshaw!' "

"I believe it's he who describes marriage as combining a maximum of temptation with a maximum of opportunity. He's quite right — it is a sensual institution. I've half a notion to get married myself," I added vagrantly, stirring my coffee.

Nickie's problem was to get back in the conversation. I could sense him mulling my gambit as he sipped, keeping his lean, handsome face averted. At last he appeared to have something worked out, and I knew that what he said next would determine whether I would have to blow my brains out or not.

"Yes. The logistics of adultery are awful. Matrimony is a garrison, but one that has its appeal to a man out bivouacking every night," said that probable virgin.

Freeze it there, I told myself. I knew that if a neat way of putting a rebuttal had occurred to him first, instead of a concurrence, he would have taken that; but it hadn't and I was to that extent in luck. My object was to get Nickie into a good frame of mind for my armed nuptials, if any — a viewpoint from which he could see me, not as ridiculous and bourgeois going down the aisle, but heathen to the end. I had to come out of this making sense as a *boulevardier* who had said "I do." So I let him pick up the marbles.

"That's neat, Nickie. By God that's neat. Put it in the play. By the way, how did you make out in New York?" I asked him. Nickie had decided to become a playwright and had spent the summer revising *Wise Acres* (and running into New York to see producers).

Instead of showing pleasure he looked at me peevishly and sucked at his coffee. "You've been to see my old man again. That's how you know I've been in New York."

"No, I haven't, Nickie," I lied, for I had been back to see his father in response to another S O S (Save Our Son). "You told me you planned to go — remember?"

"I can tell by your pants you've been there. He's got this crotchet of pressing pleats out, because he hates them so. It's his trade-mark. Yours are pressed out."

"Sweet jumping Sherlock Holmes," I said. "Why don't you get a job as a detective? You don't miss much, do you?"

"So what did he want this time?"

"He's worried about what's going to become of you. I told him not to — you'd come out all right. This running off to New York all the time shows initiative. So what's happened so far on the drama?"

23

Nickie crossed his legs and turned away from me, a sure sign that something intimate was coming.

"I gave *Wise Acres* to an agent. His name is Al Roquefort, and he's very acute. He's already sent it back for revisions. Evidently you do have to compromise with popular tastes — put in movement, plot and that sort of thing. It needs a lot of work. Are you game for it?"

"That depends. I'm going to Dartmouth next year after all." I could have kicked myself, for I had to add mentally, through mentally clenched teeth, "If I don't have to get married."

Nickie nodded. "Well, we'll see what we'll see. Meanwhile if you don't want to fuss with it any more I'm sure it's O.K. with you if I go ahead on my own? Roquefort tells me royalties are amicably worked out between collaborators on the basis of how much each has done."

So I was able to purchase further tolerance from Nickie by permitting the shrinkage of my already dwindled equity in the play. I didn't care if I ever saw the script again but I didn't let him know that. Instead I answered handsomely, "You go right ahead, Nickie. And as you say, we'll see what we'll see. I've got to toddle."

As to my sex life, I was to see what I was to see that evening, the interval of suspense being then, calculably, over. I had a date with Crystal at seven-thirty. As I left the Greek's, a clock in a nearby church steeple struck four. In three and a half hours I would know what I was leaving purgatory for — heaven or hell.

Crystal was upstairs dressing when I arrived, so I sat down alone in the living room to wait. I twiddled my thumbs at a rate not normally associated with that act. Nobody came. I rose and walked to the window, from where I could look into the back yard. The hammock was occupied by a saucepan half full of string beans; another Coke bottle lay on its side on the grass. A woodpecker drilled into my head from a maple outside, pausing every now and then to spit wood over his shoulder. A door opened behind me and Crystal's father, the shirtsleeve philosopher, entered from his study. He was in shirtsleeves.

"I'd like to talk to you," he said after a greeting, and made for a chair.

"Yes, sir."

Chickering was a red-haired man of medium height, with horn-rimmed glasses and a forelock derived from Sandburg. He took a Cogswell chair facing the one into which I sank, frowned, and revolved in his fingers a cockleshell ash tray on a table beside him. It was, like the resort pillows and wall thermometers in the shape of keys to cities which also garnished the living room, a souvenir of some past family holiday; together they left me ill with premonition.

"What do you want to talk to me about, Mr. Chickering?" I asked.

"I think you know."

I met this with a gulp and the word "What?" brought out in a dry treble. I heard the ceiling creak under a footstep overhead. That foolish girl had confessed her condition to her parents! Even now she and her mother were together up there, hysterically promenading.

"I think we can fairly say now that you're a young man with a problem," Chickering said. "And there are some folks who think that's my field."

"There are? I mean I am? What's my problem?"

It was from her mother Crystal had got the liquid brown eyes (now obscured by tears?) — Chickering's were green. He had been sun-bathing recently, except that his was the

25

type of skin that never browns but only turns the pink of mouthwashes. I tried to nurse a part-skunk indifference to the whole family, a kind of moral coma which gave me for just a moment the clearest insight into that stupor into which the insane protectively slip.

"Why, that you're about to enter college without a clear idea what you want to be when you come out of it: butcher, baker or candlestick maker," he said in the American grain. "Now wait a minute. I know education is for the mind. But at the same time, you want some general idea where you're headed. I just want to leave this thought with you, for what it may be worth."

Chickering's reputation for sagacity was based largely on a way of looking at you over the tops of his glasses. He fixed me over their rims now as he said: *"Whatever your lot in life is, build something on it."*

There are times when Fate seems to be heaping mockery on us with a trowel. Just then the Chickerings' two collies, Amos 'n' Andy, trotted in, like supers in the travesty gathering fast about me. As they circled and sniffed me to see whether I was a candidate for Sunday dumplings and hymns around the old piano, there was a footfall on the hallway stair and Chickering said, "We'll talk about it later. Here's Crystal. Isn't she blooming tonight?"

"More than ever," I answered tonelessly.

I had been reprieved and not pardoned, the more bitterly to taste my doom. Now it was sure. Now I would never bicycle down the Palatinate sampling wines; never sit at the captain's table opposite a woman returning to the States after some years spent in a novel by Henry James. I would see Niagara Falls, possibly from the air, where it would look like the kitchen sink running over. I might at the end get to visit some land of amazing contrasts if, like the man of the elderly couple at ship's rail in the annuity advertisements, I had invested wisely. Or there might be just the one in the picture — the widow who has been left so well off.

Clapping a hand over my mouth I bolted for the bathroom. Nothing happened though, beyond an inconclusive wave or two of nausea, and after splashing cold water on my face I came out and assured them I was all right, and could go on with the evening. *No priest, thanks. I'll take the last mile alone.*

Crystal and I were to go to a party at the home of a girl friend of hers, a quarter of a mile away. The girl's fiancé was a fellow named Pete Hart who had gained a vogue as a wit by greeting everyone as Frisbie. In order not to get there too early, I suggested we walk.

As we strolled toward our destination, Crystal slipped a hand into mine, and from time to time turned to smile at me. "This night." What I died to hear I feared to ask. There was a new likelihood of my sickening, but I fought that down again.

At last she said: "I suppose you're anxious to know."

"Know?" I said matter-of-factly, and put the lighted end of a cigarette in my mouth.

Crystal stopped in the middle of the sidewalk and swung around to me. Amos 'n' Andy had followed along, and now they stood still and watched, like alert shrubbery.

"You must be out of your mind, like I've been, so I won't keep you on pins and needles any longer, darling," she said. "Anything is better than suspense."

That was a point that could have been argued, but I didn't stop to do so. I said, "What's the dope?"

"Everything is all right."

Free! Free! The very word went winging and singing through my heart, like a bird sprung from a cage. I was a

27

free man. The hours in purgatory were almost worth it, for the joy of this awakening in heaven. I that had been dead lived again, the master of my fate again — I was absolutely and completely FREE!

I turned, seized her in my arms, and, in an ecstasy of gratitude, asked her to marry me.

Three

I COULD have kicked myself. Here I'd had freedom in my grasp and let it go, victim of my passions again. For I'd lost my head in a passion of thanks scarcely worthier than its more sensual counterpart of a few weeks ago, judged as a gauge of self-control. What a jackass! Now when I confronted myself in a glass it was to twirl a finger around my temple to indicate, "Nobody home." Well, too late for regrets, especially with the girl telling her folks you were unofficially engaged; better jump on the bandwagon and tell your own parents as much before they heard it from idle gossips.

"I've fallen in love with a girl I rather like," I announced to mine one evening.

"Upstairs."

"I suppose I shall marry eventually. One does that, one drifts into stability."

"*Upstairs*, I say!"

My mother clapped her hands. "But that's wonderful!" she said. She was pleased as Punch when I reassured her it was the Chickering girl, whom she liked at least second to Jessie Smithers, and that I was informally engaged. The act showed pep, it showed downright spunk, especially when you had no prospects whatever and had to finish school first into the bargain before you could think of getting married. "Come and sit by me!"

I jollied her by joining her on the sofa, where she straightway hauled my long legs up across hers so that I was halfway sitting on her lap, and rummaged in my hair for old times' sake too.

"I remember how when you were a little shaver you'd . . . you'd crawl across the floor to where we were talking on the phone and kink the cord," she said. "As though you could stop the conversation coming through it the way you can the water in a hose. We never knew whether you were joking or serious. Did you really think that stopped the electricity in the wire?"

"Doesn't it?" I said with wide eyes, to give my mother that fun. She gave me a hug that squeezed a groan out of me, like a note out of an accordion.

"We thought for a while you might be feeble-minded," my father put in wistfully from the mantel, against which he had backed to scratch a perennially itching spot between his shoulder blades. "Well, all those things come back in a flood at a time like this, is what your mother means. I've done my best for you, I believe God will bear me out on that, but you cannot force values on one who will not have them." He fingered an onion wisp of beard which together with his harried features and embedded eyes made him rather surprisingly resemble the illustrations of depleted sensibility in the very literature with which I had outraged him, the editions of Huysmans and Baudelaire and the rest whom he had read just enough of to be sent growling back to his burly Germans. "I had some standing in the community once, a fine figure of a man too. Why, when the Sunday-school children saw me go up the church walk they would say, 'There goes Jesus.'" He drew a deep breath and resumed immediately, "And humor. Where is that? Where is *it* today? Paging humor, ahoy there, paging humor. Why, in my day we would get up to speak at Thanksgiving banquets, to give just one example, and begin, 'A moment ago you could have said the sage was in the turkey. Now the turkey is in the sage.' That was humor. Well, I've tried to do my best."

"And you have, Popper," I said, looking over from my mother's lap. "I appreciate everything you've done for me."

"It's a tradition I've tried to give you, not bread alone. The rest is up to you. You have imagination, brains, but these in themselves are not enough." He squared himself a little and we understood more was coming. "Imagination without discipline," he said, looking the aphorist straight in the eye, "is like a pillow without the ticking."

Cries of praise and thumps on the back declared he was a success. He pinched his nose and smiled shyly at the floor. "I only wish I had a financial heritage to leave you as well as a cultural. If certain usurpers of the editorial office . . . Ah, well, perhaps we can manage a wedding check of a thousand dollars when the time comes." More thumps and outcries attested to the tide of good feeling created by his knack for the right words, and my father opened a bottle of Madeira and toasted my eventual departure from his board in lambent words.

Over at the Chickerings', the feeling that they were gaining a son rather than losing a daughter generated a mood correspondingly sober. "I hope you find out what you want to *become* at Dartsmouth," said Mrs. Chickering (who persisted in pronouncing the name of the college I went to that way).

At "Dartsmouth," I got letters daily from Crystal. I answered — oh, weekly. "I feel more than ever that one must burn with a hard gemlike flame, as good old Pater said," I wrote in the winter of my sophomore year. Crystal wrote back, "I wish you wouldn't call your father that. That's high-school talk, Chick, and you're in college now."

I must not marry this girl. I must absolutely not marry this girl. But how to break off the engagement? With chivalry and tact certainly.

"I'm not what you want," I said one evening during the holidays. But we weren't having any of *that*. Another time I told her marriage was a corral for a man but a tether for a woman — a real trap — and I couldn't bear the thought of that April heart caged in a kitchen and dressed in defamatory aprons. "I will not do that to you," I said. Her eyes were heated rivets securing me to the basic social structure. There was the delicately planted idea that her parents knew how far we had gone, and they would help see to it that I wasn't going to return any unused portion. I had on occasion expressed a vague interest in journalism, and this was presumed to be crystallizing, at Dartsmouth, into fixed purpose. Chickering had a plan of his own all worked out. Failing any successful descents of my own on the New York dailies, after graduation, he would use his influence to get me something on the Decency *Pick*.

After graduation I spent two years trying, by correspondence and trips to New York, to get something on a daily there, without success, and, to be truthful about it, any real stomach for the thought. I was also presumed to be "finding myself." I saw a lot of Nickie, who had gone through Cornell on scholarships and some help from a grandaunt of means. He kept sending repaired versions of *Wise Acres* to Al Roquefort, the agent, who kept sending them back. The dialogue in it was now too recherché even for me. "There's Ronnie Ten Eyck," someone remarked in one scene. "He's living with his mother." "Oh, really? I thought that was all over." A little later on there was a joke about a masochist who gave up tight shoes for Lent. "All work and no play," was Nickie's account of his time, and, brother, he could have said that again! Meanwhile he worked on shorter things. The Salome legend attracted him as it had so many artists before, but he sensed the importance of exploring fresh facets of the theme rather than pursuing those exhausted by Strauss and Wilde. His dramatic version dealt with what happened to the *rest* of John the Baptist. "Swell," I said when he told me about it, glad to hear of someone bent on projects even more idiotic than my own.

Uppermost was still the attempt to get out of the engagement. That was growing harder and harder, as it had run almost six years now. We celebrated its anniversaries as other couples did that of their weddings.

"Don't you think it's time you two got married?" Chickering put to me one evening when we were alone in their living room.

"Oh, no! There's Crystal's future to think of," I answered with a winning laugh. Which provoked its usual dark glare.

The Lamplighter had evidently been working in his study, as he fixed me under a green eyeshade he had on, askew at an angle which diluted the severity of his gaze. "What this country needs is more wise men and less wise guys," he said flintily. He shuffled through some papers he had in his lap, and then cleared his throat and revealed what he had on his mind.

"I'm going to be given a trial on the radio — a weekly half hour over WCBR, just to see how it goes — and I was wondering if" — he bent over to pick up a dropped pencil — "if you'd be willing to let me do you."

33

I rose and danced, beside myself. "You mean on the *air*?"

"The fact is good cases are hard to find, cases that will air well I mean. The thing would come in the form of a letter from you, though naturally I know what your problem is and I've made some suggestions how it might be put to me. After all, it's my problem too, you know," he added pointedly.

"What is my problem?"

"You're like the Butterscotchman in the story. He couldn't run till he got warm and he couldn't get warm till he ran," he said keenly.

"And you really think I would write you a letter addressing you as Dear Lamplighter and ask your advice and all that?"

Chickering became testy and injured.

"Haven't we always done the right thing by you? I don't see why you're so proud. You wouldn't have to sign your name. At the mike —"

"You'd expect me to *be* there?"

"An interview, naturally. We could call you 'Upset' or something of the sort."

"But I'm not upset!"

"Well, *I* am, goddam it!" he returned, tugging the visor to rights. "We all are. Me, Mrs. Lamp — I mean Mrs. Chickering — Crystal. What's to become of you and Crystal, will you tell me that?"

"What would you have suggested?" I asked, curious.

He became himself again as he went through some notes he had made on my "case." To consult them he replaced his regular glasses with reading ones. To be fixed not only over spectacles but under an eyeshade was an experience even for a man prepared to find the speaker graphic. But

34

such was the gaze fastened on me as Chickering, after reading aloud some preliminary material, finished by saying: "*There's no substitute for Push — not even Pull.*"

"I'm glad to see so many of the old Pepigrams still holding up," I said. "*Ars longa.*"

"I'll thank you to watch your language. We don't hold with smut in this house." Chickering crossly pocketed his notes and cleared his head of props. "You know I can wangle you a job on the *Pick* any time you want. But you can't help someone who won't be helped, and that's the truth."

The mood the exchange left Chickering in gave me an idea. I had been going about it all wrong, in trying to extricate myself from the engagement chivalrously and graciously. It would be much easier for me to break it off — the family might even try to get Crystal to do it — if they thought less of me than they did. So I set about trying to lower myself in their esteem. I sat with my arms hung down over the sides of my chair to suggest an informed satiety, an implication that the species was exhausted and had only been an experiment in any case, and a refusal to pin my faith on technological progress. This evoked nothing to them but a lack of get-up-and-go. I cursed and swore, took snuff, professed atheism. Waiting for Crystal one Sunday evening, I remarked to her parents apropos of some worshipers hurrying by the house on their way to church: "There, but for the grace of God, go I." No cigar — too nuancy. The ring of the cliché meant to them only some latent piety in the lad after all, just as the snuff had a certain down-to-earthness which might save him yet. I hinted at insanity in my family. They praised my frankness. I planned one last stratagem. I would turn up stewed to the gills.

I drank heavily at a party Crystal and I went to, one evening. She stiffly ignored my behavior, and on the way home spoke instead of what a wonderful conversation she'd had with a forty-year-old man who was a house guest of the host.

"I hope you had as good a time there with Shirley Bates. Why, he's a hotel manager in Toledo. He was very amusing about the kinds of people you meet in that business," she said, ignoring the fact that I was pacing off the footage of the city with heel-to-toe steps. "He's very scornful of conventions."

"You mean he hates gatherings or he lets people up he knows aren't married?"

"Take me home."

"I am!"

"Then walk faster. I never want to see you again."

"Why not? What have I done?"

"You make a joke out of everything. And shall I tell you something? That's a sign of immaturity."

"Maybe you'd better marry an older man."

"I will at the rate you're getting yourself organized!"

I did not dignify this with a reply. When we reached her house I headed straight for the liquor cabinet and poured myself a stiff nightcap. Crystal laid me out with such eloquence as to fetch her parents down in bathrobes. Mrs. Chickering stood on the bottom step and wept.

I wove my way over to her.

"I'm very sorry," I said, and bowed gallantly from the waist. Only the bow got lower and lower, till finally I lay curled up on the floor — out cold.

I awoke in a bed in the Chickerings' guest room, with Chickering bending over me and Mrs. Chickering looking over his shoulder, a wadded handkerchief in her hand. Sliced sunlight lay across the counterpane. When I blinked, Chick-

36

ering stepped over to the window and twitched shut a Venetian blind.

"It's morning," he explained. "We've given some story to your folks, so at least they'll be spared this. But that isn't the important thing. What is our daughter, to you?"

"A dish who can cook." I was trying to lose ground with them to the end, but my tongue was a piece of bent tin and it was doubtful whether they understood, or even heard. And I was stung with remorse as I spoke. More elements were at war within me than I could have sorted out on the soberest day of my life.

"She has more than looks," said Mrs. Chickering, who had apparently heard but not understood. What cut me to the quick was the fact that she had been sunburned through a straw basket she had covered her face with while lying on the sand, and looked as though she had the measles. I knew then that I would marry into this family.

"You're a human being," Chickering was saying. "And the question to be settled right now, in this room, is what are you going to become. A decent self-respecting member of society, or a hopeless, useless, penniless sot?"

Obviously a multitude of alternatives lay between these extremes, but at the moment his words had a frightening cogency, especially since the sound of each one was like a hammerblow threatening to divide my head into segments, like those chocolate apples which you sunder with the tap of a spoon. "Which of the two will it be?" Chickering repeated. Then he blew his nose imprecisely into a checked handkerchief, in a moment that seemed somehow to signify the end of my youth. I decided for the more savory of the two prospects. "I'll wend my maze," the piece of bent tin brought out as best it could. A promise was a promise. I went with him down to the *Picayune Blade* as soon as I

37

could be washed, fed and deodorized back into shape, which was about quitting time. I took a job as cub reporter and married Crystal Chickering, in that order. (I remained adamant about the invitation to appear on the radio version of "The Lamplighter," which went off the air at the end of the month.)

The fifty dollars a week I got as a start wasn't enough to rent an apartment and live comfortably on too, so, on returning from a honeymoon in the Poconos, Crystal and I moved in with my family. This arrangement was understood to be temporary, like my job on the *Pick*. The house was, thank God, as large as I've made out, and we had what was practically a separate apartment in it, refrigerator and all. My mother offered to send up any meals we wanted but we usually did come down for dinner, which made, with my parents and my sister Lila, five of us around the table — and two objects for my father's chivalry. For he accused me of being as oblivious of my wife's want of intellect as I had been of my mother's (leaving out my younger sister, who didn't count in this connection). One evening at dinner, for instance, my mother and Crystal had a discussion about the inevitable early adjustments of marriage — very cozy, for the two got on fine.

"Yes," I remarked at length, "all couples must bear the strain of getting acquainted, having been, up to then, merely intimate."

"Upstairs."

"Roebuck, the boy's *married* now," my mother broke in, "you can't do that sort of thing any more."

She went on to say that though still at his table I was out of his jurisdiction, and that if exceptions were to be taken to my subtlety it was up to my wife to take them;

38

she added that this was in any case the kind of marital problem that would have to be worked out with patience and understanding on both sides. But sending me up to my room was not the way.

"I'll go up," Crystal unexpectedly said, dropping her fork, and flew away. I found her in our quarters in tears.

"We've got to find a place of our own," she said. "I like Lila, and your mother's a lamb, and even your father means well, but this won't work."

I agreed that we would look for an apartment immediately. That decided, she calmed down, and we settled ourselves for the evening. I read for an hour from an author of only middling literacy while Crystal sewed at a table runner she was getting ready for my mother's birthday. At a quarter to ten, I stretched and said, "Let's go to bed, darling."

"Oh, God, no," she said. "I'm too tired."

The honeymoon was over.

That winter we had a baby boy. He was named Mike, and he looked like Madame Ouspenskaya. I began to feel the pinch of my modest salary, and put my mind to the problem of supplementing my income. (There had been no wedding check from my father, who had sunk all his spare money in a Western mine devoid of metal.) Al Roquefort's computations left me now only a 12 per cent equity in *Wise Acres*, which I knew would never be put on the boards anyway. I was racking my brain about how to get some extra money when my father-in-law came through with an unexpected suggestion:

"Write some Pepigrams."

Now Chickering had been manufacturing these fibroid maxims for the better part of a decade. That he had a witty memory was evident from the familiar ring of many, such as "If you're a self-starter your boss won't have to be a crank," but the bulk were his own and the name they bore was his own, and patented. He told me the *Pick* bought Peps from anyone who could deliver the goods, at twenty dollars per. He assured me he normally frowned on the practice but would make an exception in my case, in fact would do all in his power to help me break in — by which I understood that he was pumped dry and starting to suck air.

"They should be a cinch for you," he said. "You *talk* in epigrams. Pepigrams are simply epigrams of an inspirational nature. They should be on the theme of success — in its widest sense, that is, successful living — and be designed to spur and uplift."

I prided myself on thinking that I could not possibly write a Pepigram. But when Crystal told me one night that we had four dollars in the bank, I decided to try my hand at them, just for the money.

But making a sow's ear out of a silk purse isn't any easier than the other way around, in case you think it is; and all I could evolve was the likes of "Woman is a door of which love is the hinge and flattery the latch," and "Thoreau said he never saw a man 100% awake, just as Freud, fifty years later, was to find no one ever wholly asleep."

"No, no, no," Chickering said when I showed him those, together with a few of the mots I'd had in *Wise Acres*. "They're too . . . I don't think you're *trying*. These aren't Pepigrams, and you know it." I felt a little like the young advertising copywriter in the cartoon who is being told by his superior, "Oh, come now, surely you can write worse than this."

I tried to write worse but it was no good; my generalizations came out as before, each more exquisite than the last. I grew discouraged. I was on the verge of giving up. Then I got a Pepigram by pure fluke.

I was roosting over a cup of coffee at the Greek's counter, one afternoon in the early fall, when Nachtgeborn reached up to turn off a radio he'd had going back there. The announcer was just saying, "All work and no play makes Jack a dull boy," but was snapped off in the middle of the sentence, so what I heard was, "All work and no play makes Jack." I straightened on the stool. If that wasn't a Pepigram, what was? I jotted it on my note pad and hurried over to show it to my father-in-law, who was still in his *Pick* office. I had to hand it to him in writing as it would have broken every tooth in my head to say it. He read it, kept his head thoughtfully lowered a moment, then looked up at me.

"You've just made yourself twenty dollars," he said.

The pump was primed. I got the hang of it, and was off. A few of my early Peps were: "If you keep your sleeves rolled up you won't get so much on the cuff"; "To turn stumbling blocks into steppingstones — *pick up your feet*"; and "If your wife is a crab maybe it's because you're a jellyfish." The last was a free adaptation of the self-starter-and-crank one, and introduced the idea of private initiative into the home. It was on that ground that it was ruled a Pepigram, even though not strictly on the theme of getting ahead. My personal favorite drew a rejection. It grew out of a story I covered which involved a report of a Peeping Tom from a home in the suburbs where a party was in progress at which, it turned out, the guests had been playing strip poker. I distilled a drop of wisdom out of the incident which ran, "People who play strip poker shouldn't report

Peeping Toms." It was ruled not strictly a Pepigram.

Everybody was gratified with me. The publisher of the paper, Harry Clammidge, a stout man whose belt creaked every time he drew a breath, had the elder Chickerings and Crystal and me up to dinner. He opened a bottle of champagne and toasted my emergence as the new Pepigrammatist and white hope of shirtsleeve philosophy. "To the new Abe Martin," he said, and they all drank and looked at me as I lowered my own eyes. Later we played games and were given a liqueur that tasted like nose-drops.

Well, I got my Peps by hard work, not by sitting around the Samothrace waiting for the Greek to turn the radio off. I stole here and there, sure; I'm perfectly honest. I admit it. But I did it knowing my hands were in the pockets of thieves and that others were picking mine. I was still also a reporter — but that was all changed suddenly, and Destiny gave me another shove forward in the direction I was being hustled, when Chickering died.

For as long as anyone could remember, he had played in an annual benefit softball game for a welfare organization known as "the Big Brothers." It was a worthy social service kind of cause, and he was president of it, but each summer he played in the face of his wife's reminders of the thousands of middle-aged snow shovelers and imprudent athletes who keel over annually from such exertions. This year the fate befell Chickering as he was running out a home run. The excitement itself was probably a contributing factor. He died on third. I feel a little foolish putting it that way, but those are the facts. Clammidge called me into his office the day after the funeral.

"I just can't imagine it," he said, shaking his head. "The place will never be the same again. It seems funny around here without him cracking his jokes."

"I believe it," I said.

Clammidge heaved a long sigh, as though the past were something to be realistically exhaled; then after a short pause, broken only by the steady creak of his belt, like ship's rigging, he said abruptly: "What I called you in for was the question of the column. Of course 'The Lamplighter' must go on. It will go on. In fact, this comes just at a time when there's talk of syndication. There's only one man I know of who can fill his shoes. You."

"I can no such thing!" I answered resentfully. "Why, I could never turn out that column."

"I know better." Clammidge looked at me shrewdly, as a man who could judge talent. "Anybody who can write the Pepigrams can write the column, because the Pepigrams are the heart of it."

I declined vigorously but he told me to sleep on it. "Give it hard, clear, sober thought," he said.

Crystal gave it that for me, twisting a damp handkerchief and interrupting herself with frequent and copious tears. "Oh, it would be so wonderful, you stepping into Daddy's shoes, carrying on his work," she said. "It's this sense of continuity that, I suppose, a woman feels more strongly about than a man. But there's also the fact that it's your big chance. Chick, there's no telling where you might end up."

Well, all this was temporary — had been from the start — and meanwhile a steady job, with enough salary to relieve me of financial worries as father as well as husband, would give me a secure footing from which to look around with intelligent leisure for something more up my alley.

So I became the Lamplighter.

The job, as I found on diving into the mass of correspondence accumulated since Chickering's death, was just

43

a job; but it did afford that sense of human perpetuity Crystal had stressed, and which I had further reason to appreciate with the passing, that spring, of my own father.

He had written a beautiful will leaving us everything: the blue sky, the sun, moon and stars, the Mind. In addition, I was to have one advantage he himself had been denied: the opportunity to develop character and fiber through hardship and having to work for a living. Thank God the house was free and clear, though in need of repairs. I had become overnight a young man of proliferating responsibilities. The insurance did leave enough money, not only to repair the house, but to remodel it, a move on which we decided when Crystal agreed to stay provided absolute privacy could be devised for both households. My mother insisted the roles be reversed: that the main house was Crystal's and mine, and that she and Lila were regarded as living with us rather than the other way around.

That was another responsibility. For Lila was of age now and, instead of in my hair, under my wing — for who was head of the house if not I? I tried to be relaxed and tolerant in this matter, but such proved impossible. It was out of her affairs that our next crisis brewed.

I was in bed early one evening on the third day of a bout of stomach flu. The doctor had ordered me to stay there but the mail hadn't heard I was sick, and so I'd had a stack of accumulated letters from my readers sent over from the office and, propped up against two pillows, was composing replies into a bedside dictaphone. I had on a flannel nightgown (I had come not to like pajamas, no freedom of movement) and I guess a green eyeshade — for the glare from my bedside lamp. "Dear Lamplighter,"

44

one reader had written: "My husband and I have a perennial argument about vacations. I like to get away to as distant a place as possible, but he doesn't like trips and isn't very keen on vacations anyway, so each year he has argued us into making less and less of a trip. This summer he says he wants to stay home altogether. Isn't that going too far?"

"Yes, Mrs. M., that is going too far. But you must remember that marriage is a give and . . ." I had begun to dictate in answer, when the bedroom door opened and Crystal came in, looking as though something were up.

"Well, you've done a lot of grumbling about the beaux Lila has hanging around her," she said, "but wait till you get a load of who's down there picking her up now."

"Who?" I asked.

"Nickie Sherman."

"*What?*"

Crystal nodded. "He's taking her to this supper dance somewhere. Nobody here knew it but they seem to have been seeing a lot of one another secretly. It looks pretty thick, too, the way they're smooching down there."

I threw the covers back and sprang out of bed.

"Get me some clothes," I said, unbuttoning the nightgown and doffing the eyeshade. I flung the latter off like a catcher throwing off his mask to go after a high one. "Then go downstairs and head them off in case they start to leave. Don't let them go till I get there. A stitch in time sometimes saves nine."

I was breathing heavily from this little exertion, for after all I'd had a fever of over a hundred. Crystal hurried into the closet and dug about for some duds. Dear God, I said within me, must there always be something?

"Do you suppose there's anything between them?" Crystal asked from the door, presently, as she started out of the room.

"You're damn right there is," I said, drawing on trousers. "Me!"

The Lamplighter could spot a risk when he saw one, all right.

Four

LOVE'S BLINDNESS consists oftener in seeing what is not there than in not seeing what is. Anglo-Saxon to his finger tips (though of mixed Latin, Celtic and Semitic strains), Nickie liked undercommunicativeness in women, not realizing that Lila had nothing *to* communicate. A nose coming down from her forehead in a straight line was enough to make our nonesuch speak of her Grecian profile — and her walk! She was a goddess, he said, a veritable Diana. I never noticed any arrows myself, but he must have liked her quiver.

Lila saw in Nickie the last word in sophistication and a future in the theater, surrounded by stars who Luxed their things and would call her "Darling" from the start. What I saw was an improvident brother-in-law on my doorstep if not at my board. This was a full-time vexation, coming when I already had saddle sores from overwork in the editorial chair. I tried first to queer the union in a nice way. I took Nickie aside and reviewed the incompatibilities. He was an egghead and she had a *soufflé* for a brain, and I put to him whether that was enough to base a relationship on. He smiled and replied that no marriage could be gone into with open eyes: it was quite precisely the plunge we proverbially called it, and every diver always instinctively shut his eyes just before he hit the water.

"That's a lot of crap," I told him, "and besides I said it first. It was so long ago I'd forgotten it, but I put that line in *Wise Acres*."

"I took it out," he answered dryly. "And now if you'll excuse me, I have a date to do the same with your sister."

And this was the kind of dialogue on which their future security must rest!

More drastic sabotage was clearly called for.

To oppose the match would be useless and it might be disastrous. I had a better plan. I would invite Nickie to dinner and give that bastard, in one evening, such a dose, such a caricature of married life that he would take to the woods and never be heard from again.

I lost no time in getting to my preparations.

First, I told Crystal to get out the resort pennants and souvenir pillows at which I had first boggled, on our setting up housekeeping, and distribute them as she wished — the more heavily the better. "Not in our living room up here — the one downstairs that Mother wants us to have from now on," I said. Crystal fell gratefully to the mementos, which included not only the handful she had collected on our honeymoon and one vacation, but the masses her family had accumulated over twenty years of hackneyed holidays and to which her mother had invited her to help herself.

The parlor was a horror when she finished with it. There were tasseled cushions from the Wisconsin Dells, representations of regional sunsets off which I could not take my eyes, paint-dipped encomiums of the biggest little town in every state in the Union and bunting with humorous legends from as far south as Texas and as far west as Seattle. "This is sweet of you, Chick," she said as she screwed a bulb into the jaws of a plaster alligator from Florida, the

48

other end of which was plugged into a socket of my brain, such suffering. "It makes the place more homey."

The setting ready, there remained the farce to be enacted against it.

I suggested to Crystal we play games the night we were going to have the sophisticate in, and she got a book from the local branch library entitled "Fun in the House." I myself confected a batch of japes that would set us back at least fifty years. Even the dinner dishes were chosen with a view to their very names striking terror in the heart of a *boulevardier*: beef stew with dumplings, peas and carrots, cottage-fried potatoes; and for dessert, I thought, a nice apple pandowdy. Crystal agreed to everything.

Before our guests arrived, I took a tray up to my mother's room. She had caught a heavy cold in a movie air-conditioned for her comfort, and preferred to dine apart. Crystal had recently disclosed to me that she was going to have another child, and I took the chance to break the news to my mother when we were alone, knowing full well the scene that would ensue. I did so after setting the tray down on a table drawn up to a small settee on which she was seated, reading.

With my back to the wall, I shut my eyes and said through gritted teeth, "I'm going to become a father again."

"Come and sit by me."

I let her displace my hair and chafe my bones a bit, this being after all her house, then climbed down off her lap and said, "Nickie will be here any minute, and I guess Lila's already gone down."

Lila was nineteen now, and desperately worldly. If reminded she had once been a tease she would not have known what you were talking about, and I'm sure she was ashamed that her brother was the Lamplighter, though

49

temporarily. Her attitudes derived from the cinema: expressive tics of lip and eyebrow, a way of looking at you out of eyes bisected by their lids, in the manner of Bankhead, or sitting with a cigarette held burning over one shoulder, with rather a play of the fingers, as who should be Claudette Colbert. Anybody would have recognized her sources — except Nickie. He never went to the movies. She thought the worst of everybody in order not to be considered naïve. She spoke with a nasal tone and a rational indifference. "What hempened?" she asked when Nickie arrived half an hour late, as though nothing could matter less. "The cab had a flat," Nickie explained, bending down to kiss her, his lips reaching a little toward her as I had seen them reach toward the countless cups of coffee which we had drunk, in vain it seemed, at the Samothrace.

On straightening up, Nickie got an eyeful of the living room and glanced at me. Then he looked at Lila with enlarged eyes, and the two exchanged a charitable smile. "They've done the room over," she said.

I moved in with a plate of small cheese dreams, carrot sticks and codfish balls on toothpicks; scalloped paper napkins reading *Name your poison* followed closely. Cocktails were tendered in glasses bearing the legend "You don't have to be crazy to get along with us but it helps." I saw Nickie take this in, and I read my own with a smile.

"I get a kick out of these," I said, waggling a foot on which was a Congress slipper.

Crystal said, "Excuse me a sec, I've got to look at my meat," and bustled off to the kitchen.

"Won't we be eating awfully early?" Lila said.

"It's not what time people eat that counts," I said. "It's what they are inside."

Nickie wore the Brooks Brothers gray flannel, with a

knit blue tie hitched between the easily flaring wings of a white button-down collar, and I thought as I watched him that if he could have been wedged without unreasonable pain and sacrifice into one of those time capsules, the future would have a good notion of our ideal of the fastidious offhand.

My conversation so far had been preparatory. I cleared my throat to get the main show under way.

"Chris had a little accident in the kitchen today," I began. "She, uh, she was waxing the floor when she slipped and sat smack down in the polish. She said she didn't mind the fall so much, but it put her behind in her work."

"Who?" Nickie asked.

"Chris. Crystal."

"Was she hurt bad?"

"No, I said she wasn't hurt at all. . . . The thing—" I slid up in my chair and got a grip on my drink. "The thing she complained about mainly was that *it put her behind in her work. Her behind.*"

"Please don't let her go to any trouble on our account."

"No, it's quite all right. Hell . . ." I turned and yelled to the kitchen, "Anything I can do to help, sweets?"

"No," Crystal called back, "thanks just the same, darling. Everything is okie doke."

I glared at Lila for not having offered to help out there, because after all she lived here, too. Of course she did work. She had a job as stenographer in a downtown office, and there was a mischievous story circulated there that on her first day the boss called her into his office and said, "Miss Swallow, take a letter," and she answered, "Where to?"

Crystal came back and sat down and picked up her cocktail, smiling at us with a flushed expression as she smoothed back a damp strand of hair.

51

"Chick here tells us you had a nasty spill," Nickie said to her.

"What?"

"I *said*," I said, sliding up still higher in my chair, "that you slipped and sat down on the floor wax and that it put you behind in your work. Put *your* behind in — Oh, skip it." The conversation was like some crazy folding chair I couldn't get straight. And by now I didn't give a good goddam who got what, and was ready to bail out. Then Crystal laughed heartily. She got the joke even in its mangled form, lacking, I suppose, the subtlety of mind that barred my guest from grasping it. At this point the parody began really to take hold.

There was a brief silence, during which Lila looked out of the window and said, "Getting dork." I suggested to Crystal that we time dinner so we could hear Henry Aldrich, which I told Nickie was our favorite radio program. Throughout dinner, to which I invited Nickie to sit down with his coat off like I was and pitch in, I subjected them to the hail of corn I had prepared and whatever I could inject impromptu.

"Why," I asked, ladling out gravy to all, "do we know that the Pilgrim women used make-up?" When they could not say, I reminded them of the compact on the *Mayflower*. I recalled the darky who thought that a fortification was two twentifications; asked what the one strawberry had said to the other strawberry. "Give up?" "I certainly do," said Nickie, who was wilting nicely. "The one strawberry said to the other: 'If we hadn't been in that bed together, we wouldn't be in this jam.'"

"Chick!" Crystal was choking with laughter. "You make me blush from top to bottom."

"That's only halfway."

I gave them no quarter. I offered to use the word "miscellaneous" in a sentence, and though but scantily encouraged, went on, "Of the two Axis dictators in the last war, Hitler is still remembered but miscellaneous largely forgotten." My electrician phoned during dinner about some imminent work, and on being asked as I returned to the table what that was all about, I answered: "We're having extra sockets put in. My psychiatrist says I need more outlets."

Crystal helped give our worldling a view of the mucilaginous whole that lay in wait for those who wed. There was an old family joke of the Chickerings' to which I'd been subjected countless times when seated at their board, just as Nickie was now at mine, and which might have scared *me* off had not a stronger cable bound me. "Dear," I remarked, buttering a roll, "I must say you don't make the biscuits Mother used to." Her answer came as expected, "No, and you don't make the dough Father did."

Nickie Sherman was visibly on the ropes — blanching at the vistas I had laid open. I gave him the *coup de grâce* over coffee.

We had that with dessert in the living room. Crystal had baked an apple pie instead of the pandowdy, and I had worked up a little dido for that. When she was in the kitchen getting it out of the oven, I glanced furtively back there and whispered with a chuckle to the others, "See this?" I was holding in my hand a splinter of wood about two inches long and a quarter of an inch wide. "When Chris answers a question I'm going to ask her about the dessert, watch what I do. This'll be a good one on her. I hope you've left room for pie."

I put the splinter back in my pocket and was whistling innocently when she returned with the pie. I cut everybody

53

a slice, and when I came to Crystal I looked over questioningly at her. "How big a piece do you want?" She was watching her weight and I knew what she would say. "Oh, just give me a sliver."

I reached into my pocket and handed her the splinter of wood.

Nickie smiled, but it was the kind of smile with which money is cheerfully refunded. Lila tossed a lock of hair out of her eye and said, "Mreally."

I sat with my legs stretched out after coffee and loosened my belt and the top button of my pants. I patted my stomach contentedly. "There's nothing like a pleasant evening with friends," I said. "I suppose we'll spend a lot of them together."

After about another quarter of an hour of this, Nickie glanced covertly at his wrist watch.

"Now for some games!" I said.

I sprang to my feet and shepherded them through a sequence of parlor pastimes which included something called "Going to Mr. Doodle's," and another named "Getting your partner's goat," of which I will forgo the details. At twenty minutes to eleven I looked at my own watch and observed unhappily that we had missed Henry Aldrich. "I get a kick out of that kid. He gets into more trouble."

"Mreally."

"Sis?"

No answer.

"Sis, be sure and lock all the doors before you come up, won't you?" I said. "Chris and I had better get along to bed. Leave the dishes till tomorrow, dear," I told Crystal.

Crystal rose and joined me, and as we paused to say our smiling good nights, our heads were in that juxtaposition which is favored in advertisements of male hair oil.

54

I had done my best. The picture we made standing together capped the climax, a tableau of Domesticity beyond which Nickie's own imagination must carry him; beyond which lay the changeless dramas of incarceration, the certain family reunions at Christmas time and the annual motor trips on which were acquired the mementos that encircled him, and the rumpus rooms finished in that wallboard that resembles Ry-Krisp.

The effort had left me spent. Upstairs in our bedroom, I sat slumped in an armchair, breathing heavily, like an actor after a taxing performance. But I was happy. Everything had gone off beautifully. Now surely I could get that sonofabitch off my doorstep, and for good. I glowed with inner satisfaction. The seed had been sown. There remained only to gather in the harvest.

The harvest was not long in coming, and it was twofold.

Before undressing, I went back downstairs for a book I was reading, which I'd left on a table there. The living room was empty. A murmur of voices from the back porch indicated that the lovers had slipped out to where it was "dork." Perhaps a critical meeting? Nickie breaking it off without losing any time? Nickie explaining that marriage wasn't for him? Ha! More than likely, that. I chortled to myself as I stole eagerly into the kitchen, a maneuver lubricated by the fact that I was in stocking feet, and stood in the shadows by the open door to listen.

"He's oaful," Lila was saying. "Just oaful."

"I know." (Pause.) "You hear of people getting stodgy after marriage, but my Christ, I never dreamed it could happen this fast."

Perfect. I chuckled to myself, there in the dark, imagining the pained frown on our hero's face as he groped for a way

55

of leading up to the break. Get you back where you belong to the fictive halls of Wise Acres, I thought, not without sympathy. Of course I was doing *him* a favor too; and Lila. All of us.

"Is he that bad all the time?" Nickie's voice came next.

"All the time."

It was a lie, but why mind her adding a few strokes of her own to the caricature? It was the cream of the jest. The whole thing was rich. I held my sides with laughter.

"And, Nickums, it's getting worse every day. Oh, Nickie, there are times when I think I'll go crazy in this house."

"It just didn't seem *him* I saw in there tonight. I mean what it can do to a man."

Swell. All beautifully according to plan. I had done what I'd set out to: given him a glimpse of convention as that omelette from which the egg of Individuality can never again be retrieved. Well, we wouldn't be seeing much of our Individual around here after tonight, I'd be bound. But let's hurry this thing along; I was getting tired, standing there, and a little cold.

"I understood it could be deadly — marriage I mean. But to become fossilized so soon . . ."

"It isn't just that. He acts like — like such an American!" Lila brought out in a sudden burst of emotion. Rare for her, all this. The dam had broken. "Oh, Nickie, I can't stand it here another day!"

Here a slight irregularity in the sequence as I had foreseen it began to creep in. There was a sudden soft rustle on the porch, as of head taken to breast, of Youth caught up. "You won't have to. I'll take you out of all this, *Liebchen* — NOW," said my hero.

"Oh, sweetest Nickie, right away?"

An affirmation softly gasped. Then another rustle with its sense of increasing voltage, out there.

"Nickie, lamb . . . But — Nickie, how'll we — I mean what would you . . . ?"

An interesting question and I'm glad you asked it, thought I, clenching my fists. One fist rather, for I had the book tightly clutched in the other.

"I don't know, but we'll manage."

"Of course I have my job, which I can keep — for a while."

"We'll work it out. But I know one thing: I'll see you die in the cold before I let you rot in this drizzle."

I drew back my arm and hurled the book down the length of the corridor into the dining room, where it hit the wall with a *splat* and dropped to the floor, causing a window shade to fly up. I had the feeling of having had my head bashed in with bad Scott Fitzgerald.

"It'll never happen to us, will it, Nickie?"

"What we saw tonight? Never!"

Feeling my vascular condition to be such that I probably glowed in the dark, I turned on my stockinged heel and strode out of there. Leaving the book where it lay, neatly halved, on the floor, I padded through the vestibule and on upstairs.

Halfway up, I paused to consult at a wall mirror hanging there. I was arrested by the face which confronted me. Only yesterday it had belonged to a youth who never doubted he would tour the pines of Rome and the Swiss Alps, up which last he would go in the spirit of the *real* Scott Fitzgerald, piling into a funicular with a gay party carrying bottles of Neuchâtel to settle a bet whether the

57

wine had more *spritz* on the mountaintops. Now it was that of a community figure who pointed the stem of his pipe at people and made them define their terms, and who would eventually lead motorcades to the state capital on behalf of much-needed legislation.

I dragged myself upstairs by hand as much as by foot, pulling myself along by the balustrade toward the bedroom, where I received the second reward of the evening.

Crystal was sitting at the dresser brushing her hair.

"You were wonderful tonight, darling," she said. "Such a card, and so nice to me. I think we've finally got the house looking like a home, too, don't you?"

"Yes," I said, going into the closet to take off my clothes. I stayed in there quite a while, reflecting guiltily that of course the souvenirs would have to stay where they were: I couldn't tell her that it had all been a burlesque. You couldn't tell a pregnant woman that. I emerged at length in my nightie and bitterly adjusted a few windows. Crystal was already between the sheets. She was gold as midday, and when she stretched she suggested fruit about to burst its skin.

"I couldn't be happier," she said.

"Nor could I."

I pulled out the light and skulked into bed beside her. I lay on my back with my hands laced under my head. She stirred against me with a contented sigh and said, "I must get out those cups and saucers from Lake Pontchartrain. Mother's got them packed away in the attic somewhere and I know she'd love to have me use them. Still worrying about those two?"

"I most assuredly am," I said.

"Not now. . . . Think they're in love?"

"If they aren't I'll eat my hat."

58

She lay a moment revolving the thought.

"Well, it's a porkpie," she said, and laughed indolently. When I did not join in, she poked me under the covers. "Your wit is infectious."

Relax, I told myself, everything is hopeless.

Five

THE AUTUMN days closed down, driving the lovers into the parlor and me back up half a flight of stairs to do my listening. I would crouch, cold and miserable, near the second-floor landing and strain to catch the flushed exchanges below. One night about one A.M. (Crystal was long in bed, she knew nothing of these taxing vigils) I heard Nickie say in response to some contentedly droned query of my sister's:

"Of course I want a home, children, all that sort of thing. You know — the eternal severities."

"Will you look at other women?"

"If you've seen them all, you've seen one."

I thought, "Oh, my God," and rocked my head in my hands. I rose from the step where I'd been sitting huddled in my nightgown and yelled down over the banister: "Doesn't that young man have a home of his own?"

He left, but he was back the next night.

"Taste is the morality of the senses."

"Why isn't morality the décor of the soul? And go on home!" I barked.

They lowered their voices, making their words at last so indistinguishable that I had to steal down to the foot of the staircase to make them out. The pair were dimly visible through the vestibule doorway, lying back among the sofa cushions as in a drifting canoe. Standing there in my bare feet I heard Nickie remark that being creative and happy, both, was impossible — even undesirable. "It would be like a slice of bread buttered on both sides."

I beat my head on the newel post. That all was not urbanity on the love front was hinted in certain wretched mails that came accidentally under my gaze, letters from Nickie in which, among other things, the recipient's thighs were likened to warm snow and her bosom to a halved honeydew. Two things seemed urgent: they must not get married, and they must get married right away.

They ran away and got married. That much at least was considerate, as it spared the expense of a wedding which I would have had to foot. Lila would keep her job till Nickie's plays were produced (a prospect which was perniciously anemic). "They can move in with us," my mother said to me. This was arranged over my dead body, and with three provisos laid down by me as head of the house. One, it was temporary. Two, Nickie must get a job, part-time or full, while he worked at his plays. Three, no children. Crystal was in the hospital at the time giving birth to our second, another boy, who was named Fillmore (also over my dead body).

The newlyweds had a honeymoon of which the expenses were defrayed in part by the wealthy great-aunt who had seen Nickie through college and who fancied herself, in all this, as nourishing the arts. The trip took in the Tanglewood Music Festival, and they arrived home in glowing spirits and in time for dinner. Our opening table talk took, under Nickie's example, a civilized and leisurely turn.

"They played Scriabin rather badly I thought," he said. "But then how can you tell when Scriabin is being badly played?"

"Ah, Tanglewood," I said, hunched over my plate. "The

61

soft summer nights, the lovers strolling, the Brahms bursting in air." For the aim to sicken and subdue had never wholly left me; just as I had once fought tooth and nail to keep him out of here, now that he was here I would fight to the last ditch to drive him back.

The maid, thrusting in a bowl of viands over my shoulder, laughed like the horse she resembled. Just so had the stenographers at the *Picayune Blade* at the same joke. Alone in my office later, I had slumped in my swivel chair, utterly discouraged at my success with this type of material. Was it, after all, my speed, rather than the Continental wit on which I had once preened myself? It seemed now second nature to me. I had undergone a sea change: the parody wagged me — not I, any longer, it. What hurt was not so much that I was the Lamplighter, but that nobody appeared to find anything odd in the fact.

When the newlyweds retired for their first night together under my roof, I stood in the vestibule and called, this time up the stairs instead of down, "Remember — no children!"

Chris and I went on a few days' motor trip into Vermont, and when we returned it was to find that Nickie had made no efforts to get a job. The steady clatter of a typewriter in his room was no consolation, especially when I learned he was recasting *Wise Acres* into verse. He was experimenting with a new kind of rhyme which went even farther than the techniques which had impressed him in the early work of Auden. He showed me some manuscript.

"Assonance is partial rhyme, or half-rhyme," he explained, "like, oh, 'lady' and 'baby.' Well, my line ends are as much beyond assonance as assonance was beyond rhyme. Call it half-assonance."

"I will," I said, handing him back the samples I had read.

"Now, look. I've been giving this job thing of yours some thought."

So I had, all through Vermont. What, I had asked myself, would be an industrial niche for Nickie? What were his qualifications? A certain opalescence of mind coupled with an amused skepticism, a sense of life's random substance and of its charming cloud formations, all adding up to a fine tensile play of thought and a knack for drawing conclusions. Any employer in the market for these, and with a taste for the personal bond to which such lambency of mind might additionally conduce, could do worse than hire him on the spot. Pending the discovery of any application blanks calling for their specification, however, more prosaic proposals seemed to me indicated. I was going to make a suggestion when Nickie said:

"I see you have the Indian point of view — let the squaw do all the driving." He nodded at my right arm. "That's the only one that's sunburned, meaning it's the only one the sun got at through the car window. *Ergo*, Crystal did all the driving on this second honeymoon of yours. If you'd done any yourself the left one would have got some sun — you old tyrant you."

"You ought to be a detective," I said, packing a pipe from a jar of tobacco on the mantel. Nickie's whole future, and a calamitous slice of my own, had passed before us in a word, as they had once before when I'd made that dry rejoinder, but neither of us dreamed it then. Then, I watched him as I sucked the match flame into the bowl of my pipe, squared my shoulders and said: "What would you say to taking a crack at a little selling? You'd have your own hours," I hurried on, "no clocks to punch, turning on the charm from door to door for the housewives — "

"Why not?" Nickie engagingly enough returned. "I see no harm in giving it a whirl, certainly."

In the course of the next months, Nickie handled many items. They included vacuum cleaners, matched sets of aluminum cookery, encyclopedias, electric mangles, and cemetery lots. He sold one of each — to me — before going on to the next "line."

Meanwhile he got squared away on a new play, of which he regaled us with bits at dinner one evening. "There's this country house in Essex with a wonderful retired Scotland Yard inspector living alone in it except for servants," he said. "And this Dalmatian dog. Every time he sits down to write a letter, the Inspector calls the Dalmatian and shakes his fountain pen out over him to see if there's any ink in it."

He and Lila smiled at me expectantly. When I had thoroughly masticated a mouthful of food, I asked: "Any other action?"

"Oh, yes. The letter he starts writing when the curtain goes up is to tell a cousin not to come, but the cousin turns up as he finishes it, and he has to write another letter summoning his son back home to thrash out some family matters involving the cousin."

"Calling the Dalmatian back to shake the pen out over him."

"Right. It flows poorly. The theater is visual of course. And no more than he's sent the cousin off to post the letter, he realizes he needs his lawyer there, so he has to write *another* — "

"Look," I said, still irritable from having that afternoon purchased the plot of ground in which I would be laid to rest, "plays vary in the amount of story they need, but you

64

can't splatter a Dalmatian for three acts." I suddenly gestured at Lila and said, "What does she think of all this?"

Lila was making nervous, fidgety movements most untypical of her.

"He was never meant to be a salesman," she blurted out. "Oh, if we only had a decent connection," she went on with a deploring glance at me, "somebody who could get him a decent job! If we only knew some people who count!"

"I can introduce you to a couple of bank tellers," I said, mashing peas into the tines of my fork.

"Maybe that's what he ought to be!" Lila said and burst into tears. My mother and Crystal rose and hovered cluckingly over her. "You should know better than to talk to her that way," they said, glaring at me. "Don't you realize she's pregnant?"

"Pregnant! But that's expressly —" I began, and broke off and looked at Nickie. He hung his head. There was a long hassle, at the height of which Nickie rose, and what we saw now was pure theater. He put his napkin down with a martyred look and said:

"I know what you're all thinking. Why doesn't he write something popular? Well, shall I tell you something? That's just exactly what I'm going to do. I'm going up to that room and write a series — for television!"

He stalked upstairs and stayed there for five months. He emerged with a popular program, which nobody wanted. That summer Lila gave birth to a baby girl. It, too, looked like Madame Ouspenskaya.

"Now let's pull ourselves together and stop this," I said to everybody. "We've just simply got to get hold of ourselves. Now I must ask you to regard this as final: *No — more — children.*"

A fat lot of good my laying down the law was going to do, I thought to myself. I had learned that this crazy great-aunt of Nickie's, who lived alone in a huge house where it was rumored she spent her evenings stitching obscene needlepoint, had offered to give the young couple a bonus of a thousand dollars for every child they had. A standing offer. Now I could never retire without wondering, as I hurried past the Shermans' closed bedroom door, whether some fumbling lark in the dark might not at that very moment be compounding the miserable errors of existence. I could not police this place forever! I decided to put my foot down once and for all.

We were looking at television in the main living room, the five of us adults, one evening. We were watching all the junk there was, to see where Nickie had gone wrong. "He needs a good kick in the tail," I muttered to my wife in the gloom. "There's a time and a place for everything," she whispered back as she clawed the rind from an orange. When there was a brief pause for station identification, I rose and gave my belt a hitch. "I'd like to talk to you," I said to Nickie. "Come to the silo."

"For some more corn?" he said with a guffaw, as he followed me to the library. Was his own humor beginning to thicken up? That would certainly be a step in the right direction. Nevertheless, I was ready for him with a no-nonsense attitude when he sauntered into the silo. I was planted squarely before the mantel with my feet apart, having hurried ahead a little so I could be striking that tableau when he entered.

"So now you're a father," I began with just the proper blend of astringency and sentiment.

"Yes," he said. "It's a great experience. It's already knit Lila and me closer."

66

"It's knitting us all closer!" I gave back to him. "That's what I want to talk to you about. Our little *ménage à* — I make it *huit*, now."

"Not that we needed it. We've always had that fine respect for one another's — oh, call it one another's Individuality that true love is based on."

Hm, true love. Another good sign of schmaltz. I watched my man as he browsed along a row of German philosophers my father had left behind. Nothing had been touched here since the day of his death.

"Have you ever read Rilke's *Letters to a Young Poet?*" Nickie asked.

"Steady," I said, backing into the mantel stone to scratch the itching spot which I had inherited from my father along with this house in which I ruled.

"*Der Liebe die darin besteht, dass zwei Einsamkeiten einander schützen, grenzen und grüssen.*"

"You don't know what you're saying."

"Love consists in this, that two solitudes protect and touch and salute each other."

"Rilke, Schmilke," I said, attempting to recover the offensive. "You don't have to tell me it's congested around here. Now here's what I've done." I drew a long breath which had the quality of a gun being loaded and cocked. "I talked to old man Nothnagle today, and it turns out luckily that he needs an all-around esthetic handy man for his department store. You know — window dresser, sectional decorations, one thing and another. How would that suit you, eh? . . . Ah, I thought you'd find it rather amusing. I took the liberty of putting in a word for you."

"Thanks a lot. Yes, it might be worth a whirl. I'll go see old man Nothnagle."

67

Nickie's maiden window was a crate of rich stuffs turned open on its side and its contents sprawling higgledy-piggledy toward the glass: the art of the haphazard. Old man Nothnagle saw him from the street as he was touching up the disarray, getting the right note of easy dishevelment, and rapped on the glass. "Keep in heaven's name the curtain *shut* till you're finished," he called, gesticulating. "It is finished," Nickie informed him. The display, he pointed out, was in the tradition of understatement, very like something he'd once seen in a Lord and Taylor window on one of his trips to New York, as a matter of fact. That had been simply a gored bale of cotton signalizing the washable print season to all who had eyes to see.

"It's what they call inverted snobbishness," Nickie explained to Nothnagle, who was now dancing with passion.

"That's all right for Fifth Avenue," Nothnagle said. "Our customers like things pretty. Get those dummies in there and put the aprons on them. And you might go and get some leaves to tack up. That's always nice."

Nickie's next conception was even more abstract: a single vase from the ceramics department set on a width of black velours. Pedestrians thought the Nothnagles had had a death in the family (as they damn near did when Nothnagle with his bad heart clapped an eye on it) and that the store was closed. Nickie was shifted to the toy department and put to work demonstrating a Tinker Toy. He was a charming success, but after the holidays toys went dead and he was switched, in a kind of free association of the management's own, to furniture-easily-assembled. But that palled and we knew the end was near. Nickie was fired one morning for telling the sectional manager, "There is nothing so monotonous as unrelieved novelty."

Now it was imperative that some hard, cold thinking be

done. I did it — and reached a conclusion that took my own breath away.

The answer to the question, "What ought Nickie to do?" had been under our noses all these years. We'd missed the trick because it was so obvious. The solution came to me like a kind of epiphany. I got the inspiration in the morning and phoned him right away to come down to my office at the newspaper, which was where I was when the light struck. We agreed on half past two.

He was punctual. He drifted in and asked *was los* was. My own mood was no longer so buoyant. Tension over the approaching interview, which I sensed to be absolutely critical for both of us, had given me a bad headache, and his knock on the door had found me searching under my desk for my last two aspirin, dropped as I'd nervously fished them out of their tin. On raising my head to call "Come in!" I'd cracked it an awful one on the underedge of the desk. I skipped the aspirin as my headache was now so splitting, fore and aft, that I knew they wouldn't touch it anyhow.

"Have a seat," I said, waving to a leather club chair I had for visitors who came to see me in person about their problems.

A fresh copy of the day's edition of the *Pick*, folded open to my column, lay on the chair, and Nickie couldn't get out of glancing at it a moment before setting it aside. It featured an anecdote which ran:

There was once a great artist who got into his canvases a red so dazzling that painters from many lands came to look and to marvel. How did the man achieve such a crimson? No pigments known to them contained it. It was only on his deathbed that the artist revealed his secret. Into the squeezed-out paints he mixed — a drop of his own blood. . . . If there is anything to be extracted from allegories, we know what we can extract from this: that the secret of success is, *Put something of yourself into your work.*

Nickie hitched a leg up over the arm of his chair and settled back.

"I notice you've got yourself a pair of glasses," he said, looking, not at the glasses on my desk, but at the indentations in the bridge of my nose. "Let's see how you look in them."

"So you think," I said, donning the spectacles to humor him, "that you might make a good detective."

"*What?*"

"We've had it under our noses all the time and never realized it. This brilliant knack for observation; that keen, analytical mind . . . How could we have kept your light under a bushel all these years?"

"Is this what you called me down to say?"

"Inclinations are there as well as the talent," I continued, bustling round a file to adjust a window blind, "and maybe you've *been* realizing it, moving toward it, all along. Sub-consciously, I mean. The detective in *Wise Acres* — your creation. And now this wonderful inspector in your new play, who shakes his pen out over the Dalmatian all the time!" Since my spectacles were for reading, I had a little trouble getting him into focus. So it was over their rims that I fixed him as I finished: "You could be another Fabian of the Yard."

The alacrity with which he'd acceded to suggestions we knew were only stopgaps was missing. He rose and walked to the window, where he stood looking thoughtfully down into the street three floors below. He scratched the foil from a roll of fruit drops. "Do you really think so?" he asked indifferently.

An ambition had indeed, I sensed, been born in him. An enlargement, say, of our old dream of dexterity, a sort of private ideal too intimate for him to discuss (as I might have put it in one of the paradoxes for which I had used to be sent up to my room) in any way but casually. I, however, pressed the point with zest. I asked his leave to let me think of him as one who would indeed always find "some way incomparably light and deft," as our old friend Eliot had put it; to preview his destiny as unfolding under skies more splendid than we had yet dreamed, and in this most glittering of contemporary lights. Oh, I could see him in his coming prime, summoned at midnight to decipher the hieroglyphs of violence; stirring from funks as fabulous as Flaubert's to resolve perplexities in a dressing gown.

"It so happens Frank Carmichael, our Chief of Police, is a friend of mine," I said. "I got to know him well in my reporter days, and I'd be more than glad to — "

"Oh, come now," Nickie said, extending the fruit drops to me. I declined them with a shake of my head.

"You'll go far, but of course you'll have to start at the bottom. You'd *want* to start there: the experience on a city plain-clothes force would be terrific. I mean a doctor begins as an intern, a lawyer chases — "

"You know this Carmichael well?" Nickie asked, grinding up the last of a fruit tablet in his fine teeth. He immediately tucked another between them, and then with his thumbnail prised a third lozenge away and offered it to me as being of another flavor than that which I had rejected. I shook my head again.

"Frank is a prince. Hiring in this city is open and above-board, but that doesn't mean that a word dropped into the right ear by someone with influence . . . I mean you'd go on to become a brilliant detective, but meanwhile it'll be a job you can support a family on, with a steady income on a city payroll, with regular increases for years of service and a pension for your widow. Well, what do you say?"

"Perhaps I can discuss it with the Captain over lunch one day."

"Frank takes his lunch. So unless you feature carrying one of your own to his office and sitting down there and eating it with him, why, forget that part of it. I think the way to go about it is for me to take you down to headquarters and introduce you personally."

"Why don't you make a date with him then, if that's what you want?"

"How's tomorrow afternoon at three?" I asked. That being the time for which, squaring my jaw, I had already set up the appointment before his arrival.

"That will be O.K."

"Done and done. I'll stop by the house for you at two-thirty. And if I don't get a chance to talk to you about this later, for God's sake be on your toes. This can be the turning point of your life."

I paused a moment to regard my brother-in-law, who presented once more, from the window, a dorsal view. I had removed my glasses some time ago, but had been fiddling and gesturing with them ever since. Now I set them down on my desk. Then, going over to where Nickie stood looking into the street, I slung a hand rather urbanely round his shoulder and said: "Whatever one's lot in life is, one ought, you know, old boy, to build something on it."

Six

DRIVING NICKIE down to headquarters in my Olds, I chatted about an article I'd read on interplanetary travel.

"There's more than an even chance we'll go to the moon in our time," I said.

"What for?"

"What?"

"What does anybody want to go to the moon for?"

"I feel we've been put on this earth for a purpose," I said, trying to control my temper. What the hell did I care whether anybody went to the moon, or when? I was only trying to make conversation. I was tense over the impending interview, with another of those headaches that fought aspirin four ways. Nickie seemed a bit mumpish, possibly out of a feeling that he was being railroaded. He had on a green corduroy hat of Alpine derivation and a tweed jacket from a pocket of which protruded a volume of Sartre which he had been commissioned to review for a quarterly which had meanwhile become defunct. He had the blackthorn walking stick along but I made him leave it in the car. That was for later, when he had arrived. That was for when he would be retained by a family of means anxious to prove that the father had not been a suicide, or flown to England to examine the spot where a village postman had been beaten to a jelly on the moors above Ipswich.

Captain Carmichael's office was of the kind that is known as comfortably cluttered. Sunlight slanting through Venetian blinds lay in bars of dusty gold across a carpet from which the figure had long since been trampled. Carmichael's scoured face rose like a moon over a parapet of papers on his desk as we were shown in. He was of medium height and wore a suit of a shade of brown resembling a mustard of intermediary strength. After introductions and handshakes he was a few minutes removing stacks of paper from his desk to the floor, so as to make himself visible in his swivel chair. "Cleaning out a lot of old records. Takes forever," he said.

"Frank's not afraid of work — he'll go to sleep alongside of it any day," I said.

"You old bastard," Carmichael returned with a grin. "Still the same old goofer." We had a few reminiscent didoes while Nickie turned to inspect a series of etchings of noted cathedrals. Then Carmichael asked what he could do us for.

"Well frankly, Frank, I want to get this boy off my hands," I began humorously. "I can't make a move but he knows where, can't turn my back but he knows what I'm up to. I figure get the pest into something where his talents'll be taken up eight hours a day where they belong, and maybe he'll get his eagle eye off yours truly. Seriously, though, the thing is he's been running a small business, sales agent for more lines than you can shake a stick at, but he's so damned — modest may not be the word exactly — and from what I read in the papers police forces are *after* a better type of personnel. Won't you bear me out on that, Frank?"

"Yes, I will, Chick. We're endeavoring to attract a better grade of apple. We definitely need new blood." Carmichael

74

unsheathed a fresh pack of cigarettes from its cellophane and looked at Nickie. "Had any previous experience at all along those lines? House dick or anything?"

Nickie was watching the Captain's hands.

"Had your after-lunch snort at Steve Kitchell's, Captain?" he interjected, crossing his legs and leaning back in the chair he sat in.

Carmichael regarded him blankly. I sprang into action.

"Oh, come now, Nickie, how in the world could you know that?" I said, my eye on Carmichael.

"Simple matter of deduction." Nickie pointed to the cigarettes the Captain was opening. "They tell me the whole story."

"Surely you must be fooling," I said, watching Carmichael like a hawk. "Nobody could be that observant, acute, quick to draw logical conclusions from insignificant details that would escape other people and I don't know what all. Tell us how you figured it out."

"There are two pennies in the cellophane wrapper. It is the method by which cigarette vending machines give you your change of a quarter. Steve Kitchell's is the only place around here that would be likely to have a vending machine. *Ergo*, the Captain undoubtedly got them there."

"But how does that prove he *drank* anything at Kitchell's? Explain that."

"You will observe that the ashtray on the Captain's desk has only two cigarette butts in it. At three o'clock in the afternoon, that means he's anything but a heavy smoker. He'd never be 'dying for a smoke,' and so it's unlikely that he'd go *out* just for cigarettes. But he might pick some up if he happened to be in a place that had them. Such as a tavern."

I laughed and shook my head, to confess myself utterly

75

floored. "If you knew what it was living with this man! Nothing gets by him."

There was a sense, however, of Captain Carmichael's not yet having been heard from. The cigarettes now lay on his desk, nor was he smoking. He sat in his swivel chair with his hands clasped behind his head, estimating the caller.

"Go to Biddle?" he asked at last.

"Yes, I went to Biddle High," Nickie answered.

"They stop teaching them manners there?"

"What do you mean?"

"I don't see that a shot now and then is anything to apologize for; certainly not anything for anyone else to put their two cents into — speaking of that amount of money." Carmichael's eyes, normally the lusterless gray of pellets of chewed gum, glittered sharply. I rolled mine to the ceiling.

"He doesn't mean it that way, Frank," I said, maneuvering my way around behind Carmichael where I signed to Nickie with a slicing motion of my hand to cut it short, drop this method of approach. "What he means is that most people see but do not observe. You know — inference. So important in criminal detection. And he's not saying but what you only had a glass of beer."

"No, I rather think the vehemence of the Captain's response rules that out. I'm afraid we must lean to the theory that it was for schnapps that he called on Mr. Kitchell," Nickie put in affably.

I shook my fist and made a mouth at him over the Captain's head. Then strolling once more into view of the latter I said, "Of course he's pulling your leg. He knows the police aren't supposed to drink on duty. Heh heh heh."

That did it. Or it might have if Nickie hadn't put in, "The Captain wouldn't have been on duty during lunch hour. He

76

usually, of course, takes his lunch, but he didn't, I notice, today."

"That boy!" I struck my brow in what was now quite bona fide despair. "Come now, Nickie, how did you know that?" I asked, playing to the bitter end the role for which I had long ago lost all stomach.

"No paper in the wastebasket. And no lunch pail in evidence."

By now it had been borne in on the recovering Carmichael what this was all about, and he took it in somewhat better part. He understood at last that he was "auditioning" an applicant. Swinging from side to side in his swivel chair, his hands still laced behind his head, he sat assessing the talented prospect.

"I suppose what you had in mind was something in plainclothes," he said, taking in the pink shirt, black knit tie and Tattersall vest for which this term would have to do.

"That is correct."

Carmichael sat a moment tugging thoughtfully on a verdant eyebrow. Then he rose and, crossing the room slowly with his hands in his pockets, said:

"Decency has eighteen men on the detective bureau and we're thinking of expanding it to twenty or more. Yes, we need new blood. There's a future in this growing town, sure enough." The Captain paused and studied Nickie again — as did I, only I was wishing Carmichael would stop using that word "blood" all the time. "There's of course tests to pass, physical and others, and, assuming he'd do all right on them, which I see no reason why he shouldn't, why, yes, I'd be personally happy to see a fellow of his caliber in the department."

"Done and done," I said, reaching for my hat, which hung on a rack.

"There's just one thing." Carmichael pulled his eyebrow a moment again, and looked at the floor. "See, we have a rule, a kind of seniority. See, I can't hire my detectives cold. They have to advance to that point."

I was uncertain. "You mean . . . ?"

"I can only promote them there from my boys in blue."

Nickie was on his feet and reaching for his own hat. "In that case we needn't waste any more of one another's — "

"Now wait! You wouldn't have to be a cop long. It's just a formality. I'm the one who kicks them upstairs and I can kick them anywhere, including on to a special training at the National Academy in Washington. You could go far," the Captain said, shouting now, for Nickie had already gone far: he had sailed out the door into the hall. "I could almost guarantee, I might even personally — "

On the sidewalk, it was Nickie who led the way this time and I who galloped in his wake. I trailed him with preachments, taunts, Pepigrams, anything that came to my mind as I addressed that adamant back.

"Can't get started for fear of failure," I said. Then: "There are dreams we must follow, others we must wake up from" — backsliding to a less modish day as I grasped for ammunition. Then (satirically): "Quite a hustler when you're running away, aren't you?" Then nothing for fifty feet. I swung from side to side of that brilliant chap, expostulating with spread hands like a merchant of ideas, and always a step behind. "You're driving me crazy. There was once a farmer who was advised on the latest scientific methods by a representative of Uncle Sam. At last he said to the government man, 'Don't bother to advise me. I ain't farming as well as I know how to now.' Are you that farmer . . . ? *Just a minute! I will be heard!*"

We had passed my parked Olds and I went back for it,

78

letting the genius fly on. I turned the car around in the street in a series of violent maneuvers, caught up with him and continued the guerrilla warfare from inside it. Slowing at the curb, I cranked the window down and hooted through it: "All wishbone and no backbone just about says it for you, brother! And I'll tell you one more thing. You'll get out of my house and not set foot inside it again until you've got a steady job. That's final. I believe this is yours." And I flung through the window the blackthorn stick which I had edited out of his getup earlier in the afternoon.

Now he was within an inch of being a cop. For God does indeed write straight with crooked lines, as the Portuguese proverb has it. Nickie ran a bookstore for a few months with backing from his aunt and some financial chaperoning from myself, and it was in that brief loop in the divine beeline that I was gathered into a train of events bearing us on to theft, blackmail, adultery, and some days in hell for everybody. Oh, Nickie Sherman got his chance at Euclidean logic all right, but in forging its propositions for the Captain he cooked my goose. That would never have happened had it not been for the bookstore; more particularly, had I not left my office and dropped in for a look at the books (not the ones for sale) at the precise moment when a woman named Mrs. Thicknesse was on her way there too, to ask for one that was. What makes life seem such a rigmarole is its being a whole. But it is only after a private or domestic ruin that the elements leading to its manufacture can be seen coming together, as, from the vantage point of the chastened present, I can see ours coming together now, and even, in the corporate peace of restitution, begin to savor them a little.

Nickie's view of a bookstore was that of a place where

79

ideas were exchanged, not merely merchandise sold, and among the hangers-on at his were a youth named Rupert Blue who was writing a novel about an impotent stallion, a sort of allegory of our time, entitled *Poor Splendid Loins*; an in-between kind of artist (he was better than a Sunday painter but hanging was too good for him); and a burgeoning composer whose name I have also forgotten, who claimed to have first heard and been unable to stand Bartók, then liked him, and finally outgrown him, all in the course of a single composition. He felt himself personally to be going a step beyond current modernity while at the same time taking one back to his native American roots, just as Bartók had for inspiration to his native Hungarian folk rhythms. He was at work on a Western Suite one movement of which, for instance, was marked *Pronto.*

I had but to enter the shop to send any or all of these scuttling, and I sent them all scuttling when I went in to look at the ledger. I was browsing over it when the front door opened and this Mrs. Thicknesse walked in. She wrote musical criticism for the *Pick*, and I knew her to nod at, from the few times I'd seen her bringing her copy to the office. We exchanged nods now and I returned with a frown to the ledger, which showed a profit of nineteen cents for the month.

Out of one ear, I heard Mrs. Thicknesse ask for the latest novel by a writer of historical romances, and Nickie answer that he didn't have it, in a way that hinted that he *wouldn't* have it.

"It's a best seller," Mrs. Thicknesse reminded him somewhat stiffly.

"Not alone that — " Nickie began in explanation of his viewpoint, but I clapped the ledger shut and revolved smilingly into view.

"I'm sure Mr. Sherman can get it for you, Mrs. Thicknesse," I said, removing and pocketing my cheaters.

"Of course I'll get it for Mrs. Thickness if she likes," Nickie chaffered from a hot plate on which he was brewing tea, "but I'll have it on my conscience. How about a cup of tea, Mrs. Thicknesse, and we'll talk the whole thing over. Here's a novel I like, just out. It's about a Southern girl and a young schoolteacher who, entrusted with her defloration — "

"Why oughtn't Mrs. Thicknesse read the book she asked for, eh, Nickie?" I asked. Having drawn his attention with these words, I shook my fist at him from behind a stack of volumes which screened me from Mrs. Thicknesse. "I can well understand this taste for historical novels," I then chatted remedially, sauntering into view of the latter again. "They recreate a bygone era into which we can escape from the tensions of our own. What century does your man write about this time, eh, Mrs. Thicknesse?"

"The eighteenth," Mrs. Thicknesse replied a shade loftily.

"For a picture of the eighteenth century, read Fielding," Nickie said. "These historical novels today," he continued, pouring hot water into the teapot and all down my neck and shoulders, "are supposed to be reflections of other eras, but in reality they are reflections on our own." He felt the conversation to be going well; this was what a bookstore should be, a place where ideas were aired, ruminations gracefully traded over cups of tea, in an atmosphere of civilized ease. Not so I, off whose hide this was skin just as much as it was off his aunt's, though indirectly.

"Have you *read* this author your customer is asking for?" I asked him with a wink at Mrs. Thicknesse, who smiled back at me under tautening nostrils.

81

"Yes," Nickie said. "He combines the humor of Dreiser with the tragic insights of P. G. Wodehouse."

"Don't go, Mrs. Thicknesse! Mrs. Thicknesse — " But she *had* gone, and I turned on Nickie a face from which the color had drained. "I swear I have *never* in all my *life* . . ." I said in a rapture of exasperation. "And what's more I won't put up with it any longer. You think you're being idealistic about everything but you aren't. You've got to take people and things as they *are*. Surely this town can support another bookstore. There's a great hunger for books in this country."

"The more hunger, the less taste."

I wished I had said that, and so there was real anger in my voice as I answered, "*When* will you grow up!" — and clapping my hat on my head, darted through the door in pursuit of Mrs. Thicknesse, to tell her we would be glad to order the volume in question.

More of that in a moment. Suffice it to say here that we closed the bookstore when Lila had another baby, and, tiring by now of doing without, threatened to leave Nickie if he didn't get a steady job. Meanwhile, the seeds of my salesmanship had begun to do their work, and the life of a sleuth secretly to tantalize him, so much so that he was finally prepared to swallow its requisite preliminary — a brief apprenticeship in blue.

Thus it was that the trio principal to this were once again assembled in Captain Carmichael's office, to which Nickie had flown on the first glimpse of himself in uniform — for a clarification of the terms and some estimate of the speed with which he could get out of it. What was there for the Captain but to say that he would keep an eye on him and kick him upstairs the minute he could; and for the Lamplighter but to remind him that promotion was two-thirds motion? The Captain circled his new rookie for inspection as the latter stood stiffly, then sat despairingly, in the middle of the room; the Lamplighter, sitting on the window sill with his legs hanging down, slipped his hands under his thighs and beamed approval of the scene. It was the moment for which he had waited, a dream come true.

"How soon will I be eligible for nomination to this Academy you say you can get me a scholarship to?" Nickie asked. That was the F.B.I. special training school in Washington, concerning which I had earnestly besought Carmichael to keep using the terms "academy" and "scholarship."

"Everybody has to cut his eyeteeth," the Captain said. "You wouldn't expect to get a Ph.D. no more'n you matriculated, would you?"

Nickie dug out his nightstick which had got wedged under one haunch. "I believe I saw a statement of yours in the paper recently about the trouble you have getting young men to go into police work. These lures aren't part of your *modus operandi*, are they?"

"What are you talking about? And isn't this better than burying yourself in some damn burg like New York and having all that corruption to buck?"

"Meanwhile there's the transfer to plain-clothes, of which, of course, you have given me your word," Nickie reminded him as he rose and walked to the window. A sudden sense, from it, of the public daylight he would daily have to brave sent a shudder through him. "This uniform is traumatic."

"They can alter it. Where does it bind, or whatever?"

The Captain closed the interview by extolling the beat for which Nickie was to report for duty at eight the next morning, under the guidance of a veteran patrolman named Pilsudski. He sent him off with a hearty handshake and an earnest "Good Luck."

I was by Nickie's side as, setting his face like steel, he marched down the station-house stairs to the sidewalk. There his spirit failed him, and he gasped "Get me a cab," which was the way he had come. "No," I said, "walk in it *now*. I'll stay with you for a bit. I'll watch with you one hour."

"I can never do it. There's Mrs. Sleet, our high-school teacher."

"It isn't either. You're getting hallucinations. Now pull yourself together!"

We took a turn around the block, a sort of dry run. I had to support him. He said his sensation was like that of dreaming you are walking naked in public, only more so. "You'll get over it," I said. I told him that my faith in his future had never been more firm, nor my pride in his courage more keen, than this hour. I assured him that I would always walk his beat with him in spirit if not in fact, and that I would stake my professional reputation on the counsel which had brought him to it. "After all, Vocational Guidance is part of my field." Then I said it was time he went it alone, and, enjoining him to avoid all agitation and to faint not, I took leave of him with every good wish and hope for an early fruition to these proceedings. "Praise waits for thee," I said, gripping his arm with great emotion. "Go."

He shot from my grasp and went, as one well might who had the sensation he had described, as fast as his legs could carry him without actually running; till he realized that nobody was paying him the least mind, while he himself was shuttling through the crowds more furtively than perhaps became a cop, and slowed down. He practiced strolling, as though already on his beat. Standing there watching him, I remembered his having once called Life "a carnival at which one should throw the balls at the prizes." "How about two?" I'd asked him, for he was courting my sister at the time.

84

"What?" he'd said, and I'd explained: "These epigrams are all about what 'one' should do. What if there are two? What are they supposed to throw the balls at?" Then there'd been three, and now of course there were four Shermans. But I had no doubts about the idealist — he would come through in the end. He strolled convincingly out of sight, already "picking 'em up and laying 'em down," and I suppose the rest of the afternoon passed without incident for him.

Not so for me. As I spanked my hands together, like a man who sees a job well done, or at any rate well launched, as Nickie's figure melted into the noonday throngs, I saw materializing from those across the street a figure also, by now, familiar. It was that of Mrs. Thicknesse. I hurried over to greet her.

Seven

I HAD CAUGHT up with Mrs. Thicknesse, the day she flounced out of the bookstore, about half a block away. I pursued, in that interval, an imperially borne cornshock figure of a woman somewhat in excess of medium breadth but with the height to carry the surplus, and dressed, in addition, with such a fine sense of requirements — she was all nip and tuck in an azure summer print — that I slowed appreciatively a moment. But at last I was abreast of her, hat off, and apologizing for my brother-in-law. "Oh, it's all right," she answered with a laugh, "I suppose he meant well. I talked that way when I was his age, too." "So did I," I said, half in a comic nuance not entirely clear to me, half out of the true calcification that had already overtaken me as a result of my being Lamplighter.

Mrs. Thicknesse gestured to a black Rolls-Royce parked at the curb and said, "May I drop you?" "Yes," I said, an instinctive desire to ride in a Rolls limousine relegating as secondary the question of where I was going. I opened the back door for her to get in, at the same time glancing about for a chauffeur. "No, the front," she said, and, going round, sprang in behind the wheel herself.

I got in beside her and she slipped that automobile into gear and glided smoothly into the stream of traffic.

"Your chauffeur off today?" I asked, neglecting as best I

could the stares of the curious coming in at us from all sides.

"I have no such thing. It seems to me an obscenity to be driven about when one is able-bodied. Don't you agree?"

"Absolutely," I said, sliding down a little in the seat.

She piloted us deftly around and past a prowl car, honking at the cops in it as we went by for some stupid move or other they had made. I slouched down farther in the seat, also dipping my hat over one eye. I could sense us sliding among the flanks of autos less princely than ours but not therefore any less aggressively driven, and at last I peered gingerly out over the window ledge. "This is the rush hour," I observed keenly. Suddenly confronted, eight inches from mine, by a phalanx of massed faces looking in at me from a bus stop, I submerged again. The aristocratic life was evidently not for me.

With Mrs. Thicknesse it was patently otherwise. She dilated on a variety of themes and I learned, in the course of our brief journey, a number of her cherished peeves. They included abstract Christmas cards, clocks embedded in cubes of lucite, and fiction in which the emotion is obliquely revealed. I peeped out again to take our bearings. Mrs. Thicknesse asked, "Where is it you're going?" Just then I spied the familiar shopfront of the Greek's. "There," I said, pointing to it.

"Oh, that's that wonderful old ice-cream parlor I've heard about. I've always been meaning to visit it. Do you know the proprietor well?" she asked. And I suppose because the death wish is strong in all of us, I answered, "Yes. Would you like to stop in for a soda?"

Mrs. Thicknesse backed the Rolls into a line of parked cars with unforgivable skill. As I crawled out I saw a newspaper on the back seat, open at the financial page on which was a story caption saying that cocoa prices had eased but had stiffened later.

It had been hot as hell for days and was muggy even in the normally cool interior of the Samothrace. My seersucker, of which in deference to my position as shirtsleeve philosopher I declined publicly to shed the coat, was limp and shapeless as a surgical habit. But not a rill of perspiration stained my lady's face. We ordered chocolate sodas, and as we bent over them we made hydraulic noises. Mrs. Thicknesse spoke a patois which on closer hearing turned out to be correct English: "Had I but been she," she would say, and "anyone's else" (could *that* be right?). As the ceiling fans whirled overhead, she imparted a further sense of her disfavors, adding to those of which she had already given notice, fabrics which are derived from legumes, store-window lettering from which the capitals are omitted, and eating matter produced by adding water to something. The desire to "rate" with so redoubtable a woman is natural, and some allusion of hers to popular thinking suddenly made it imperative that I know what she thought of me.

"Just what can any one person do to *better* this world?" I began, circling cautiously toward the subject. "Of course the way to improve it is to improve the people in it— that goes without saying. But should you try to *pull* people up from your level or get down there and *boost* them up from theirs? Becuz, because progress seems to me a tree up which we all help one another shinny." I sipped at my straws, watching Mrs. Thicknesse. "I don't know whether you've caught my stuff."

Mrs. Thicknesse nodded, sucking at her own straws. Then it was to be a cat-and-mouse: she would not yet be drawn out. I executed a series of retaliatory dance steps under the table, and wrote an obscenity on the roof of my mouth with my tongue. These are both expedients to which I resort in moments of stress. I said aloud:

"You have to take any approach the individual case calls for. The aim of modern — "

"More mere mechanistic rot."

I inscribed another off-color retort on the roof of my mouth. Mrs. Thicknesse was evidently a wing shooter, aiming, like a hunter, a little ahead of the ducks in flight so they would be there when her shot arrived.

"The semanticists," I said very rapidly, "have of course pointed out that thinking isn't the purely rational process we think it is but a form of *behavior* in which everything takes part, including the glands."

Mrs. Thicknesse discharged a small digestive bolt against the tips of her fingers. "Bologna," she said.

"Then there's the psychological approach."

"A snare and a delusion."

I scrawled a harrowing rejoinder with my finger on the knee of my trousers as Mrs. Thicknesse developed her point about science.

"It is a pack rat which, as you know, leaves something in return for what he steals from you but of considerably less value. It has taken our soul and left us a psyche — a zircon for a diamond. That's the trouble, the whole mess we're in. There's only one ideal," she continued earnestly, "that has enabled man to get as far as he has, and you know what that is." I busied myself spooning up a gobbet of ice cream. Mrs. Thicknesse stood out, clearly now, as one of those people in whose eyes one stands in mortal fear of flunking. "It's the aim to be greater than the sum of his parts."

"Naturally," I said, crossing my legs. "We have to keep that constantly in mind."

"But you can't do it on a psyche. You need the sense of a Soul for that."

I swallowed the spoonful of ice cream. Then I said, "My problem is, how to use that in my work? Now, for instance, I have a young fellow who's been probationed to me. Not just somebody who's written in for advice; no, this is somebody I've got quite under my wing. I'm one of the officers in this Big Brother Association you may know about," I said, referring to the cause for which Chickering had died on third, and which I had inherited along with my job. "He's robbed a candy store and a few other things like that. His name is Pete Cheshire, and how can I tell him to be greater than the sum of his parts?"

"You don't have to."

"What?"

"It isn't necessary to use those words," Mrs. Thicknesse smiled. "People don't have to *know* they're being more than the sum of their parts, any more than your chap had to know he was less than the sum of his when he stole something, thereby taking something from himself. Make him understand he's a *moral* being, don't in the name of God tell him he's maladjusted! I hope you haven't done that."

I dropped my eyes guiltily into my soda and said nothing. Anyhow, it was the case workers; they made me do it; I had to build on what they'd told Pete Cheshire before he got to me.

"These psychiatrists!" Mrs. Thicknesse said as though divining my reflections. "Trying to make people mature by puddling about in their infancies. Why don't they get people's minds off themselves, in order that they may have what is revealed unto babes and sucklings?" She ate a gob of her own ice cream, studying me, and at last said, "Have you read any of the Eastern philosophers?"

To answer affirmatively on the strength of the Chinese and Arabian proverbs in which I rummaged for fillips in which to package my counsels would be stretching a point. But Mrs. Thicknesse was so formidable, and my fear of flunking now so great, that I didn't dare admit complete ignorance. So feeling myself momentarily less than the sum of my parts, I answered, "Some."

"Not everyone can read the philosophers, of course, but those responsible for influencing others ought to drink at the purest springs."

"I thoroughly agree. Wasn't it Confucius who said that the first step toward learning anything is to know that we don't know anything?" I said, looking Mrs. Thicknesse squarely in the eye. Then I laughed and said, completely rhetorically, as I pulled a paper napkin out of the dispenser, "Maybe I ought to have *you* talk to Pete Cheshire."

"I should be happy to. When will you next see him?"

I looked over at the Greek, feeling he must come over and break this up if I was not to go out of my ever-loving mind. Nachtgeborn liked to stop at tables if given the least encouragement, and I managed to catch his eye and dabbed the paper napkin to my brow as a humorous comment on the weather.

He nodded. "Do you know how hot it is?" he chatted from the cigar counter at which he had been perfunctorily paging through a newspaper. There were no other customers in the place. "It's so hot I can smell the frames of my glasses."

"I believe it," I said. "How are things, Nachtgeborn?"

He pocketed his spectacles and shuffled over. I introduced him, and Mrs. Thicknesse complimented him on the flavor

91

of the soda and said it was a long time since she'd been in a bona fide ice-cream parlor. The Greek nodded and looked at the floor, pinching his nose. He had an announcement to make.

"I'm going to fix the old place up," he said.

Mrs. Thicknesse became instantly alert. "Just what do you mean?"

"Modernize." The Greek executed gestures of demolition and revision. "I'm going to tear out that and that and that. I'm going to get rid of that. I'm going to put in booths — "

"Hold on there." Mrs. Thicknesse moved her empty glass aside and folded her hands on the table. "Am I to understand that these wireback chairs and marbletop tables, that counter with its delicately decayed hues, like a fine old Camembert," she said, with gestures caressive where the Greek's had been dismissive, which put back everything the Greek had thrown out, "am I to understand that all these period pieces, the *mise en scène* of a time that will be no more, are to be scrapped in favor of garish booths covered in leatherette and trimmed with deplorable chromium?"

"Yeah, and upholstered in red I was thinking," the Greek beamed. He was tickled to death with the scope of the other's response.

I sprang into the act. I rolled my paper napkin into a ball between my palms and dropped it into my glass. "I have this to say to you, Nachtgeborn. That if you so much as lay a finger on this ice-cream parlor I shall never set foot in here again."

The Greek looked blank. "Why not?"

"Because, man, you'll spoil it."

"Spoil it." The Greek ran a baffled eye around his worn interior. "*This* place?"

"Certainly," Mrs. Thicknesse answered. "My dear man, don't you see that 'fixing this place up,' as you call it, would destroy something quite wonderful? Most nostalgic."

"That what that is?"

"Not a stick that doesn't delight the eye and refresh the spirit."

"How about that?" He pointed to a flaking mural of a maiden with bare feet and one fat braid, reading a love letter by a fountain about which doves flew, entitled "Tidings."

"That above all," I put in, for Mrs. Thicknesse and I operated as a team. Here was ground on which I could "pass" with her. "That's your *pièce de résistance*. Believe me."

"But isn't it what they call corny?"

"Precisely it's charm."

"Because it's olden times."

The Greek nodded, reappraising everything with a thoughtful pull on his lower lip. Then he pointed cattycorner across the street in a forensic way. "My competitor's been talking about modernizing. All new fixtures, a jukebox — "

"Jukebox!" The cry was torn from Mrs. Thicknesse and me simultaneously. She went on: "You mean you'd put in one of those horrors and throw out that nickelodeon? Surely you appreciate better than that what you've got here." Nachtgeborn listened with bowed head as Mrs. Thicknesse and I together scored the current dissolution into a plastic wasteland, and urged the Greek to resist the stampede by preserving at all costs the endearing bower that was his. "Let's hear that marvelous old thing," Mrs. Thicknesse said, giving him a nickel to put into the piano.

The strains of "In the Good Old Summertime" filled the room. Mrs. Thicknesse shut her eyes and rocked restrainedly to the oncoming rhythm. Lightly, she massaged the air with her fingertips. "How a sound like that mocks all our mechanistic civilization," she said.

"It takes a special mechanic from New York to repair it," I said.

She warily opened one violet eye, to judge if some irony had leaked into the discussion; decided it had not, and closed it again. I watched her. How old was she? Not yet forty. Thirty-five? She emitted a costly musk which, together with the deranging metallic squalls of the music, stimulated me to pieces.

I shifted nervously on my haunches to relieve the sense of glued trousers there, and just then the song came to an end. My companion opened both blue eyes and, drawing a sigh which inflated at length a bosom which it would be useless of me to deny was warm snow, smiled her great appreciation of the treat. She thanked me and gathered up her bag and otherwise assembled herself for departure. I said that I would walk home from here.

"Very well." She paused to take a drink of water from her glass, rolling her eye at me as she gulped. She set the glass back on the table. "This Pete Cheshire, when did you say it was you were to see him again?"

"Thursday night at eight. In my office."

I didn't think Mrs. Thicknesse would come. Pete Cheshire at any rate showed up on time. (He had been put officially in my custody by the probation officer, you understand, and had to report to me regularly.) I was standing at my office window looking down into the street below when I saw the familiar form in a tight suit and a brightly banded straw boater come into view. I heard him walking up the wide frame stairway to the third floor

94

and then his footsteps approaching down the hall to my door.

"Hello, Pete," I said, letting him in.

"Greetings. Greetings and a bit of a howzit."

"You look sharp tonight."

"Well, I'm working steady, and when you make it you might as well look it."

"Sit down."

I got into my swivel chair but Cheshire stood. Having hung his boater on a wall peg he drew a cigarette case from the breast of his coat, and from a pants pocket under its long skirt, a lighter. "Still working for that wrecking company?" I chattily began, watching him set fire to the fag. Cheshire nodded, sucking back a cloud of smoke.

"Yowzuh. It's nothing I'd care for permanently, but I appreciate your getting me the job, because I sure like the sound of things ripping apart." This was a leading reply designed to excite the words he loved to hear applied to himself — "sublimation," "vicarious," and the rest. They were not forthcoming now, the Lamplighter having wearied of this aspect of things. "Wanna make anything out of it?" he grinned invitingly.

"No, Pete," I said, with something of the granite smiling quiet with which Spencer Tracy has done his settlement work, blinking as I spoke, "we all have outlets of that kind. Me, I like to bowl. Sound of patterns being busted up and all." Cheshire's face fell at this hint of exile from a special category. "You're lucky you're getting your release from the work itself."

Cheshire took the leather club chair to which I had initially waved him, and with a pondering frown, another tack. "I have these awful guilt feelings about what I've done. You know what?" he went on when I declined the

95

gambit, "I get them *while* I'm doing wrong." And he looked at me as if to challenge me to tie that for intricacy.

I was consulting a dossier in a Manila folder open on my desk, which gave a rough history of this youth's exploits. The first had been panning pennies from a local wishing well, using his mother's flour sieve and wearing his father's hip boots at the age of nine. In late adolescence he had come under the sway of a certain Mike ("Agony") Lammermoor, so nicknamed because of the suffering he went through with and over women. Lammermoor was a connoisseur of billfolds but he was not averse to prospecting in shops after quitting time, and it was for one such job that the two had been convicted and sent up for six months apiece. I knew the story of Pete's meeting with Lammermoor by heart but I never tired of hearing it, so under the guise of excavating data for analysis I jogged him into telling it again. Lammermoor was probably the man I wanted more than anyone else to meet. Pete rose and struck a narrative tone.

"I'm standing on the corner of Updike and Ruby, minding my own business, when up walks this Damon Runyon character. He stems a smoke and we get to chewing the tallow, and first thing I know we're double dating a couple of snipe. Friends of his. He's interested only in the nighttime kitties with the choice cuts, which takes capital, so the first thing I know we're climbing in this store window. Like a fool, I should have stayed home. But there we were, and I gets this terrific guilt feeling right there on the job, also one hell of an anxiety. Crawling through the window it dawned on me, I said to myself, 'Pete, this is crazy. This is all wrong.' It dawned on me like anything." He cleaned the carbon from his nails with a file long enough to have sawed his way out of jail with, also extracted from under the skirt of his coat. I asked him just as a matter of interest which way he'd been crawling when the light struck him, in or out, and he answered, "Oh, out. But by that time it was too late, him having the boodle and all. The rest is in your report. What a guy goes through."

"Are you in touch with the Agony?" I asked.

"He writes me from stir, which he's in again, but I don't answer him."

"I wish you would, Pete. He may need your friendship, and besides," I said, closing the folder and setting it aside, "I'd like to meet him when he gets out."

"I'll see if I can arrange it. He never got in with the right crowd. Hey, you know why you and him might hit it off? He likes books."

"Perhaps we can have lunch one day."

Pete reached for his cigarette which he had left burning in one of the soup ramekins which constituted the management's idea of ashtrays. "That brings me to my subject." He took a last drag on it, and twisting it out said, "There's no future in wrecking unless you own the business, and I've got something else cooking. I'm supposed to report to you."

"Nonsense, I'm not your Sunday-school teacher, I'm your friend. If you want to tell me something man to man, shoot, Pete."

Cheshire frowned a moment. "I've always thought I'd like to run a restaurant. Oh, I don't mean just a place to put on the nosebag, I mean a place with — "

"Class."

"That's not enough." Cheshire tried to make himself clear. "The word restaurant fills me with a mood right away. I like the idea of night falling and of the town percolating all around me, into evening. I'm getting dressed and so are lots of others, good-looking men who will escort women in beautiful gowns with teeth as white as toothpaste, and some of them heading for my restaurant. Where they'll ask, 'Is Pete in yet?' A sophisticated place where the boss will be table hopping." His face clouded over and he said, "But what's the use dreaming? A man who's done a stretch hasn't got a chance. He's marked for life as a moral leopard."

"That's not true and I won't hear it," I said. "Of course you'll have your restaurant. I'll do all I can to help you."

"This idea of night, and people coming to where — Who's that?"

There had been a knock on the door and I rose to admit Mrs. Thicknesse. I was eager to have Pete resume his rhapsody about Night for her benefit, and, the introductions over, I said, "Mr. Cheshire is an acquaintance of mine, we were just talking over a business interest of his. Pete, maybe you've seen Mrs. Thicknesse's musical reviews in the *Pick*. Or do you care for music?" I slid a straight-back chair under Mrs. Thicknesse, who had declined the leather one Cheshire had offered her, on the ground that deep furniture was bad for one. "It mashes up the withins like a bag pudding," she declared. "Do you like music, Mr. Cheshire?"

"Music is the universal language. I osculate between jazz and the better, personally," Pete said, thoughtfully wrinkling what there was of his brow. "What I can't stand is this in-between, that sweet popular stuff."

"It's claptrap in the main," Mrs. Thicknesse agreed.

"Craptrap is right, and the main is just where it belongs." Cheshire navigated the room as he talked, twirling on his finger a keychain tethered to a trouser pocket. He had no end of winking gear. "The other day I heard a waltz by Wayne King. I threw up."

"You were quite right. It's not the true folk expression, as jazz is, but a bastard form."

"Bastard is right." Say, this dame was all right, Pete was thinking. "Guy Lombardo is another one."

I got Pete back on his Ode to Night, and pouring us paper cups of dry sack from a bottle I kept in my desk, soon had all our tongues a-wagging. There was a subtle balance of ingredients here. Pete Cheshire breathed a bracing air, which Mrs. Thicknesse clairvoyantly sensed herself to constitute: the social atmosphere that Cheshire, owing to obscure elements within himself, was driven to impress. She opened a window on his apocalypse. Pete's game, you see, was to be suave. As young men plan to go into medicine or law, he planned to go into suavity. The yeast that activated him was in reality the same as that which worked in Nickie Sherman, with whom he was about to match wits, and in myself too, for that matter. It was after all but the simple wish for worldly patina, so present in all of us in some form or other; in Pete's case movie-nourished, woman-haunted, bathed in swank; containing within the same circuit of associations a restaurant for smart people in which he would officiate in a tux, and a smoothie who might show up there, also in a tux, between feats of legerdemain at the customers' library safes. He could see himself in either role and the smallest shift in fate could send him into either; thus the Lamplighter was right in divining his ward to be where he considered him: at the forks.

"Of course I'll need backing," Cheshire said when he had reviewed his ambition for the newcomer.

Mrs. Thicknesse dug in her bag and gave him a hundred dollars. "Take this, Mr. Cheshire. A sort of start on all the

99

saving up you'll have to do. Take it and go thy way."

"How can I ever thank you?" Cheshire said, pocketing it. "I'll do all I can to justify your faith in me. I aim to run a mature restaurant where people can enjoy the group spirit."

"Never mind that," Mrs. Thicknesse said, as from behind her back I also gesticulated for Pete to lay off that. "It's your own spirit that's important, which if you lose it and gain the whole world, or even the local trade, you have nothing."

"Check."

I coughed, as to ask who was Lamplighter here. But it was to Mrs. Thicknesse Pete continued to give account; she who sent him off with a final word of blessing; she who watched his departure from the window as I had his arrival.

"Well!" I said ironically. "You certainly have a lot of faith in him."

"I have next to none." She turned back from the window. "It's usually too late to whip the crust back into the batter, despite what science would have us hope about remaking people in its image. You see I'm a skeptic — about science."

"Then why . . . ?"

"Bread on the waters. Call it that," she said with a smile. "Maybe it will come back after many days, maybe not." The room had begun to darken, and in the soft summer dusk her words took on a sad felicity. I lit no lamps. Every once in a while Mrs. Thicknesse drew a breath on purpose. She inhaled a lungful of air now as though conscious of ingesting a fraction of the universe, and sat down. "I have a great curiosity about people. I have a great curiosity about you."

I transferred my gaze to my blotter pad, resuming my own seat, and murmured some acknowledgment. In the muting

100

twilight I thought I had never seen a handsomer woman; everywhere persuasion of line for the journeying eye, a suppleness of posture and gesture subtly elongating, as it were, the work of a sculptor with his heart set on classic amplitudes. She had a perfection of tone about her, like that of ripe fruit. But of course there the resemblance ended, for Mrs. Thicknesse was voracious rather than edible.

"I'm so tired," she said, brushing eyes with finger tips. "So if you're not otherwise involved what about coming along home and listening to a little Chopin? I have the new Horowitz of the B-flat Minor."

As we glided smoothly toward the limits of the city, Mrs. Thicknesse deploring dianetics as she drove, I thought of Harry Clammidge, my boss, and chuckled nervously to myself. He had forbidden me to call love the lotus that turns into lettuce, forcing me to grind out the likes of, "A fellow has to pay for enjoying a woman's lips by forever after taking her lip." But now I felt the old *boulevardier* in me reawakened, given half a chance again. My wife at her mother's with the family car thought I was spending the evening bowling; no yokels gaped at us from the evening sidewalks, or very few. I was with a woman with whom I might taste again a citified communion, that paradox and nuance which I had loved long since and lost awhile, of which her own mot of a moment ago, about being a skeptic on the side of tradition, was indeed itself an earnest. That *Zeitgeist* which had been choked off in my youth was abroad again.

Mrs. Thicknesse was saying something astringent about human motives. Glancing negligently out the car window I remarked, "We know God will forgive our sins. The question is what he will think of our virtues."

It wasn't La Rochefoucauld, maybe, but then neither was she any Mademoiselle de l'Enclos. We must make do with one another, in adventures as in marriage. Still she turned and smiled at me. "That's rather neat," she said. "I didn't realize you were such a wit."

Mrs. Thicknesse lived in a large house just beyond the city's raveled end, where the country began. It was of white-washed brick, pleasantly scrawled with ivy. It had been remodeled often in its past, and was now an assemblage of added rooms and corners which clung to original sections like bridgework to surviving teeth. It was dark when we approached it from a twisting drive. I got out of the car and followed Mrs. Thicknesse who led the way into the house, snapping light switches as she went from room to room. The living room was done in tastefully chosen furniture from some bowlegged period, and as I stood taking it in a small French clock chimed ten o'clock. Bending to inspect a framed picture on the piano, I asked, "Your husband?"

"No, that is an early photograph of Rachmaninoff."

Mrs. Thicknesse got us some brandy — no more evidence of house servants than of a chauffeur — then went to a huge phonograph beside which were toppling stacks of records. I told her I wasn't terribly familiar with the B-flat Minor. She fixed that.

"Chopin's own comments about it are interesting," she declared. "Luckily we have some of the correspondence on it. 'I am composing here a Sonata in B-flat Minor in which will be the Funeral March you have already,' he wrote in 1839 from Madame Dudevant's. She was, of course, George Sand." I nodded, crossing the room to the sofa where I remained on my feet while Mrs. Thicknesse continued from the other end of the room on hers. "Much of Chopin's most brilliant work dates from his growing passion for the novelist. The first movement of this is an ingeniously developed étude . . ." She shifted her weight from one foot to the other as she stood beside the already revolving turntable, record in hand, as though patiently waiting for herself to finish. "The Scherzo is a thrilling dance whose somber tensions are relieved by a melodic middle section. The third movement is the celebrated Funeral March, and the concluding one is a Presto of tremendous eloquence and vitality."

She put the record on the turntable and set the tone arm in place.

We sat at opposite ends of the sofa, listening without speech. We leaned our heads back, Mrs. Thicknesse, on the whole, perhaps slightly more than I, and there was no stir between us for long periods. During the second movement, in the part where the somber tensions are relieved by a melodic middle section, her hand chanced to settle on the cushion between us, where one of mine already accidentally lay, so that our little fingers just touched.

Mrs. Thicknesse appeared unaware of it, and indeed the contact was so minute that she might very well have been; it was so microscopic that I had the sense of being joined to her by a single cell. It was the merest seed of sensation, there on our skin; sometimes I lost it, then there it was again, on the crust of one knuckle. I had the feeling of being myself *it*, of being reduced to an utter crumb of consciousness. The experience itself became at length monstrous.

The sonata over, we sat as we were while the needle rasped in its groove. Mrs. Thicknesse shook her head, the first to evict herself from our pentecostal trance. "What two hands can do," she said, as I went over to shut off the phonograph. I saw that there was some more Chopin and some Liszt on the other side of the record, a long-playing one of course. "How that sense of order and beauty mocks our mechanistic one."

"You don't realize it till you hear it on hi fi."

Mrs. Thicknesse rose. "Before going, would you like to play a little 'vingt-et-un'?"

"I'd love to. One should always be eager to do things about which one knows absolutely nothing."

"Don't tell me you don't know one's favorite game!" she chided, and, catching my hand, towed me into the back of the house where the dining room was. I chuckled again at what Clammidge might think if he knew that, instead of bowling, I had spent the evening trading niceties with his music critic and was going to finish it off with a little "vingt-et-un" — whatever that was.

"The object of the game is to obtain from the dealer such cards," said Mrs. Thicknesse as she dealt them across the dining-room table, "that the sum of their pips, or spots, is as near as possible to twenty-one, without exceeding it."

" 'Twenty-one'! Of course, I know that," I said, falling happily to. Like the man in Molière who learns that he has been talking prose all his life without knowing it, I discovered that I had been playing vingt-et-un all mine without realizing it. I liked the game a lot, played it with my wife as a matter of fact, under the name of "blackjack" as well as "twenty-one."

I read my face-up card, then took a peek at the face-down one. "Hit me lightly." Mrs. Thicknesse slid a nine of spades across the table and I was over and she gathered the cards laughingly back.

"Why, my husband is away a good bit of the time. Sometimes a year at a stretch," she told me. "South America mostly, where he has all sorts of interests — copper in Venezuela, a soft drink concession in Ecuador. One is practically an Enoch Arden widow."

"How much of the year is he home would you say?"

"Not more than a month or two all told, and he spends half of that taking pictures. One of your camera fiends. Not that I mind that, even as his longsuffering model. Oh, I'll not bore you by trotting any of them out. There are simply bales."

"I like to look at pictures," I said, frowning at my cards.

"Most of them are nude — studies, do you call them?"

"Hit me. . . . I don't mind. Hit me once more, ever so lightly. V*ingt-et-un!*"

Mrs. Thicknesse twisted around in her chair and looked off into a small anteroom. "Well, just a few then." She went into the anteroom and returned with a large green envelope from which photographs of every description cascaded when she overturned it.

They ranged from snapshots to cabinet-size, and were of everything from bisected leeks to empty doorways, but the bulk were of Mrs. Thicknesse and most of those were nudes. I had a furthered sense of the subject's moulding. I mean that even still I expected to find Rubens and encountered — perhaps not Cranach, but something remarkably close to it. The impression was in part fostered by the "stretching" effect that seemed to be the photographer's obsession: she was forever reaching over something, or toward something, or at something, like Eve aspiring toward an implied apple. There was one of her lying on her back with a knee arched up and one arm outflung above her head in a suggestion of lyric ruin. The eye was carried in one highlighted line from foot to chin, detained only by a soft sparkle, like a thistle of light, on one tinctured breast, and sent along the profile away to a dark smoke of hair. There must have been a rational explanation to all of this. This was the body linked by circumstance to that peculiar mind and that preposterous name; a body lying in smashed light or some damn-fool notion of vivisected space, left reaching for unincluded and probably unrenderable fruit.

"They're quite nice," I said, casually shuffling a sheaf of them into the deck of cards, on our resuming the game with me dealer.

"One should have a hobby," she said, noting my fumbles. "It's relaxing. Do you have any?"

"A hobby? Well, I used to do a bit of sketching," I said. "Charcoal and a little water color. I found that pleasant."

"As I did modeling. It *is* a change." She rose. "Would you like something to eat? There's some cold chicken I broiled yesterday and I'm kind of hungry myself." I said I'd love some and she went into the kitchen. "Well, if you ever need a subject . . ."

"Oh, I think not. Thanks just the same though."

"Nonsense," Mrs. Thicknesse said into the open icebox. "It would be no trouble."

"Well, I'm afraid — "

"I'm being quite honest with you. I enjoy modeling." She turned and smiled down the corridor into the dining room at me. She stood with her hand on the refrigerator door, silhouetted against a composition of cold viands, like Betty Furness on television. "It's perfectly the same as a hobby for me."

I laughed. "I'm only a Sunday painter."

"I understand. Would Thursday be a good day?"

"Thursday will be fine."

Eight

I HAD SET up my easel and was waiting for Mrs. Thicknesse. The room she had suggested might do handily for a studio was a large corner one with windows along two sides, on the second floor of her house. It was early afternoon and the light was rich. A couch covered with a length of Paisley stood in the widest window embrasure awaiting the model. I put a piece of drawing paper on the easel and got out some charcoal. The door opened and Mrs. Thicknesse entered, wearing a frown.

"I do hope it won't be too warm in here," she said, crossing the floor to the couch, on which she lay down. "It did turn a bit chilly and I put the furnace on this morning. Is this all right, for an attitude?"

"Your attitude is fine. Just make yourself comfortable. Lie any which way. It makes no difference."

I encouraged conversation as I worked, to induce relaxation in the subject and also to obtain those plays of animation that illuminate character to the artist. I coaxed her into speaking of what she liked rather than lamented, and there was a world of difference. At one point we got on the theme of immortality, in which she believed without being sure of its precise form. "There is no death," she said. "No, my dear lady, but there are funerals." My mouth was a taut "o" as I strove to record the living flow of the throat, a shoulder, the impact of dialogue on the human breast. Finding us momentarily back on her bugbear, psychology, I explained that nowadays a man in my profession often had the problems *reach* him in that fashion. A woman of eighty had written to me complaining that a son of sixty was still tied to her apron strings, and there had been nothing for me to advise but that she wean him forcibly away even at this late juncture, if it meant putting him in an old people's home. "Another woman wrote me letters for five weeks about her cleaning compulsion," I related. "What did you do about her?" the model murmured. "I washed my hands of it," I rather amusedly returned.

While the colloquies went swimmingly, the work in hand was another matter. Years of disuse had rusted a talent feeble at best, even for a Sunday painter. With cold tongs of fingers I evolved on the drawing paper a teat which was a criminal libel of the original, whose possessor lay stretched on her back, in turn, in a pulsing mockery of the craftsman. She was at her ease, but look at my position. The fact that I had gotten into this ridiculous trap to humor her was no help in getting out of it. I couldn't let the woman see what I was doing. Masking my inability to draw by dashing off something nonobjective would produce an even more insupportable result, because I had undertaken this work fully knowing my hostess's abhorrence of the vein.

"Oh, it won't come right," I said and, by way of displaying at least that facet of the creative spirit, tore what I had done into shreds and threw it in the fireplace. The charcoal followed for good measure.

"Would you like to take a turn through the garden?" Mrs. Thicknesse sat up with her arms clasped around her knees and regarded me as one who has a stake in another's mood.

Mrs. Thicknesse dressed and we did, coursing at random among its rustling shrubs in a way that was in keeping with the easy convolutions of our speech: for the upshot of the hour was cardinally to further one's reconstruction on Continental lines. The summer was cooling observably toward autumn, as the afternoon toward evening, prompting Mrs. Thicknesse, with a toss of a flannel scarf, to remark that the air was like wine. "That accounts for the nip in it," her young friend rejoined. Nothing much, you understand, just the small change of intellect we were jingling, not its gold coins. Up among the bypaths we went, and there was a brewing sense in it all, for me, of old remembered Henry James, of choked fountains starting, of muted desires and passions ranging in the afternoon. What infinities are in the mind! The idlest thought teems like a waterdrop with microscopic life, and no day's awakening but renews that long symbolic dream that is as dense and haunting as the sequences we know to be compressed into a wink of sleep. I was not oblivious to the air of financial weal my lady breathed, that sense of real money that lubricates so much. I dallied secure in the knowledge of not being expected home for dinner, and of being regarded as bowling after that, as on Thursday last. The name of Thomas Wolfe was dropped, and swinging a birch stick I had picked up from the grass, I said, "If it must be Thomas let it be Mann, and if it must be Wolfe let it be Nero, but let it never be Thomas Wolfe." This of course my friend appreciated as a paraphrase of the old Viennese coffee shop mot, "If it must be Richard let it be Wagner, and if it must be Strauss let it be Johann, but let it never be Richard Strauss."

I divined in her mood, as she took my arm with a shiver of pleasure and the leaves overhead went *shrdlu, shrdlu,* that blend of peace and disturbance which comprised my own. "I like crowds, people," she said, "but true intercourse is possible only between the pair."

"That's so true," I answered. "I believe Emerson has said something of the sort, though of course his choice of words is slightly different."

It's hard to isolate the elements that went into our rather complex relationship. In part, Mrs. Thicknesse undermined me by praising the character in my face. Which compliment did not precede by long my head's landing in her lap. We twisted tassels with voluptuous woe, listened to Sibelius with an air of shipwreck. We had our chocolates, sadness, kisses. Mrs. Thicknesse, apart from being rather more interesting than was really necessary, was a most attractive specimen of her sex. In part, she deepened our bond by ostensibly formalizing it.

Among the vanished graces mourned by Mrs. Thicknesse was letter writing. What was it that made the great friendships of history seem that but the very epistolary woof in which they have come down to us? Letter writing was communion, phone calls mere communication, and that further alloyed by "Is so and so there? Oh, this is just a friend of his. No, no message." Too, in privacy one pulls out stops at which one might in person shy. "How beautiful you looked as the Palestrina flowed remorselessly on last evening," the Lamplighter wrote to Mrs. Thicknesse in the winter of that year, when his work was going poorly and he sought repeated refuge in her home. (The *Pick* had dropped its "Musical Notes," so we never met in the offices there any more.) "You have not only a good ear but a lovely one," he wrote in the spring of the next. And in a lighter vein: "You ask whether I ever observe Lent. I do, from a distance, and find it one of the more diverting aspects of the human pageant." So I sat scratching away like Voltaire in the office in which I received my replies, thinking that some of this seemed as good as a lot I'd read in "collected correspondences." It happened that the Swal-low-Thicknesse exchanges, too, were destined for a wider audience than its parties — thanks to those two great editors, Cheshire and Lammermoor — but that was still some months off. Now the Lamplighter's one disquiet was his wife — for it was useless of me to go on pretending that it was Clammidge I was two-timing. To make it up to her, I gave over my entire fantasy life to her, so that she was its heroine rather than I its hero.

I wish to comment.

If you think that small amends, try gathering wool for somebody else sometime. Just try it. For the Self, which activates all revery, naturally clamors that it be wish-fulfillment. What my restitution consisted in was imagining sequences in which my wife outdid both me and Mrs. Thicknesse as a wit — and greater sacrifice could not be asked of me. I made her the Dorothy Parker of our generation. How sick she made me and my inamorata look one night, for example, when our imaginary set had foregathered for cocktails preparatory to dinner on the town and it was asked around whether a woman could be got for an unexpected man. "How about Clara Thicknesse?" someone suggested; "is she dated?" "Dated, she's antique," crackled my spouse. Another time a man admired a new dress Clara had on, a risky combination of colors about which she'd been worried. "Oh, it comes off," the man assured her, and Crystal was heard to say behind her hand to a group nearby, "Easier than he dreams." A woman chatted about her husband's casual air travel. "Last week he went to Paris with an overnight bag." "Anyone you know?" That one got into the columns and was known by the inner set to refer to Mrs. Thicknesse. Oh, how I built her up in these fantasies, and how those arrows quivered in their marks! Asked what the Lamplighter was like at home, what kind of barbs *his* were, she answered promptly, "Phenobarbs." By mid-spring she was the rage of Wise Acres, for it was most convenient to lay these expiatory ordeals in that English country seat remembered from the play of the same name, in that youth of mine which had been cut off. I have often wondered what the two women would have thought of one another actually, for they never met in real life, but only in my now fevered and self-flagellating fancies.

I hammered out some of the best of these sequences when my head was on the pillow assigned to me by law, and their principal slept peacefully on hers. As I lay wincing and groaning wakefully under the lash of laughter unloosed against me by her acid wit, I wondered where all this would end. I did not think I deserved such punishment for my peccancies. I felt the person against whom any "infidelities" were technically committed to be actually far more in my moral debt than I in hers. What had I done less than sell my birthright, for her? For her I had suffered my talent to be buried, my wit to be pickled in platitude, I had taken a job. We have seen all this. The gulf between us was a cross, moreover, which I alone bore, and nothing showed its breadth so much as her opinion of what I ground out for groceries. She liked my stuff — at least I might have been spared that! There was now no longer any question of "educating" her away from that level without treading on the delicate memory of her father, in whose mantle I was thus doomed to walk the earth awhile. And what purpose is served by relating that I heard fall from her lips, in a discussion with Clammidge's cultured wife, the name of Edna St. Vincent Benét? Except to indicate the stresses from which Mrs. Thicknesse vouchsafed me at least intermittent relief.

So being already my wife's moral creditor, the additional immolation of myself in reveries enabled me — after perhaps a scowl in her direction — to turn over in the darkness and go to sleep secure in the sense of being treated shabbily.

One evening Mrs. Thicknesse thought she would like to give bowling a try. I took her to Pulsifer's Alleys, where I actually did continue to go, nowadays, in the afternoon whenever I could work it in. She wasn't very good but gave it another fling the next week. It was then I bowled my best game in ages, making seven strikes in a row, and people crowded around from other alleys at the prospect of a perfect game.

I heard a familiar voice behind me: "Bowling the ladies over?" It was Pete Cheshire.

He was wearing a green double-breasted chalk-stripe and a tie with actual trout flies hooked into it. I missed on the next roll, getting only three pins, and the tension relaxed. My score was two hundred and seventy. Cheshire invited Mrs. Thicknesse and me to be his guests in the supper lounge adjoining: he hadn't seen me for three months and Mrs. Thicknesse since they'd first met, and he had news for us.

We wound up over hamburgers. Mrs. Thicknesse confided a great passion for these and remarked, as she stirred her coffee, what an industry this country had made of forcemeat. Cheshire frowned and said he doubted whether Pulsifer, a guy he knew, would use horsemeat in his sandwiches. "Not horsemeat — forcemeat," Mrs. Thicknesse said; "the generic term for ground flesh." Pete had if anything more aplomb than last time, and he smoked a Be-

113

tween the Acts and fingered the dry-flies on his tie as he told his news.

"I've got eight hundred dollars saved up" — how we widened our eyes at that — "and I'll slip you some more tidings. I just put a binder on a lot. To build my restaurant on."

"Pete, where is this lot?" I put down my bitten sandwich and demanded to know.

"Corner of Buchanan and Jericho. I can see the scene already. Women with teeth as white as toothpaste clinging to men's arms — "

"What?" I looked at his head as though it were a gong that had been struck and given forth no sound. "A street that runs dead a few blocks away, a lot overgrown with weeds? What ails you?"

"Buchanan runs dead but Jericho don't. That's the coming *rue*."

Mrs. Thicknesse, who was piling condiments on her hamburger from every container as an indication that she fitted in with all classes, asked, "How can you erect a restaurant in a residential zone?" Cheshire smiled calmly, and, twisting out his cigarillo, drew his sandwich toward him.

"Buchanan's residential but Jericho was once an old business street — so? I build on a Jericho address. No zoning there. Humdinger, that German with the chain of restaurants, he's bought the old Cobbett mansion on Jericho to make into his latest. If a smart operator like that . . . I mean I see it as the street to get my stinger in." He bit into his sandwich and, with a quid of food in his cheek, said: "I've already taken out my liquor license. I'm twenty-one, now, you know."

This was so feeble-minded that I didn't even stop to argue about it, but only, studying the two-finger span be-

114

tween his eyebrows and his hairline, asked whether I hadn't read in the paper that they were rushing plans to restrict Jericho Street. "Yar, and I'm in under the wire with my permit. I have a mutual friend in Orlando Heights who explained it all to me. It'll be what they call a pre-existing nonconformity." That shut us up.

Pete looked away with too much innocence and inquired, "Kind of a fellow is this Humdinger? Anybody here know him personally?"

"Slightly," declared Mrs. Thicknesse, "and I am not impressed by philanthropists who can't get to their appointments on time, and pillars of society who knock people up in the middle of the night and think nothing of it."

Pete pricked up his ears and set his half-raised sandwich down. "Who *what* people in the middle of the night?"

"Knock them up. Which is what he did to the Everly sisters, out there in the country. Frightened them half to death." I fidgeted on my chair. "Mr. Humdinger was lost on the road in his car, and instead of taking the trouble to find a lighted house he knocks up the poor Everly sisters."

"*Both* of them?"

"I think what Mrs. Thicknesse means is the English usage — " I began miserably, pressing Pete's foot under the table. Except that by mistake I got Mrs. Thicknesse's. Who in turn thought it was Pete who was squeezing it, because she stared at him and said, "Really!" The confusion was utter. Peter continued with excruciating relish, "This I got to hear about. How did he go about it? What gave?"

"Well, they were both in bed of course — "

"That was convenient," he said with a shattering laugh.

I *thought* I would go *out* of my one and only mind. "Oh, good God," I said, and signaled for the waiter. "We really must go."

"This is on me," said Pete. He tore the check from the waiter's pad when it was figured up and rose, digging into his pocket. When we thanked him he said it had been his pleasure. "Au reservoir," he said humorously, and made off with great urbanity.

Mrs. Thicknesse and I agreed that a business of his own was probably the only solution for him because he was obviously unemployable. "He's up to something," I murmured, watching him stop at a table to pump hands and slap backs, as though already grooming himself for proprietorship. "I'd give a lot to know what."

I found out soon enough.

I was paging through the day's issue of the *Pick*, one afternoon at the office, when my eye was caught by a story caption with "Old Cobbett Manse" in it. My feet came slowly off the desk as I read:

> Louis Humdinger, who has just completed conversion of the old Elihu Cobbett home on South Jericho Street into a restaurant and had announced plans for a grand opening next month, has run into a zoning snag that may doom his long-cherished project. He has been denied a liquor license because one has been recently issued for a site eight hundred feet from his, to a Peter Cheshire, of 718 Marble Street, for a café and cocktail lounge which he plans to erect at an undisclosed date. A city ordinance forbids more than one liquor-dispensing establishment within a distance of fifteen hundred feet . . .

I had Pete in my office inside of three hours.

"The whole thing is a ruse now, isn't it? *Isn't* it?" I demanded.

"I don't know what you're talking about."

"Somehow, somewhere, you got wind of this zoning gimmick, and the minute you were twenty-one, snuck in

116

there first to get poor old Humdinger over a barrel. You plan now to milk him, blackmail him, something, because you know restaurants break even on the food and make their profit on liquor. Is that it?"

"Blackmail's a nasty word, and why is Humdinger 'poor old'? Because he's an advertiser in this rag? Why should I waste sympathy on a guy like that? He pays his help lousy, and you heard what Mrs. Thicknesse — "

"Oh, to hell with that! And never mind the cracks about advertisers. I just want to see everybody get a square deal."

"They will," Pete said with forbidding calm. "Including me." Then he became injured. "Here I try to do my best, and all I keep is getting snide remarks. I never asked to be trailed and checked up on. All I ask is to be left alone. But no, that's our society. Once you're marked as a moral leopard — "

"I never called you that."

"Keep up the good work. But business is business. Vanderbilt and J. P. Morgan both own railroads and have a cutthroat price war on freight rates. So Morgan buys a ranch, raises cattle out west, and ships them east on Vanderbilt's railroad at freight rates ruinous to the latter."

"Where is the Agony? Where's Lammermoor now? Who's advising you in all this?"

"Fasties are an important part of American finance."

"Just what fastie do you have in mind for Louis Humdinger, Pete?"

Pete reached for his hat and walked to the door. "Wouldn't you say that's between him and me?"

"I thought I was your friend."

"Yar, I did too. But friends don't call one another on the carpet. Anyhow, I'll report this to you: that I'm taking

117

that new job you got me with the Jolly Fisherman restaurant — a little bit of everything, to learn the business. Well, *auf wienerschnitzel*. Give me a clang sometime."

I gave him a clang the very next day after getting one myself from Humdinger, who called in tears to say he couldn't "hond dot guy Cheshire up anywhere," and that he'd been told I was the man to get in touch with, to unravel this. I arranged for the two of them to meet in my office at eight o'clock sharp the following evening.

I stayed down for a bite of supper and then, back at my desk with a few minutes before my visitors were expected, wrote a note to Mrs. Thicknesse:

> Well, our fox is about to show his hand. Shall tell you the instant I know any more — and do my best to mediate the nuisance intelligently. Always remembering — as one, I suppose, alas, must — that you can't coddle a hard-boiled egg.
>
> How you do continue to worry about curing the tobacco habit. My dear, I have a suggestion. Smoke exploding cigars.
>
> Your De La Mare's "twin-born cherries shaken on a stem" keeps running through my head. I think no lips deserve the metaphor more than those which recalled it to me.
>
> I hear the first of our foolish mortals on the stairs now, and have time only to end and address this before donning my umpire's uniform. Fair woman, *Vale!*

It was Cheshire who arrived first, and I finished pasting down the flap of the addressed envelope as he took his hat off and hung it on a wall peg. He was spiffy as ever in a mélange of hues best ignored, except to note that he had on the tie with the rod lures on it — his lucky piece.

Pete drifted past the desk and glanced down at the letter. I put it out of sight in a desk drawer. Humdinger arrived as I was kicking the drawer shut, for it stuck like everything else in my office.

I had never seen Humdinger before and was now not entirely sure I wasn't looking at Gustav Von Seyffertitz, the character actor whom you may remember. Humdinger lacked about three feet of being a ten-foot pole, with a cleaver of a face and eyes like an umlaut. Next we must talk about a man with a martial bearing who cried. The military air was furthered by short-cropped hair, a black triangle of it that came to a point at the front between deepening bald wedges. It looked like half a slice of burnt toast.

He led off with a sentimental preface about how he loved this country for the economic opportunities it had afforded him. "I have what you call great squash on America." (I figured out after a moment that he meant he had a crush on it.) "I have only ordinary restaurants in my chain till now — good but not ze real fine place I've dreamed of. Real German cooking and ze best wines. Finally I find ze spot I have my heart set on and bingo — no liquor license. Can't open wizout it. All my money sunk in it. Ruin." He brushed a tear from his eye and sat in the attitude of one who truly sees despair before him, vanity behind.

Now it was time to hear from our next contestant, and so I turned with a smile to him. "Well, Pete, what have you to say?"

Cheshire rose and circled the room, drawing on a Between-the-Acts.

"Never have I too wanted anything so bad as a good restaurant," he began, choosing his words carefully. "It's been *my* life's dream. Night falling, people — " We had the nocturne again, a rival ode which fairness obliged Humdinger to hear out as fully as his had been; but when Pete came to a new part in it, how he had all along had this neighborhood spotted as *the* coming thing, skepticism was in order. Humdinger knew he was lying in his teeth. We could only wait to hear his price. It wasn't long in being stated.

"I know you're on the hook," he said, standing over Humdinger. "O.K., I'll get you off. Give up my spot. For a consideration, of course."

"*Natürlich.*"

I got a firm grip on the arms of my swivel chair.

"What would you consider fair, Pete?"

"Oh, I don't know. Five thousand."

Humdinger uttered a protest that can't be phonetically rendered beyond suggesting a sustained animal cry rich in German gutturals. He got out of his chair. "Five hundred. Not a penny more."

"Then I'm afraid there's no point in our wasting one another's time."

"You — swinehound!"

"Call me Pete," Cheshire said, strolling to the wall where his hat hung.

Humdinger launched another appeal to his sympathies, but Pete's receiver was off the hook. Humdinger looked helplessly to me. I went over and laid a hand on Pete's shoulder.

"Wait. Maybe we can compromise — or find an alternate solution. What about a job of some sort with Mr. Humdinger?" I said, grasping at a straw. "On top of the five hundred maybe. The training would be invaluable to you, till you got squared away yourself."

Pete turned a brightened eye on Humdinger, in whose face a ray of hope had also been kindled. "Well, now, why not?" Humdinger said. "I have lots of jobs in my chain. Driving trocks, maintenance — "

"I was thinking of something more at the top," Pete said. "You'll need somebody to take charge of the new Cobbett one. Greet the guests, see that — "

"A *maître de!*" Humdinger gasped. He drank in with fresh horror the two-inch chalk-stripes, the tie with the insects on it which might even possibly be changing positions, the tab-collar shirt. All that was hard enough on the layman; to someone steeped in the Bemelmans tradition it must have been a nightmare. Humdinger turned away with another stricken look and stood dabbing at the umlaut with his handkerchief.

"That's the way it reads," Pete said, and now really got his hat.

Humdinger whirled around. "*You hoof!*"

"If you mean heel," said Pete, who was quickest this time, "don't stand on ceremony. I'm easier than that to know. Thank you, gentlemen, and good night."

I detained him forcibly at the door. "Now hold on," I said, just a little sicker of his crafty double-talk than I was of the Prussian's sniveling. "Let's cut out the weasel words. You know you rigged this from the start. Now be fair. Mr. Humdinger is — because — well, damn it, he could probably pull the rug from under you easily enough, considering."

"Considering what?"

"Oh, don't be a rummy. Considering how quick the state liquor commissions are to crack down on people with any record. Any sign of irregularity and your license would be revoked like *that*. When they see how long it'll be before you can raise the money for your place — Oh, don't be a fool. Take the five hundred and put it in your savings."

"That's right, kibitz for *him*. Feed him gimmicks," Pete said, pointing to Humdinger whose expression had taken an optimistic turn. "Is this what you call being neutral?"

"Now just a minute, friend. I'm only tipping you off to possible embarrassment."

"It's like I say," Pete observed after a moment, like a man who finds repose in a conclusion to which he has come, "about a person who's marked as a moral leopard. He's got no chance against the forces of respectability. There's a higherarchy that runs every town — "

"I wouldn't say that, Pete."

"I will. I'll say it again and again. There's a higherarchy that runs every town, and they're hand in glove. Sitting around in their snug complacency, pulling wires for one another, keeping society the way they want it — their way. Well, if you think I'm going to cut off my nose despite my face . . ." Feeling us now to be so swimming in nuance that I hardly knew where to begin, I stood staring at the rug. "I wouldn't say you're such a shiny example yourself," Pete went on, "and if you think you've got *me* over a barrel you've got another think coming. There's enough gimmicks in the world for everybody," he said, looking me in the eye, "so don't count me out yet. Good evening, gents."

"You haven't said anything about my suggestion for curing the tobacco habit," I chatted from a pond of pillows on which I lay watching Mrs. Thicknesse pour us tea in her sun room. One foot was flung up on an arm of the divan on which I was thus disposed, and a cigarette burned in an indolent hand. "Either in your letter or now."

"What was that?"

"Smoke exploding cigars."

She laughed, holding her finger on the lid of the teapot as the Oolong flowed in a tawny spout into the cups. "That's marvelous. You're growing more a wag by the hour. I shan't try it though, thanks just the same. When did you write me that?"

"Week before last."

"I got no letter from you then or last week. I wondered why. I thought you liked our little notes as much as I have come to."

I swung my foot to the floor and sat up. I watched her set the teapot on the trivet.

"Your mailbox is pretty far from the house. Things could easily be taken out of it without anybody noticing, couldn't they?" I asked.

"What do you mean?"

"I hope not what I think I do. Pete Cheshire may have seen the address on one letter in my office. I finished it as he arrived."

Mrs. Thicknesse sat down and leaned back with her hands in her lap. "He's really hopping mad with you?"

"Worse than that, by now." The higherarchy (not including me) had indeed cracked down on him since the evening when I had heard the term coined. A few influential citizens had got the liquor commission to look into the situation, analyze it for what it was, and revoke Pete's license. "Well, if you didn't get either of the letters, he helped himself at the mailbox and is about to graduate to blackmail."

"Good God." Mrs. Thicknesse rose and walked the floor as our tea cooled in its Limoges cups. "There are of course two alternatives. Get the police after him is one. Do you know anybody on the force?"

"Only too well!" I exclaimed, feeling danger blowing like

a cold wind from a fresh quarter. "What's the other alternative?" I asked her quickly.

"Why, pay him what he wants. I don't know what you wrote," she said, her dark lashes sweeping downward as she cast her eyes to the floor, "but if there were — things in them . . ." My own expression told her there were. "Oh, well," she said, collecting herself with a determined sigh, "money will be his object, which needn't worry us as it won't be ours."

A tour of my eye about the sun room and on into the living room, from whose brocaded depths De Falla's notion of Iberian gardens blew across our leisure like a tonal scent, assured me how true that was; and rejecting, as resolutely as my friend, any tarnish on this golden afternoon, I was able to pick up my tea and, strolling to the mantel, drink it with at least a measure of the aplomb with which I had watched it poured.

"Well, you know, my dear Clara," I observed, standing there, "conquering a woman is like climbing a mountain. Getting back is half the danger."

"That's marvelous. It really is, you know. . . . Darling, you're stirring your tea with the *handle* of the spoon."

Nine

PETE CHESHIRE was wearing the bait-flecked tie. Everything else was wearing him. The tie floated an anchor on a blue bay of shirt, which in turn lay between the lapels of a jacket the color of tomato soup, from whose buttonhole sprang a pink carnation. He was drawing on one of those cigarillos of his, and walking around my office.

"Get it through your medulla obligato that you're over a barrel."

"How much do you want for the letters?" I asked, fingering a stiletto used hitherto only for slicing open mail, now possibly adaptable to cutting out somebody's tripe.

"Not a red cent. I just want a little favor."

I laid the letter knife aside, along with my dreams of mayhem, and did something in a more practical vein. I got a firm grip on my knees and asked: "Just what kind of favor did you have in mind?"

Pete took another turn around the room before replying, then did so abruptly. "Just say that I was here last Thursday night, between eight and ten, in case anybody asks."

Watching my spiffy friend out of the tail of my eye, I recalled certain thieveries which had occurred in the city of late, whose enactor always left a calling card signed "The Smoothie" at the scene of the crime. On the Thursday night for which my cooperation was requested a hardware store

125

not far from where we were now matching wits had been entered and robbed of three hundred and some dollars. Now I guessed I was expected to rise out of my seat and exclaim, "Then you're — the Smoothie!" I was damned if I would. I would tell the other principal in this gathering dream to go soak his fat . . . Steady, I warned myself, taking in his two fingers of brow: you're in the clutches of a shrewd moron. A smart dumbbell. Don't lose your head. Stall for time.

Shooting my sleeves back, I laced my hands behind my head and said with an understanding smile, "Pete, the game isn't worth the candle. This will be what they call a Pyrrhic victory. A success that's really a setback. One thing like this leads to another, because habit is a cable. We add a thread every day, and at last we cannot break it."

"Blow the spit out of your valves and try another chorus."

"This is a mighty strong thread you're adding — blackmail, Pete — and, Pete, let me put it this way. He who rides a tiger finds it difficult to dismount."

"Who's riding one?"

I brought both palms down on the desk as I rose.

"I won't stand for this — goddam it!" I added, to show that the Lamplighter could get along with the common people. "You were going so fine. Going straight."

"We both know why I changed. You're such a shiny example. And I know you'll cooperate to the fullest to keep your respectable standing in the community from getting any blot on it."

Before he could give his spiel about the "higherarchy," no doubt augmented this time with cynical inclusions about their private lives, I went on, "You're going straight now all right — straight to hell! This operation is so full of bugs

I hardly know where to begin, but I'll do my best. In the first place, Pete, this Raffles act. Aren't you aiming a little high?"

"Hitch your wagon to a star says you to me."

"Let alone that a Raffles would be a man of *honor*. Gallant. *He* would never take advantage of a lady who once befriended him."

"You'll notice it's not her I'm putting the squeeze on, though I could get all I needed in one lump out of her. Because my goal is ten thou'. I figure that's what I need to make a fresh start in a restaurant business in some other town. It'll take quite a while unless I make a strike, say with some member of the local nobility's jewels."

"In a tuxedo?" I asked him dryly.

"Meanwhile it's nice to know I have a standing alibi. Or rather a pacing one" — and he laughed heartily.

"You mean you expect me to cover for you *every* time? Never!"

"We'll see," said Pete inclemently. Then he seemed to relent; after drawing on his cigar with a *savoir-faire* that made my teeth ache, he smilingly went on, "Of course I'll do the same for you, any time you need an alibi. See, the Smoothie always fares forth on Thursday nights, which I believe you have a standing date. You probably give out the story you're working late at the office, so it works out nice for both of us."

"And what if I tell you you can go to the devil?"

"Guess."

I looked straight at his numskull. "If I can ever get it through that thick — "

"Watch it." In a dead calm, Pete bent to twist out the cigarillo in an ashtray. "You know I could put the bite on you direct for a few thou', but I'm not. I figure you probably haven't got that kind of money lying around. All I ask is that you back me up any time I need it."

"Of course you may not need it," I said, wishing aloud.

Pete frowned. "That's hard to say. I have an idea I'm being followed. So I thought I'd better brief you and put you on a round-the-clock alert."

"Who's been following you?"

"Somebody who's vaguely familiar but I can't place. I will though, when I can get in a little tailing of my own. Not my old probation officer. Maybe it's just my imagination. I hope so."

Pete strolled toward the door.

"So-o, that's the way it reads. I was here last Thursday night, having one of our heart-to-heart talks. Next Thursday the Smoothie will strike again. There's a pattern in these crimes," he said with a grueling smile, and was gone.

I stood looking at the closed door for some moments after his footsteps vanished down the hall. Then I charged my desk and snatched up objects from it and hurled them in all directions. While most of me did that, part of me went *tsk, tsk*. This was so unlike me — like everything else I did. Where was it all leading?

It was here the Lamplighter had his first intimation that he was marked for martyrdom. That he had preached no cliché so homely that it would not be found, at last, incarnate in himself. That he must be thrown to the wolves in order that moralities grown stale, virtues long withered into phrases, might live again, and blossom in purple and gold. The seed packet of dried bromides which he must water with his blood were ones he had inherited against his will, but that was beside the point, if it was not the heart of the matter. For a day of propitiation had been ordained, and he was the designated bullock.

The hero was not yet ready for glory. From his typewriter he ripped a sheet of paper on which was begun an answer to a letter beginning: "Dear Lamplighter: When we first got married my husband used to say I slept with my lips slightly parted. Now he says I sleep with my mouth open. How can I bring back . . . ?" He tore the letter and the answer to shreds and flung them away. A tumbler full of pencils shattered against a far wall. A jar of rubber bands, a handful of memo pads, a box of paper clips followed. I can't vouch for the exact order, except that the paper clips were last. Because the door opened just then and Clammidge got a spray of them in his face.

"You need a rest," he said, stooping to tidy things up somewhat. "I've been watching you." I stood over him breathing heavily as he retrieved paraphernalia. He gave this up after a moment, and, rising, began combing office equipment out of his hair. "Why don't you take a little trip?" he asked.

I laughed hollowly. "How far? It's nothing," I said. "If only people could manage to be a little adult . . ."

"I know lots of the letters are silly, and shall I tell you something?" He dropped into the club chair. "Don't waste your time with those. Concentrate on the people in real trouble, who need help. Doing a good job of analyzing people and their troubles takes a lot — which brings me to what I came to see you about." He drew a breath so deep his belt groaned like a spike being drawn from a plank. "You ought to tighten your column up as a *psychological advice feature*. That's the coming thing. I've been going over several columns in the big city dailies, New York and so on, and the trend is definitely to psychoanalyzing the readers who write in. Their family patterns and all."

"I've been giving it that slant."

"But not enough. Read these." Clammidge tossed over a sheaf of cuttings. "You've got to practice psychiatry to run a worry column these days. Correspondents are patients, is what I'm trying to say, and they want to be treated as such. We've got to go along with the times."

"What about the Pepigrams?" I asked, soliciting outrage in order to enrich my grievance. "Will they have to be clinical too now?"

"It goes without saying you'll have this whole new field to explore."

"Like: 'Say *Stability* and you've also said *Ability*'? Like that?"

"Write that down before you forget it!"

He rose and started for the door. But I wasn't through rubbing salt into my wounds.

" 'You may not be suffering from a real depression — just a recession.' "

"By *George!* Don't let those get away from you." At the door, Clammidge paused with his hand on the knob and glanced concernedly down at the shambles. "You're happy here, aren't you?"

"I couldn't be any happier."

"And you like Decency as a whole?"

"As a hole it's fine."

He nodded. "Well, carry on. I'll send you a full memo with my thoughts on the change in the column. Meanwhile, get some recreation — you'll need it. The missus wants you and your missus for dinner next week. She'll probably have all the social heavyweights in town, including the new Episcopal minister and his wife. I think your wife will want to meet them." He smiled and added, "I guess we all become climbers in the end."

The climber is a creeper, I wanted to say. A nice thought-for-the-day — but the right day. When I collected my severance pay, perhaps.

Clammidge gone, I turned the key quietly in the lock and had a nip from a bottle I kept in a bottom drawer, now whisky rather than sherry. I sat with my feet on the desk and looked down at the litter with a detached interest, and saying "Didley-boo, didley-bah, didley beedy-o-day." I spat on the rug. I would do this everywhere, I would have no consideration. I would be a sonofabitch indoors and out. I would pursue every facet of nonconformity until my name, rather than provoking amusement, would excite respect.

Sipping the whisky slowly, I ruminated on that "trip." I would go, but as for coming back, that was a horse of another color. For the hero was now in training; now began the rehearsals for glory:

After many days of travel, footsore and weary, driven from villages by barking dogs, the Lamplighter reached the blue Pacific. He set sail across her broad waters, and settled at last among islands fragrant with Eastern spices and no paper clips. The natives were friendly — but the tribal chiefs were not. For he taught the people new ways, which the jealous chiefs said were evil.

One evening there were soft footfalls without and Ola-kanoa slipped into his tent.

"You must flee for your life."

"Why?"

She drew a long, sad breath.

"The Lamplighter's words are wiser than the wise men's and they are angry and have stirred the people up to kill

131

*him. Here is some food and papaya juice. I have prepared
them with great danger to myself, for my father is one of the
higherarchy here."*

"Tell your papaya simply won't stand for this."

"Do not joke. The old men have great power."

"Yes . . . Your toothless sharks are the deadliest."

*"Such words enrage them — they fear your wit. They
have roused the populace with rumors that you were driven
from your own land, where you were once nobly thought of,
even one of the higherarchy."*

"I've got to think."

*"There is no time. Someone has taken down the tribal
drum and is beating it."*

"And I must do the same?"

*"Olakanoa has smiled many times at the Lamplighter's
jokes, and the many ways of humor he has taught her. But
in her heart she will never smile again."*

"I won't go."

*"A boat is ready at the water's edge. Under the palm
which slants toward the setting sun . . ."*

*And so he became a legend among the islands. For though
he was never seen in those parts again, many recalled his
words, and even those who had never laid eyes on him or
even heard of him still speak the many proverbs which he
taught them, and which they cherish to this day.*

I shook my head to break free of the daze which enveloped me, and, finishing off the drink, went downstairs to
my favorite bar.

I didn't tell Mrs. Thicknesse what was afoot, for the time
being. I would keep it off her doorstep as long as I could.
My own first wrestlings with my dilemma (a dilemma with
only one horn, the familiar "or else" dilemma in which no

alternative need be stated) were resolved with the plan to wait. Take each problem as it came. Obviously I must weigh what I owed society, in the form of the cops (if they called), against what I owed my wife and family. The question of one's probity is who it's *for*. One's wife is the beneficiary of more than one's insurance. Morality is the premium paid Respectability for benefits accruable, and computed on the actuarial tables of social . . . uh . . . uh . . . well, what I'm trying to say, I guess, is that conscience is a lightning calculator as much as it is anything else, including a small voice.

I hadn't formulated any plan, except to let the spirit move me when the time came, when my office phone rang and it was Captain Carmichael asking whether my ward, Pete Cheshire, had spent the preceding Thursday evening with me there.

"Let . . . me . . . see," I said, reaching for my engagement calendar. "Thursday evening . . ." I was intensely curious about what I was going to say. I hung on my every word — you could even put it that way. "I have seen him recently, but I couldn't swear to the day. I don't keep my appointment sheets — I throw them away. Why do you ask, Frank?"

"These jobs that are being pulled by someone who calls himself the Smoothie. Cheshire's been picked up for questioning on the latest — he's here with me right now as a matter of fact — and he claims he was with you at the time of the crime. Is that right?"

"Well, that reminds me of a story," I said, just like Abraham Lincoln, the way *he* met many of his crises. Good old Honest Abe. "It seems there were two Swedes — "

"I know. I read that one in your column yesterday. Just tell me whether Cheshire was with you then."

"That's a hard question for me to answer, Frank. He was in here *some*time last week, I know." That's it — stall for time.

"Were *you* in the office working last Thursday night?"

"Oh, yes. Yes, I was."

"Will you swear?"

"Yes, I will," I said, and did so under my breath.

"And he could have gone up to see you?"

"He *could* have."

"He's been reporting to you regularly?"

"Oh, faithfully. In fact he comes in to see me oftener than the probation rules require."

Carmichael paused a moment.

"Well, as long as you give him a clean bill of health, that's good enough for me," he said at length. "God knows he's walked the chalk line up to now, as far as we can tell. Except for that liquor permit shenanigans, which I thought was pretty clever of him. In fact I think he's got a kick coming, on that. But that's neither here nor there. I was pretty surprised when one of our men put the finger on him."

"How did that happen, Frank?"

"Oh, some extra fancy detective work. Highfalutin' deductions. Too highfalutin' to suit me."

A prickle of anxiety went up my spine.

"On whose part, Frank?"

"As if you didn't know! Look, that relative of yours is one smart apple, and I'm tickled to death to have him on the force. But I wish he'd come down out of the clouds. If there's anybody who has to have two feet on the ground it's a cop. All these beautiful patterns he weaves. I wish you'd talk to him."

My mouth suddenly felt as though it were full of peanut

butter. It was a moment before I could manipulate my tongue.

"I will," I brought out at last. "I'll check into this whole thing and call you back."

I hung up, already sliding the bottom drawer open with my other hand.

I was pouring a second drink when the phone rang again. This time it was Nickie.

"I'd like to talk to you," he said. "Can you meet me at the Greek's in fifteen minutes? Be there without fail. It's urgent. There's something very peculiar going on."

Ten

I T'S A RUM business. The reason I hedged with the Captain was, I'm in a bit of a box. You see, this Smoothie you've got by the scruff has got me by mine. He's got hold of some letters I wrote a lady in question, and you know how it is to have them come to light. The embarrassing metaphors, the overwriting. The hazards of the Renaissance man, old boy. I was prepared to sit tight, weather it out somehow, but now that I learn what this means to you, Nickie — *well*." And I parted my hands in a gesture of knightly grace.

The gesture provoked some consternation in the Greek who was watching from the soda fountain, for it was executed across a table at which no one else as yet sat: I was rehearsing for Nickie's arrival. He hadn't come yet.

I was installed inside, and from time to time glanced at the door, wishing the sight I dreaded would hurry. It was a sight all too familiar to me, nor one of which familiarity had, over the long months that lay behind, ever quite managed to abate the shock.

Patrolman Sherman had plied his rounds, from the start, with every insistence on the primacy of the intellect. But opportunities for the stylized sort of thing he did seemed rather few, somehow, and it was my task ceaselessly to shore up his faith in the advice which had steered him into this line of work. Nickie had set himself a period of six months for the promised advance to plain clothes, and that time up without a sign from Carmichael, he went into the Captain's office and asked him bluntly whether covenants made were to be honored by those party to them, or whether he was to be left in Limbo.

"I thought you were in Kenwood," Carmichael said, slapping about in his everlasting papers. "But let me check into the civvies setup again and see if I can spot an opening coming up. They didn't enlarge the detective bureau like they promised me," he said, crossly appropriating half the grievance.

Six months became nine. The seat of Nicky's blue pants was now shiny, and "reflected the chicanery of elements which could be named." These undoubtedly included me. The next time he applied to see Captain Carmichael he was told by the secretary in the outer office, "You mean Captain Quagmeyer. Carmichael took a job in the state capitol."

Buckling in with a bit of a grin, we arranged for an interview with this new superior with whom we would now have to start from scratch. I went along as Nickie's chief counsel, to see that he got a square deal.

Quagmeyer was a blond mountain of a man with a hand like a ham. We both shook it, and then Nickie turned and sauntered to the window.

"Cook breakfast every morning do you, Captain?"

Now, all of us have semantic land-mines which a single word will trip. "Breakfast" was one of the Captain's. Each morning since his wedding he had had to rise while his wife spent a last hour in the sack, "dozing to"; then when he had the orange juice quite squeezed, the coffee brewed and the eggs and bacon on the table, she would appear and, her hair looking like last year's bird's nest, sit down to them. At first Quagmeyer's relatives and friends kidded him about this aspect of his henpeckedness; then no longer dared; and now this rookie cop.

"Oh, yeah?" he said, which already tipped us off that this was haywire, because what kind of answer is that to a sentence which is itself a question? "Who are the smart alecks around here that they can't give a new man time to take his coat off before — who told you I fix breakfast every morning?" he demanded.

"No one had to. You see, the finger and thumb of your right hand tell me the whole story. The stains on them resemble the dye used on oranges, which comes off under pressure sufficient to squeeze them. True, they're faint now, but to the incisive eye — "

"Oh, yeah? Well, get this. Who makes breakfast in my house, or why or when or how often, is none of anybody else's goddam beeswax! Is that clear? Is that clear!"

"Yes, sir. I was only — "

"All right. Never mind what you were only. Just remember what I say, and tell any other snoots around here that goes for them too. My private life is none of anybody's business." Quagmeyer, who had risen, sat down. "Now then, what did you want to see me about?"

"It can wait." Nickie started out, but he paused at the door. "It's just that I entered the service with a sort of understanding with Captain Carmichael, which you might feel you inherit. It's that the very first opening on the detective force — well, he promised to keep an eye on me."

"Don't worry. I'll do that!"

I snatched up my hat and scuttled out behind my protégé.

Days afoot in Kenwood gave Nickie an appetite with which he could legitimately indulge his taste for food, for he had become a full-fledged gourmet. "When they saw how tight his pants were they thought they'd split," seemed soon a more relevant version of the glossy backside than his own mot. After a day of pounding the pavements, he liked to relax with a spot of pâté, or maybe a swatch of smoked salmon, and a glass of chilled vermouth, or white wine when he wasn't having that for dinner. His wit increased in dryness like the wines of his prospering fancy. Asked one evening what he'd had for dinner at a party from which flu had kept his wife, he answered curtly, "Provisions." "You're so stuck up," she'd said.

Lila had changed, as was blessedly inevitable, for the better, under the role of wife and mother. No motion-picture chic or embezzled gestures now. She was realistically bent on installing Nickie and herself in the solid country-club set — which, Nickie said, had two subjects of conversation, Martinis and tennis, and even they were indistinguishable because what you heard of either was:

"Five to three . . ."

"Four to one . . ."

"Three to two . . ."

He often sat on the sidelines trying to guess whether they were talking about scores or strengths. His wife asked him if that was his idea of putting down roots, of acquiring that sense of belonging in a community which he must want for his children if not for himself or her. They had an apartment of their own now, and it was time they had some of these people up. She said they *did* talk about other things than Martinis and tennis. She loved to hear the wives discuss the servant problem, a vexation to which she aspired. She had them in for bridge on Wednesday afternoons, but that wasn't enough; they must repay some dinner invitations.

In the process of making Nickie into an acceptable member of society she had extracted repeated promises to swear off aphorisms and nuance. But making a sow's ear out of a silk purse was much harder in his case than it had been in mine, and all his guarantees were vain. At the first of the dinner parties they gave, he said at one juncture, "Failure is the tragedy of being shot to death by one's lover; success that of being bored to death by one's wife." There was an embarrassed stir around the cocktail table, and mutters of resentment from many. An all-star fullback rose and went out on the terrace. Thank God they had one to go out on, or he might have gone home.

"Do you *have* to talk like that?" Lila asked when all the guests had departed except Crystal and me, for we were there too.

Nickie shrugged. "A man is what he is."

"That's a defeatist attitude." Lila appealed to me. "Can't you speak to him, Chick? Get him to talk English?"

Nickie awaited my words with a twisted little smile of anticipation, as the girls went off into the kitchen to make us some midnight coffee. Nevertheless I said what had to be said: That we must all of us make our peace with life. That we cannot linger on mountaintops but must descend into the valley and live on daily bread, on that humble plane of which my own remark at table that I eschewed gum — which had gotten such a laugh — was the clearest of illustrations.

"You mean life is a give-and-take?" he said sardonically.

"Why not? Is it Huxley who says — I believe it's in *Point Counter Point* — that no matter where we've been, we must all come back to truism at last? Is it in *Intruder in the Dust* that Faulkner remarks that all the wisdom of the world can be summed up in half a dozen clichés? You may recall that in *The Wild Duck* Ibsen emphasizes that we can't go on dunning one another with the claims of the ideal — "

"You mean that, of the two class exquisites, since one became a cracker-barrel philosopher, the other might as well be a cop. Is that it?"

"Now just a minute, baby."

"Don't misunderstand me. I don't say that selling out in itself — "

"All right, shall we step outside for a minute? The terrace will do."

He finished off some white wine and seltzer he had in a glass and took another tack. "I think platitudes have their place. They are like the lower teeth in a smile."

I took a meditative view of the draperies. After a measure of silence, I turned to him. "Epigrams are parasols and platitudes are umbrellas," I said, grinning fixedly, "and which of the two is of more benefit to mankind I leave to you."

This so irked him, especially as coming from a character whose conversation had been written off as scratch corn, that he suddenly lost all reserve, and began to pour out his grievances in a bitter indictment of me as their source. Tie that! I had duped and bamboozled him into a walk of life from which there was now no turning back, due to domestic living standards undertaken on the strength of it. He saw himself as a Jason who, in order to be kept from his rightful throne, was sent off on a wild goose chase for a Golden Fleece. "But he got the fleece," I reminded him. "That was mythology," he answered. "This is life." Half an hour later we were still at it, raising our voices to such an extent that our wives warned us of the danger of the neighbors' calling the police.

I drove home in a smoldering fury. That bastard and his

classic allusions. What had *I* not given up! From what kingdom had I not endured exile, or any of us, for that matter? Who is there past his first youth for whom the gold has not long since turned to straw, the snow to slush? Be grateful for small talents; one does not flog his goat because it isn't a faun. Thank God if you have an Argosy to distract you, the lure of a Magic Fleece which might still professionally exist for you to find, as it did in Nickie's case but nevermore, alas, in mine. Here I was pushing thirty and no sign whatever of fame and fortune. I wasn't getting into *Who's Who* and I wasn't getting into *Who's Who*. Nobody wanted to meet me, nobody asked what I was like; celebrity did not necessitate my slipping through the town in smoked glasses, as I had once no doubt it would. That was all over now, unless I might be imagined hurrying into New York, New York, in a mackinaw and cap with earflaps, to catch the premier of the latest Ma and Pa Kettle.

I gave Nickie's beat a wide berth, as well as avoiding him socially. It was more than I could bear to see the Sad Sack on duty, lounging along with his truncheon or standing with that abject brilliance on street corners or before shop windows; perhaps gazing into Nothnagle's, for which he had once done displays requiring exegesis. Once I saw him selling tickets to the Policemen's Ball. At such times I felt he was right, and wanted to run up to him and tell him it was all a ghastly mistake. I wanted to throw my arms around his neck and blurt out the words with which Blücher had embraced the British officer at Waterloo: *"Ich stinke etwas!"* But what purpose would it have served? It was imperative that his faith remain unshaken in the wisdom on which his life was now founded.

Once I saw him approaching unexpectedly — he had apparently been shifted to a new and less populous precinct.

He was twiddling the nightstick on its thong, and walking with that peculiar flat-footed waddle that cops seem to develop. I ducked into the entranceway of a deserted shop and flattened myself against the door, hoping he wouldn't see me. He might not have, but a woman across the street did, and recognizing something cops-and-robberish in the tableau, made a sign to the officer and pointed at me. I heard his footsteps drawing measurably closer, slowly, cautiously.

"Boo," I said, smiling as I came out. "Hi, Nickie. How are things? I saw you and thought we might have a bite of lunch, if you're not tied up."

"No, I'm free. The Greek should be having chicken and pilaf — it's Tuesday."

"Oh, let's not go there. I don't like chicken and pilaf. Let's take a cab and go to that Armenian place you discovered. Where they do the shish kebab so well."

There was a tale behind my avoidance of the Greek, whom I was steering clear of too, those days.

You will remember that the Greek also was a recipient of my wisdom. Along with Mrs. Thicknesse, I had urged him not to spoil his place. His respect for me as a person superimposed on my prestige as Lamplighter had moved Nachtgeborn to heed my words. The result? The teen-agers on whom his trade increasingly depended swarmed into the remodeled, juke-boxed and chromium-plated Sugar Bowl across the street, while the Greek tottered on the verge of bankruptcy. Even the adults went to his competitor.

"They're not adult in the matter of taste," I explained to the Greek. "There, they're immature."

"And what do I use for money while they get mature?" he put to the man who was almost his sole connoisseur. "Where are you going?"

143

"I have an engagement. We'll discuss it another day."

"Is tomorrow too soon?" he called after me. "Maybe you don't like the echo in here!"

The Greek did not take the role of curator of Americana in very good part, and he made no bones about it to the man who had saddled him with it. I would drop in for a sweet or a sandwich, only to have him mosey up as I bent over my food and inquire ironically, "How are things with *you?*" his dark eyes liquid with reproach.

"Well, spoil it then, damn it, spoil it!" I snapped at last.

"Now he tells me," he said, flapping his hands at his sides. "The other guy's got the trade now. What I wanted to do was jump the *gun* on him."

"These things take time," I said. "You'll be discovered."

"Yeah, with my head in the oven. Holding on to the past is all well and good, but I can't eat nostalgia."

I frequented the Samothrace with loyal regularity but flagging zest, for it is a fact that the Greek wore me thin with implied and finally outright claims that I had misguided his strategic thinking and "put him in a pool of blood," financially speaking. He would have nagged me about it now as I sat waiting for Nickie, to discuss a little pool of blood of my own, but I had given him a prophylactic glare which told him I was in no mood to be needled, or even talked to. The Greek, who knew a lot about people's business from the polite interest he took in their conversations, contented himself with calling over, as Nickie entered the door and a cab drove off outside, "Here comes another one of your clients, I believe."

"Hello, Nickie," I said.

I watched him set his cap on a chair and give his Sam

144

Browne belt a hitch before sitting down, for of course he was in uniform.

"Can you break away from your beat like this?"

"I was at the station-house when Carmichael called you." (Carmichael was back at his post, the job in the state capitol having been only temporary.) "This is on my way back to the beat. Call it a long lunch hour. Now what the devil is this all about? How can you say Cheshire was with you? How can you be sure of that? What gives?"

"I didn't say I was sure," I said, crossing my legs. "Carmichael's got it all twisted up. It's all a skimble-skamble anyhow because Cheshire sees me regularly — the parole thing — and I can't think on the spur of the moment when he's been in. I had reason to hedge for time in this case because . . . Well, hold on to your hat. Here's the whole story. I think you'll find it rather amusing."

I related my little caprice in the Continental manner that had become more or less second nature with us here, pausing occasionally to wipe sweat off the palms of my hands. I told him everything, leaving out only the name of the lady. I punctuated the narrative with sips of coffee which the Greek had at one point interrupted it to serve.

When I was through, Nickie said, "Sweet Lord almighty."

I don't know whether he felt that famous first pang of pleasure we are supposed to on hearing of a friend's trouble or not; he never smiled, and he was the gentleman throughout. And why shouldn't he be? What was at stake was our separate hides, and neither could save the other's without the gift of his own. If I retracted the alibi, Pete Cheshire would scandalize me to God knew what hellish ends; if Nickie took the heat off Cheshire to spare me that, all his brilliant deductions would go down the drain, and with it in all likelihood the chance for which he sickened: to get out of that uniform and into mufti. This was his Big Break, as they say in the theater. But I was curious about those brilliant deductions.

"By the way," I asked him, momentarily forgetting my own woe in my admiration, "how did you dope out who the Smoothie was?"

He waved the question away with an airy it-was-nothing gesture. "I'll tell you later. We've got to concentrate now on pulling the fat out of the fire, and fast. There's not a moment to lose."

"You mean *I've* got to pull the fat out of the fire. Because of course I'll get you off the hook, Nickie."

"Well, now wait. What's at stake? Your domestic life, my career. *Love versus Labor.* And I think your home is obviously the more important, just as mine would be if it were the other way around. This way nobody'll be any the wiser. I mean if you keep mum, things can't get any worse; if you talk, they will."

"Look, don't think I don't appreciate this, but it's out. I'm going to Carmichael and that's flat." I nervously feared losing the chance for altruism which I now suddenly saw as cleansing away the selfsame stain which it laid bare. The poison would carry its own antidote. What the deed unearthed would put me in the doghouse with my wife; the deed itself would almost simultaneously be admired, getting me out. I might even come out a little ahead. I could hear them already saying, "He *could* have kept his mouth shut. It took guts to do what he did. No, I think you can be proud of your husband . . . Migh-ty proud . . ."

"Let's weigh these pros and cons a little more carefully," Nickie was saying. "My career could survive the setback but what of your marriage? Oh, I'm not saying Crystal

146

would divorce you, but it'd rock the old matrimonial skiff, maybe disable it for the rest of the voyage. It's easy to get another job, but not another wife."

"Now cut it out," I said. "We're also talking about your marriage, not just your career. How much longer do you think Lila's going to stand for your being a cop? Not much if I can read the signs. Not in the crowd she wants to hang around with. Your muffing this may be the thing that'll curdle her for good on you. The chips are down and all your prestige is riding on the pot. This is it, for you. Thanks just the same, Nickie."

"But I'll *have* another chance. Now that I know Pete Cheshire's the Smoothie, he's a sitting duck. All I have to do is watch his every move. I'll tail him myself if the force won't — after hours!"

What gave here? Had he too a debit he was trying to crucify himself out of? As the bidding for the chance at nobility went forward, we seemed to me like a pair of auction-goers whose each successive offer raises in the eyes of the other the value of the object being striven for.

"He'll only put the squeeze on me again and we're back where we started," I protested.

"But why should you do this — this . . . ?"

"This act of self-sacrifice?" I suggested levelly. "This deed of honor few would be capable of in these crass times?" When he did not answer I went on, "This gesture of sterling worth *so much more indicative of moral fiber than the peccadillo it exposed was of moral frailty?*"

"Well, no, I only mean — "

"That it's a far, far better thing I do than I have ever done before? A far, far better rest I go to than I have ever known?" I lowered my head and a sob caught in my throat, for heroism has always had the power to move me.

147

I thought it fitting that here, here at the Samothrace where Nickie and I had so often conceived of life as an intellectual feat, we learned that it is in fact a moral one. We had been clever so long that it was now necessary for one of us to be good.

In moments of stress, we often say things that seem to "come out of left field." An inflamed association, a forgotten but vital nerve-end set tingling like a bell in some remote corner of the house during an electrical storm, possesses the moment. Now I remembered an expression of my departed father-in-law's.

"It was one of those colloquialisms that are so much more vivid than all your fine words can ever be," I said. "Whenever something out of the ordinary, or outrageous, happened, he'd say, 'Well, if *that* don't beat the dogs a-fightin'!' He'd probably say it now."

Nickie reached across the table and laid a hand on my forearm. "He probably also used to say, 'It'll all come out in the wash.' It will."

I dropped my brow on my hand and shook my head. "Dear God, what it all comes to. And in our youth we thought everything was possible."

"Well," said Nickie, picking up his blue cap from the chair as he rose, "it looks as though it just about is, doesn't it?"

Eleven

I sat in the musty phone booth with the door open, waiting for Captain Carmichael's line to be free. I had headquarters but not him yet.

Just how much heroism would be entailed? Would I be put in jail for obstructing justice, if only for a couple of hours? Which was the corniest of the awful "illustrations" with which I had cynically batted out my column from day to day? Without a doubt the one about the artist who squeezed blood into his paints, thus putting something of himself into his work. That was what I was being called upon to do: I must put something of myself into my work. Yes, having preached platitudes I must now practice what I had preached. I must eat my own cooking.

The wait for Carmichael was a long one, and I got in a little more rehearsal.

Trailing a leaf across his cheek, the lovely Ramarosa asked: "What is a stalemate?"

"A wife who has begun to pall."

"Then what is a checkmate?"

"One who handles the spondulics."

So his legend spread from the islands to the mountains of the mainland, and from one continent to the next as eastward he flew from each new scrape. It would be hard to say from which his notoriety most sprang, his sexual prowess or his devilish wit, but together they kept him on the move, for he never, as he chaffered, "stayed for his downfall." The old men with faces like parchment feared him on both counts, having daughters as well as populaces on whom holds might be loosened.

"You must flee," he heard at last from Ramarosa. "The King my father has now been set against you."

He leaned to a bowl of fruit and twisted a grape from its stem. "The King is a royal nuisance."

"Do not. Your humor is already resented by those in high places who are the objects of its barbs."

"These are only rube-barbs. Wait till you hear my city stuff."

"Never has my father had a wise man and a jester in one, until the Lamplighter. Now the old jester and all the soothsayers both plot to kill him. The invitation to play chess was a plot. Now they have intercepted his notes, and have convinced the King that I have been made free with. The Duke is behind it all — the illegitimate son who wishes to be monarch."

"I'll crown the bastard."

"The Lamplighter's tongue is as swift as the hummingbird's wing."

"And as the hummingbird's breast, so soft is my pale one's cheek, and as sweet as the nectar of which the hummingbird rapes the flower."

The Princess turned and sighed profoundly.

"I was glad for the hours heaped with more joy than the heart can hold, and which it wishes in vain could be put by for another time. For as the Lamplighter has said, we sometimes have the moon by day, but never the sun at night." She sprang to her feet and listened at the door.

150

beyond which was the faint scuffle of feet. "I have not told you this till now. We have a yearly sacrifice for which the victim is to be chosen today. He will be the year god, but will die in the honor. His heart must be plucked out, still beating, and offered as a propitiation for the sins of all. Wear these veils, and slide down the vines at my window. Go to Smyrna, to the home of one Timon, a merchant. He is an important man in the community and knows the many wise sayings the Lamplighter has brought from Arabia, China and elsewhere. He is an importer —"

"Someone seems to be trying various keys softly in the door. Who can that be?"

"This is Captain Carmichael. Hello. Hello."

"Oh, hello," I said, snapping out of it, and drawing shut the door of the booth. "This is Swallow again."

"Oh, hello. What can I do you for?"

"It's about Nickie. Frank, I've been looking back, or rather thinking back on that Cheshire thing, and I don't think he was in my office Thursday night at all."

Silence at the other end. Then in a skeptical voice, "It was just whipped up."

"Yes — he did. I mean I'd like to withdraw that alibi. For Cheshire I mean. I was all mixed up a while ago."

Another silence. "Did you find the appointment slips?"

"Not exactly . . ."

"How come you were sure one way an hour ago and the other way now?"

"Oh, I think it's been more than that, Frank. And I didn't say I was sure — did I? Anyhow, what I'm trying to say is that I am now."

"Now that you know whose parade you peed on?"

"Frank. You wouldn't accuse me of anything like that?"

"Look, I know how you feel about that brother-in-law of yours. I've been trying to get him out of *my* hair too, and, baby, he's gum. But you understand I can't let your story cut any ice one way or another now."

"But Cheshire — "

"He'll be watched, don't worry. But the dope on last Thursday is now such a hopeless goulash that you realize I can't move on the strength of what either Sherman or you say."

"So you'd call me a . . ."

"Oh, come on. I think you're probably doing the right thing from your point of view — giving the benefit of the doubt to the person who's closest to you. But Sherman's two cents in the case was such moonshine from the start that even this couldn't bring it down to earth."

It was no use. He didn't believe a word I said, now.

"Earthen vessel, darling?" I bent to kiss my wife in the hallway, glad to be home from work early for a change. "You say someone left an earthen vessel for me?"

"No, no — an *urgent message*. From a — " She handed me a slip from the telephone stand. "Mr. Cheshire. He phoned about ten minutes ago and said for you to call right back without fail. It's important. Isn't he that fellow you've been Brothering?"

"Yes. Why don't you fix us a drink and I'll call him. Double whisky for me."

She did and I did. With the message, Pete had left the booth phone number of the Jolly Fisherman, the restaurant where he still worked as a waiter, in the split shift which let him loose at odd hours of the day. He came right to the point and it floored me. It was completely to be expected, yet I hadn't anticipated a shadow of it.

"Thought you were pretty smart, weren't you? Well, it was a neat gismo, but it won't work."

"Gismo? Won't work? What are you talking about, Pete?"

"Tipping that wisenheimer brother-in-law of yours off who the Smoothie is, and then letting him make with the Philco Vance."

"*What?* Oh, my God, I see what you mean."

"I'll bet. He *seemed* familiar, and then finally I tumbled to the connection. Never mind how."

"But it's not true, what you suspect. It wasn't rigged."

"Then how could he get on to me?"

"He's that brilliant," I said bitterly.

"Cut the hoke. You thought you could kill two birds with one stone — get me in the clink and him a medal. He put on a good act with the deductions, but I'm still in circulation — and the price of the letters has gone up."

"Habit is a cable," I began automatically. My mind skated helplessly like a square of butter on a hot saucer. Not so Pete's.

"I thought we were mutual friends, and I've tried to be sporting, but if this is the kind of pool you want to shoot, O.K. About five thou' would just about salve my wounded spirit."

"Quit clowning. You know I haven't got that kind of money around. You said so yourself."

"Dig it up. Put the bee on your relatives. You seem a close-knit group. But get it up in five days."

"Is this in addition to the alibi thing?"

"Yar, as far as I know. I might relent. It depends on how soon I've got enough for my own establishment."

"Damn it, this is a crime."

"You got it, Daddyo."

"Why, you lunk — "

I was served a stream of invective that had me alternately holding the phone away from my ear to keep it from splitting, and pressing it harder so Pete's voice wouldn't reach the rest of the house. "Pete — Pete," I kept trying to cut in on him. "Pete, let me — let me just say this. You're a very complicated person. Your societal drives are in dynamic conflict with your subliminal."

"Go bend a noodle."

"What you're doing now is giving in to your id."

"Screw the big words."

"Right." I heard footsteps approaching and hastily wound up the conversation with a dummy response on my end, and Pete adding that he craved the cabbage in fives and tens, on his.

Crystal handed me the large whisky and said, "Trouble?"

"Not to speak of."

After "eating" my dinner, I slipped out to a bar and put Mrs. Thicknesse abreast of developments by phone. "Could you loan me at least part of it?" I asked.

Her mind went out from under her like a wobbly calf's legs.

"Oh, dearest God," she moaned. "All the cash I can scare up is about a thousand dollars, it eventuates. Things are so tied up. Of course you're welcome to that, and anything else I can get my hands on, but don't be helpful. I mean hopeful. Oh, dear. And if we don't. Will everything be told in Gath?"

"Where?" I was absolutely going to cauliflower an ear, squeezing receivers against it.

"Gath."

"Where is that?"

154

"Ancient Palestine," Mrs. Thicknesse said, regaining some of her composure in the tutorial role. "You know. Tell it not in Gath, publish it not in the something of Ashkelon. Streets."

"It's beginning to look to me that whether we can stop it all depends on one thing." I got a firm grip on my bones. "Where is your husband?"

"In Arequipa."

That might as well have been in ancient Palestine too, for all the good he could do us from it in five days' time. She went on to explain that all one's convertible securities were in one's husband's name, and he would be in South America indefinitely.

There was only one thing for me to do. So after fishing in the return cup to see if my dime had come back after hanging up — every little bit would help — I finished a drink I'd had standing on the bar, pinned up my hair and went home to do it.

My mother was upstairs in her quarters, disposed on the chaise longue with a magazine. I paced her sitting room trying to make preliminary conversation. She said abruptly, "You're in trouble." She spoke with a certain eagerness, almost hopefulness, for the chance to play mother again. She was bored lately, too. "What is it?"

I flattened myself against a far wall and said with shut eyes, "Mother, I've gotten mixed up with another woman. Someone is trying to blackmail me."

"Come and sit by me."

Fifteen minutes later, we had reckoned up that we could raise forty-five hundred cash between us, including the thousand from Mrs. Thicknesse (not mentioned by name), short of going to the trouble of mortgaging something. That left five hundred to go, and I was racking my brain about

155

that when I suddenly remembered something Pete Cheshire had said, about our being a close-knit family.

"Damn it, why shouldn't Nickie do his share?" I said, rising from my mother's lap.

It was to get him out of the soup that I had risked getting in deeper myself. If it hadn't been for him I wouldn't have been in this mess in the first place, because it all dated back to the time I scooted out of the bookstore to placate Mrs. Thicknesse.

"He's not mature, Moms," I said. "And we've got to make him mature by making him face up to his responsibilities."

"There, there," she said, reaching out for me again, but I eluded her.

Taking refuge behind a large fern, I said: "He has a steady job, gotten through me. He must have a little put by, thanks to Lila. If not, there's his crazy aunt," I added shrilly.

My mother extended a handkerchief at me through the foliage. "Here," she said. "Cry. Let it out." She had shed a few tears herself in the course of the preceding scene, but what she wanted was some real precipitation, together. It was her belief that since the McKinley Administration the springs of sentiment had been drying up, to the race's loss. She often talked about the old days, mixing them all up.

"I can remember when you were a little shaver, why, on hot days you'd point to a thermometer we had nailed up on a tree outside the dining room window and say, 'What fever is it out?' So let go — cry. Tears are good for everybody, man, woman or beast. Go ahead. Cry."

"Later. I want to try this other idea first," I said, edging from behind the fernery and toward the door. "There's not a moment to lose."

"First promise me something. Promise me you'll never, never get mixed up with another woman again."

"I promise."

"Because they always blame the parents when the children do wrong. So keep your vessels clean. It always pays."

"Oh, I will. One woman is enough for any man," I said, turning the doorknob behind my back.

"One more thing. When you were a little tyke you used to talk in those what-do-you-call-thems."

"Aphorisms, Mom?"

"Yes, those. It wasn't so much what you said but the way you said them, that worried me. You'd lie around weak as a cat, as though it was all you could do to barely talk. Once you said something about letting your senses come to you instead of you coming to your senses. Have you come to them now, my son?" She clutched a pad of my hair and kneaded it reminiscently. "All these neurotic women. The world is full of them."

"I'll give them a wide berth from now on," I said. I was espaliered against the door, standing on tiptoe.

"Who would have dreamt it *then*? Never any energy. I was always trying to get a tonic down you."

A tonic was what I needed now, laced with plenty of gin; I promised myself as much the minute I could get away.

"Everything was too much for you, you said, and nothing enough. What was your Belgrade status? What did you mean by that?"

"I don't know. Loitering among the European capitals, an international polish . . . You're hurting me."

I got the door open and was able to take my leave, after a restatement of my pledges and brushing away an imaginary tear to make her happy.

I had the drink downstairs with Crystal. I sipped it with spurious leisure. Suddenly I remarked, "Oh, that's right, I promised Mother I'd pick her up a few things from the drugstore." I sauntered out the front door, but on reaching the porch, shot down the steps, into my car and off to the Shermans'.

Lila let me in.

"Is Nickie home?"

Was he home! She rolled her eyes to heaven as she jerked her head toward the living room, as if to say I could have him. I found him in his favorite deep chair where, wreathed in tobacco smoke, he was the picture of a genius caucusing with himself.

"I hate to interrupt you when you're working, especially on the Smoothie case," I said after clearing my throat. Lila flopped onto a sofa, from where she watched with slow burns and wit's-end sighs. "But it's what I've come about. Cheshire. There's been a new development which I think you ought to know about."

"I'll leave the room," Lila said, but I caught her arm. I could tell from her expression Nickie had told her everything — it's hard to fake that kind of thing — and I made no bones about my visit. "You probably know what's cooking so I won't lie, hedge, or mince matters. The Captain wouldn't believe a word I said. That's that, so let's not waste our time talking about acts of sacrifice, unusual in human relations, which had to be made and were made," I said, looking from one to the other of them. They said nothing and I went on: "I don't want to hear about it." I shook a cigarette from a package on a table, and they watched me light it. "About how honor has come home, the wasted rectitude perhaps the more ennobling because wasted — "

"Don't throw your match in there, Chick. That's a *false* fireplace," Lila said.

"Sorry. Because there I stood, I could do no other. But the upshot of the whole thing is, Cheshire now thinks I put Nickie wise to who the Smoothie is so he could make hay at headquarters. Naturally he'd get that idea if he knew we were related, which obviously he does. Now he's hopping mad and putting the screws to me for real about those letters. He wants five thousand dollars."

"Oh, good God!" Lila turned to Nickie, about to blurt something, but he cut her off.

"Let's don't get panicky," he said, wetting his lips. "I feel I'm closing in on him. Something I'm thinking through that escaped me. Just one more link in the chain of evidence and I think we can close our trap on him."

"If you'd opened your own when you were supposed to we wouldn't all be in this mess," Lila snapped. I looked blankly from her to Nickie, whom I caught in a vehement shushing motion, and said, "What the hell is this all about? How did Nickie get on to Cheshire anyway?"

"I'll tell you. I can't keep quiet about this any longer," Lila shot at Nickie. "He's my brother and I owe him as much loyalty as I do you, and the way I figure it you're both probably going to need it."

Here she told me the whole story of Nickie's connection with the case, and if *that* didn't beat the dogs a-fightin'!

Twelve

Nickie and lila were on their way to an adult British movie on the evening in question. They were making the second show. The evening was warm but fresh, after a spell of thundershowers, and they walked. Nickie was perhaps drawing on one of the panatelas to which he was intermittently partial.

As they were about to cross an alley, a car pulled out of it with a speed that caused them to step back on the sidewalk, slowed at the street, turned and made off in a splatter of mud. It happened quickly but not so quickly that they didn't get a look at the driver, thanks to the light afforded by a nearby street lamp. His face was dimly familiar to Nickie but Lila recognized it with no hesitation as that of an old student at Shively grade school.

"That was Pete Cheshire," she said. "Do you remember him? I guess he was after your time. He was sort of no good, always getting into trouble, and the last time I heard of him he was a juvenile delinquent." The circumstances prompted Nickie to make a mental note of the license number.

At breakfast the next morning (Lila's narrative ran) they heard on the local news broadcast to which they regularly listened that Jellico's, a hardware store abutting on the alley out of which Cheshire had shot, had been broken into from the rear and robbed of a cashbox containing three hundred and some dollars. The thief had left the Smoothie's trade mark on the scene, the calling card with the familiar sobriquet scribbled in red ink. The Shermans looked at one another with wide eyes across the breakfast table.

"I guess we know who did that," Lila said. "Well! Quite a break for you, seeing the getaway. Better get down and tell Carmichael."

"Yes, quite a break," said Nickie, who seemed, however, in no hurry to transmit his information. I am reconstructing the details from my imagination, but here I clearly see our prince dressing a fresh panatela as he adds thoughtfully: "One a man would be a fool not to take advantage of."

She takes him in, inconclusively, over the last of a cup of coffee. Which at length she drains at a gulp. "So why don't you get a move on? Or don't you think you've got time to go to the station before your beat? Or will phoning Carmichael be O.K. — What's the matter with you?"

"Suppose — " Nickie drops the hull of the cigar into an ashtray. "Suppose this were to be cleared up without anyone knowing the getaway was seen?"

"Cleared up by who?"

"Really."

"Oh, I see." A second cup of coffee for this; she reaches for the percolator and pours them each one. "Make it look like a what-do-you-call-it. Deduction." She sets the pot back on the range from her chair. "Well, it'd be something new in crime detection all right. Working backwards from a solution to a clue. Is that what you had in mind?"

"There's no reason to think it'll be any easier than the other way around, and it may be harder," says he, regarding her evenly over the breakfast rubble. "In case you think this is shooting fish in a barrel."

161

We see Lila immersed in separate, more pragmatic reflections of her own. Holding her coffee to her lips in both hands, characteristically, her elbows cocked on the table, she looks around the kitchen as though already spending the raise his brilliant feat of unravelment will net them. Not to speak of savoring prophetically the elevation in prestige among their set. "I guess you wouldn't get much credit at that, just being a *witness* to a crime. And God knows we need the money, in case this is your chance to impress that damn promotion out of them."

"You don't seem to be listening. The logical problem will be there just the same, and besides, there's such a thing as a sporting satisfaction," says he, his voice gaining a degree in volume in the effort to penetrate her utilitarian rind. "If you think this hasn't any dignity."

"I never said that."

"All right. This way, it'll be a play of wits."

"Of course." She sets her cup down and glances at a clock on a shelf over the sink. "Well, you'd better get over to Jellico's and dig up something that points to him."

Nickie had time for only the merest look at the scene of the burglary before getting on to his beat, but his eyes in those few minutes drank voraciously of data, and what they missed he snared with a small camera snatched up on his way out of the house. On his way home from the beat that afternoon, he dropped in at headquarters to see Carmichael. He sauntered in and (this part I later got from Carmichael) hoisted a thickening thigh onto a corner of the Captain's desk.

"I think I can promise you something on the Jellico case, Captain," said that barefaced bastard, revolving in his fingers a virgin cigar no doubt. "I had a look at it this morning."

162

"What's up? What can you give me? I'd sure like to get these heists out of my hair."

"Now, now, everything in its time, Captain. As Kafka has said, impatience is a form of laziness."

"Kafka the high-school principal?"

"No, Kafka the noted novelist." Nickie slid down off the desk and strolled to the door. "I'll try to have something for you in a few days. As soon as I've been able to correlate my thinking. I have some theories."

Carmichael studied him narrowly.

"I see your game. Taking a crack at the plain-clothes in your spare time, to show what you've got on the ball. Well, more power to you. But if you get anything, never mind the tutti-frutti — just lay it on the line."

The evening of the following Monday, Nickie's day off, Lila came home from shopping to find Nickie sunk in an armchair in the living room, staring at a wall through clouds of tobacco smoke, both cigar and pipe.

"What are you doing?"

"Working on the Jellico case." He rose and rapped out a cold briar. "There are no clues — at least none that I can use at this stage — nothing that ties in. I got a look at Cheshire's car in front of his house and the tires don't match any of the tracks in back of the store. Meaning he probably changed them. Here is somebody worthy of a man's mettle."

"I don't know how that follows, seeing he's already been caught. Or what amounts to caught."

"The facts," Nickie said, ignoring this, "are as follows. The criminal is a left-handed man in his twenties, five feet six inches tall, walks with a sort of pigeon-toed gait."

"How do you know?"

"I've been tailing him all day."

163

"Is that why your hat is pulled all out of shape? I noticed it in the closet."

"Do you remember Pete Cheshire's being left-handed?"

"Oh, I see. Your problem is to scrounge up something at the scene of the crime that points to that. No, I don't remember anything about that, or the pigeon-toed walk either. Maybe he's put that on the way he took the tires off. Maybe he knows you're following him. . . ."

It was at this point that Lila began to lose her stomach for the tour de force. When, subsequently, he told her he had spent the day going over the premises, she said, "Premises! Why the hell weren't you on your beat where you belonged?" He laughed through his nose with obscure gratification. "The logical premises," he said, "not Jellico's."

When the fifth day passed and he still hadn't cracked the case, she said, "Maybe this was a mistake. Maybe you should have told you saw Cheshire right off. That way you might have made Carmichael feel a *little* good about you, for what it's worth. Anyhow, I don't see where all this futsing around is getting you."

"I'm not futsing around," said Nickie, wheeling about on the piano stool where he had been running off some rambling melodies to relax the tensions of thought and give the subconscious a chance to work. "And I'll tell you another thing."

Deduction, he pointed out on the basis of the dictionary definition which he had taken the trouble to acquaint himself with since embarking on this intellectual *étude*, deduction was reasoning from generalities to particulars, induction from particulars to generalities. In the light of which facts mystery writers, going on about the "deductive feats" of their protagonists, were misusing the word on a scale unparalleled in the history of poor English: what they meant

164

was induction. "This is probably the only case of pure deduction in the history of crime detection," he said. "In case you think it hasn't got any dig — "

"Oh, for God's sake, I never said it didn't! And please don't play that underwater thing of Debussy's again. I've heard it so much I'm getting the bends."

"And is it so different from the problem police often face, of knowing somebody's guilty but not having the evidence to prove it?"

"No! And don't fill up that stinking *pipe* again, I can't stand it."

"That's easily remedied," Nickie said, and clapping on his hat, went out for a walk.

Then and in the hours that followed, Nickie gave the case his best, never doubting the eventual triumph of his efforts nor the respectability of his enterprise: for was its challenge any less than that put to the assembled Parisian chefs who were given a dish to eat and then asked to name its ingredients? It was while lying in bed that night that he hit on the ingredient that would point to left-handedness. It could be inferred from the direction in which the particles of glass *must* have flown when the window was smashed from the outside. Of course! How one overlooks the obvious in the quest for the obscure. Well, he needed something more than that — and he got it the next day.

Tailing Pete at some odd hour, he saw him walk from the Jolly Fisherman to Jellico's hardware store, and cash his pay check there. Nickie had Carmichael on the phone inside of twenty minutes.

"Captain? I thought you might like a little present of the Smoothie. On the basis of the direction the particles of glass flew when smashed — and this is important as the glass is that wire-mesh you really have to hit — he was left-handed. Secondly, your criminal is someone familiar enough with the place not to have had to muss it up to find the cash box. Now, suppose you were contemplating this theft. How would you find out where the proprietor kept his money? You might take him a check to cash, or save up two checks if they were pay checks, so the amount would be too big for him to handle from the till — and watch where he went for the money. I called on old man Jellico today and asked him about people who've been in to cash checks. He gave me a few, including a fellow who, oddly enough, had just been in for that very reason. Fellow called Pete Cheshire. Name mean anything to you?"

So Cheshire was run in, and he gave his alibi, also incidentally lighting a cigarette with his right hand to add to the confusion, and that was that. Nickie was back in the doghouse with Lila, to remain there even after she learned it was I who had queered his diagnosis. I never quite understood why she was as tolerant of me as she proved to be; probably because none of my part in this could make Nickie's pickle the less exasperating to her as a wife.

"You know what this whole thing reminds me of?" she said, speaking from behind his deep chair. "It reminds me of a vaudeville act I once saw where the fellow played a violin by tucking the bow under his chin and scraping the fiddle across it. That's you, you couldn't do a thing the normal way. You have to do it bass ackwards."

His eyes retained their glaze through this and later strictures, and through some of Lila's story the night I came canvassing for funds, but not much. A third of the way, along about where I began to understand what she'd meant about opening his literal trap instead of trying to close his logical one, he rose and went to the kitchen for some much-needed (by him) beer.

When she finished I looked at him, installed in his deep chair and already halfway back to Nirvana, putting pipe and beer alternately to lip, and thought you sonofabitch. Knowing all this while I sweat blood, all the while I sat at the Greek's showing sterling qualities. Then almost immediately I relented. The worse people are, the easier it is to be objective with them. We fuss at what irritates us, but try to understand real breaches of behavior. And wasn't the very absurdity of his mare's-nest a measure of his need to get into mufti, of the depth of his problem? I remembered that he had once called me "the intellectual's Mortimer Snerd." How could you feel anything but affection for a man able to go so wide of the mark?

"This is all water under the bridge," I said as the practical one who must take hold. "What we need first is to get the money lined up. I need another five hundred bucks? Can you help me?"

Nickie said quietly, "I'll give you more than that."

I thought he meant I could have the money, and after thanking him I spoke a little of Pete Cheshire. I thought it needed saying that Pete deserved a little understanding along with the rest of us.

"He was an unwanted child," I told them.

"He'll be wanted when I get through with him."

Nickie's path was vague in distant spheres again, and I took his rejoinder to be a professional promise, like MacArthur's "I shall return." In short, a boast that he *would* in time close the ratiocinative trap on our rogue. What he meant was precisely the contrary.

Lila phoned me at my office the next afternoon and said, "Nickie's made a clean breast of everything to Carmichael. Including his monkeyshines. He wanted to get Cheshire behind bars where he could never trouble you any more."

So it was Nickie who now had taken off corruptible and put on incorruptible, who had doffed the cavalier's plume for the martyr's hood. A change not unnoticed in his lady's heart, judging by the snuffle on the other end of the line.

"Gosh," I said, my own eyes misting. "And is Cheshire behind bars?"

"Well, Carmichael's promised to pick him up for questioning again, but he's not very hopeful that the testimony of a cop that he was seen in the vicinity will be enough now, especially in view of all the discrepancies Nickie has dug up meanwhile. The left-handed business and the tire-tracks and all. So I don't know . . . Cheshire might be sorer than ever, Chick. But there's one positive result. Nickie's going to be in plain clothes at last."

"That's all that matters," I answered from my heart of hearts. "Nickie's been promoted."

"That's not what I mean. He got the sack. Chick, could we move back in with you for a while? I mean till he gets something else?"

Thirteen

THERE WAS no Pete Cheshire in the Jolly Fisherman, to which I immediately sped. It was early for the dinner trade to begin, so perhaps he was still off on his afternoon break. Two or three other waiters stood about, though, flicking napkins at their tables and muttering taunts at one another.

Kitchen doors flapped open and I was borne down on by the owner in a manner consonant with his belief that he should embody the name of the establishment. Except that what he wore was faultless yachting duds, including a white cap which he swept in an arc ending at his stomach at the approach of each guest or party thereof.

"Cheshire?" he repeated in answer to a query clearly held to have vitiated the flourish in this case. "Follow me."

He led the way through an areaway choked with encumbrances, mostly vegetables on their way in and refuse on its way out, clean out of the restaurant. By now he recognized me as the one who had got Pete his job here. He made his revenge on me by breathing stertorously. Forging along behind him through odors of varying felicity, I found myself at last in a small courtyard. He pointed up to a scaffold where some painting was theoretically in progress. "Cheshire!"

Pete rose smartly into view from a sitting position and began slapping clapboard with a whitened brush.

"Hello, Pete," I said, shielding my eyes against the sun. "It's me." I thanked my usher, who nodded and, after telling Pete to hurry the job along, sidled his way back through the vegetables and ex-vegetables. "Got you wielding the brush, have they?"

"Yar." His glance at the retreating owner said "demoted." He was not waiter timber — not for the Jolly Fisherman at any rate. "Have you got the dough?" he inquired down.

I took a few steps up one of the two ladders between which the scaffold stretched, and rested on a rung. There I sketched in the new developments, including everything Nickie had told Carmichael. "So you see I *didn't* have anything to do with that part of it. Sherman's been canned, see for yourself. If that doesn't prove I'm on the up and up with you, then I just don't know."

Pete assessed me hesitatingly but not hostilely. I went up a few more rungs to repair the disadvantage of being nether to him, till we were at eye level — for Pete had sat down again. I sensed that the target of his anger had shifted from me to L'Hommedieu, which was his absurd employer's name. I pressed my advantage.

"Don't you remember a couple at the alley as you came out? Think."

"Yar, I guess."

He morosely trimmed a dipped brush against the rim of the paint bucket. His heart wasn't in much of anything. He had been wounded in spirit by the transfer to chores which argued him not debonair enough for waiting on tables; and if not that, then how debonair enough to be proprietor in the lyric nights? I took in his garb. He had on a T-shirt and a cap which bore the names of rival lacquers, and overalls so caked with dabs of different-colored paint as

170

to resemble a canvas by the Pointillist school. I took a cautious sounding of my improvement.

"What gives here, Pete? Who put you in this Schiklgruber outfit and made you work in the hot sun?"

"Goddam daisy. There's a guy I thoroughly don't think much of."

"I didn't cotton to him myself. Will he let you go back to waiting on tables when you're through painting the place?"

"Probably let me go period."

I drank in the side of the building which was being decorated. It was visible down a busy shore road which, having reached here, jogged around the courtyard we were in and along the front of the restaurant, so the name on its white expanse was a valuable advertisement. "The Jolly Fisherman" was painted in red letters over a heroic red lobster, but the paint had begun to flake and it was Pete's job to restore all this.

"Let me give you a hand," I said stepping out onto the scaffold. "I used to do a little sketching myself in my time. Your lobster is blurred around the edges, maybe I can sharpen it up for you. Sort of like Tom Sawyer, eh, Pete?" I said, taking the brush from him.

He watched me paint for a while. At last I said:

"Am I going to get the letters back now?"

Pete wiped his fingers moodily on a wad of waste.

"The thing I'll never forget most was the liquor license deal. If it hadn't been for that I might be squared away on my own by this time."

"Tell you what I'll do," I said, meticulously redefining a claw. "Give me the letters back and I'll help set you up in a dogwagon. Now wait! We all have to settle for reality. I'll loan you — now be reasonable — fifteen hundred bucks.

At five per cent, because I know you'll want it that way. You have your pride. Diners are the coming thing, the new Americana, like the ice-cream parlor was twenty-five years ago. Done and done. But on one condition: you go straight."

Pete directed my attention to a nearby cinder parking lot.

"See that heap? It's a '41 Chevvy, which's fenders are dented, which's rings need replacing, which's upholstery is beyond salvation. Compare it with the cars you see coming up that drive, and my house with those."

He swept his arm toward a vista stretching away as far as we could see. It was a prospect of shuttered mansions on opulent widths of lawn, of water breaking on private beaches, of glittering, dream-imbued Long Island Sound. On its bright sands expensive girls toasted their young limbs through the careless summer; on its whitecapped waters speedboats darted and white sails bobbed in a world of wealth at play. It all gave off a special, fabulous hum, like a hive where the honeycombs of leisure forever brimmed. A chauffeured car drew up at the curb below and two couples alighted and entered the restaurant. "That first guy is Carl Bolton, of the mayor's commission," Pete said. "He just recommended a 34 per cent reduction in crime. The other guy is a famous sportsman. He favors the return of the spitball. They're the first of the summer-theater diners." Presently their table talk drifted up to us in murmurs through an open window. I dropped my brush and sat down beside Pete on the scaffold, our legs dangling.

"I don't belong to that world any more than you do, Pete," I said. "I'm a looker-inner from the outside too. And I think you ought to stop this trick-or-treat with me, as though I'm one of your persecutors. Now how about those letters?"

172

Pete got to his feet and smartly resumed slapping the boards with the brush.

"I haven't got them. I gave them to Lammermoor."

"Who?" Then I remembered the grifter whose protégé Pete was, from the dossier gathering dust in my files. "You mean the Agony? Is he out of jail?"

Pete nodded. "I gave him the property to mind for me."

"You mean you've gone halves with him the way you always planned — is that it? What do you mean by minding them for you?"

"Minding them for me while the heat was on me, appraising them and one thing and another. He's interested in that type of operation is all."

"You can get them back of course?"

"I hope so."

"What do you mean you hope so?"

"He's a clever fellow, with a certain strain of sardonic mercy."

Not pausing to argue with him (any more than I did to explore this habit of studding his speech with fine phrases picked up from God knew where) I said, "Let's lay this on the line. How do I go about meeting him?"

"You said you'd like to have lunch with him some time. Make it dinner and you'll impress him more. He likes to operate on the social level — like the Yellow Kid. This is just a tip on how to handle him. I'll do my best to make him listen to reason. He'll be back from Chi two weeks from Saturday. I got a letter from him here. Would you like to read it?"

I improved the interval till I was to meet Lammermoor by shoring up other corners of my crumbling world.

First I went to Carmichael and pleaded with him to give

173

Nickie another chance. "Hell, you appreciated cunning in Cheshire, why not in him? Just because the fast one is on you. And he did put duty above personal gain. Besides, that same cunning may benefit you in some way later on."

Carmichael finally agreed to take him back on probation (!) but Nickie was shunted off to an outlying precinct. It was the punitive switch to the sticks, not to make any bones about it. I drove out one morning to see how Nickie might be taking it.

I scouted the neighborhood cautiously in my car, and finally made out his figure up ahead, on a street which was a tramline but where there were almost no houses or stores. It was a few blocks from the end of the trolley tracks. I drew to the curb about a block behind, and sat watching him, with the motor running. He ambled along in the old way, swinging his salami, as he called the truncheon. His uniform certainly didn't fit him any better than it ever had. He had wired Brooks Brothers in New York to ask if they could run something up for him, but no soap. A streetcar rocketed by and wobbled away to its terminal. Silence again. Suddenly he stopped, raised the nightstick over his head and slammed it down on the sidewalk with such force that it bounced over the curb and clattered into the street. The pique of his career? I waited till he had retrieved it, then put the car in gear and shot past, looking the other way so he wouldn't see me.

Next to the Greek's to see how he was doing.

That one sat equally like a succubus on my conscience, but it was more than I could do to pay the regular visits I knew I owed him. The only time I could face up to him was when I was so low anyhow nothing else would make any dent. This was one of those days. It was also the day when the Lamplighter hit on the specific for the Grecian's woes.

174

"Put in a fine lager," I threw out as I roosted over a hamburger for which I had no more relish than if it had been my straw hat I was eating.

The Greek turned with a look of slow speculation to a partner he had acquired, a brother-in-law who opened early in a new policy aimed at the breakfast trade, while Nachtgeborn came in the afternoon and stayed till one a.m. The brother-in-law's name was Constantine but he was called Al for short. "Beer has made a lot of places liquid," I said, able to laugh at the joke despite my troubles.

The two turned with a look of wild surmise to the back mirror. Flanked with fluted mahogany columns and surmounted by imaginative scrollwork and fat Cupids — well, who could fail to see in it the heart of a period saloon? A cool bower where old timers would recall close presidential races, vintage crimes, and the great rail and marine disasters.

I wet my lips nervously. "I was thinking out loud," I said, dismounting my stool, and fled after tumbling half a buck on the counter.

Deep in spates of exchanged Greek, they did not notice my exit. Eight days later they were in the same spot gesticulating toward the same mirror; evidently I had agitated them like a hot poker thrust into a mug of claret. I sped on by in my car, not daring to think about it. I was on my way to the Golden Ass for dinner with Lammermoor.

What did you expect me to expect? A reed shaken by the wind? Eyes like buckshot and a mouth out of the corner of which maledictions would be leaking? Lammermoor was a lean, handsome egg in his thirties, with perfect teeth and eyes like black jawbreakers. He was bent over a Pocket Book copy of *Moon and Sixpence* when I drew up to the booth where he and Pete were waiting for me.

175

"Know why Maugham is the author he is?" he asked me after the introductions. "He knows people."

"Yar, it's the same with everything — who you know." Pete was slouched over the table chin in hand, spinning the overturned lid of the sugar bowl on its pivot. "Good old pull."

I winked at Lammermoor, who smiled back. My spirits rose. There seemed to be a bond between us, and if I played this right . . . I glanced at a bulge in the breast pocket of his plaid coat.

"Well, what'll we have?" I asked as the waiter thrust menus between us. "This is on me, you know."

We had two rounds of Martinis and then dinner of roast beef and red wine. Lammermoor and I talked about books, and to impress him I ordered a demitasse. Pete cut in on our discussions with a disparaging opinion of the place.

"They put in fancy fixtures and some cheap wine, and dilute the people into thinking they're in a first-class restaurant."

"Recommended by Duncan Phyfe," I said with another wink at Lammermoor. But then I saw Pete glower, and not wanting him to feel left out of it I began to butter him up. I asked him to tell how he had foxed the police in the Jellico job. He opened up after a moment. The unjibing auto tracks? He had switched tires. The left-hand, right-hand confusion? He was amphibious. The indecipherable footprints? Overshoes and on the wrong feet. And how about the theft of the Van Allstyne jewels several days before, in broad daylight? That seemed the latest of the Smoothie didoes though the work had not been signed, no doubt to shed the aggregate risk of the preceding jobs. Pete denied all knowledge of the Van Allstyne affair, though praising it as a caper. "I was up on that damn scaffold at the time, painting the other side." I looked at Lammermoor. So did Pete. Could it be that all along . . . ? "How about his letters?" Pete suddenly put to Lammermoor.

Lammermoor conjured them from elsewhere on his person than the bulge I had noted in his breast pocket, simultaneously twisting out a cigarette. "These are brilliant," he said, unfolding one. "But I think editing has improved them. See if you don't."

He turned a page round to me and indicated a passage in which adroit deletions before and after permitted the phrase "we have been bedfellows" to stand out in unexpectedly startling dimensions.

"But I meant intellectual!" I protested. "This is outrageous."

It wasn't a patch on another bit of tinkering Lammermoor let me inspect — a line scissored off at the bottom of the page and a period put after the words, "our peculiar intercourse."

"Think of the position this puts me in!" I exploded as subduedly as I could in a public place. "What will people think? Why, we haven't even slept together."

Lammermoor smiled. "It shows you what a little judicious cutting will do, as I think you call it in your profession. I'd say the value of the letters has doubled if not tripled, wouldn't you?"

"Well, Pete, was this done in cahoots with you?" I demanded, blazing.

"Not at my express behest."

"Do you know what you're saying?"

"It was before I found out what you told me."

I could only vent my anger on the waiter, who happened to be passing.

"Look," I said, catching him by the coattails, "I distinctly asked for a demitasse. You've given me a large cup."

"Just drink a *little*," he said, and was off.

I sat back in defeat.

"All right. How much do you want?"

To my surprise Lammermoor snapped round the letters the heavy rubber band in which they had been originally secured, and tossed them over to me.

"I don't want any money. Just a favor I think you're in a position to do me."

He moved dishes away to make room for his arms along the table-edge.

"I'm all gummed up with a woman. A girl I guess I should say. I've got my foot in a tangle of barbed wire." His narrative and his expression reminded me of the origin of his nickname — the hell he proverbially went through with females. "I'm trying to get rid of her is the plain fact, but she's hysterical and all mixed up. She needs psychoanalyzing. I've been reading your column the last few days — are you a trained psychiatrist?"

"If you mean am I a licensed practitioner," I answered modestly, "no-o . . ."

"You wouldn't know it from your stuff." (The shift in policy had begun to be heavily shown in my recent copy.) "I'd take it very kindly if you'd try to help this girl."

"But of course. Have her write me a letter."

"That's not enough. She needs the works. Talking to."

"There are doctors in town who I'm sure — "

"She won't go to a head shrinker. But she just might see you. You wouldn't scare her, I mean it'd be different. What do you say?"

What could I say? My job was after all to help people. And I was ecstatically grateful for the letters. "I'll do what I can for the young lady," I said.

Lammermoor was on his feet already casting around for the phone booth. "I'll call Sherry right away and arrange for the first interview."

He had no more than done that than I had Mrs. Thicknesse on the wire to tell her the good news about the letters.

"Hurrah!" she exclaimed. We were both so hysterical with joy we could hardly talk. "Come on right over and we'll celebrate."

"I'll be there in two shakes."

Fourteen

WE MET with outstretched arms and embraced with cries of pleasure. We were free, free! Our being up in Mrs. Thicknesse's bedroom gave us an extra sense of seclusion, of safety from the world and all harm. She had laid a fire against the evening's chill, for the weather had turned abruptly cold, but neither of us got round to lighting it then. She asked to see the letters. I refused at first but she teased them out of me with the reminder that they'd been intended for her originally. I sat near a window while she read them. Oddly enough in the cooled weather, a storm seemed to be threatening in the west, where the sky was the color of body bruises except for one herniated cloud which let through a little sulphurous sunset light. Mrs. Thicknesse screamed with laughter at the emendations, and I laughed too.

Then came the let-down. We had been through a lot, and had discharged what energy we had in a spasm of jubilation. Now we were quite tired. Mrs. Thicknesse leaned with her hand on the mantel and her head on her hand, like a mountain climber pausing to rest on an escarpment to which he has barely the strength to cling. "Done up," she said. Her gaze wandered toward the bed.

"I know. Why don't you lie down for a bit?"

"Faint." She held out a hand which I took.

We went toward the bed arm in arm, supporting one another. The fatigue which lent sanction to our progress toward it threatened to overcome us before we had gained it. But we made it, the bed, which is to say we unmade it.

"Funny," Mrs. Thicknesse murmured from it, in the deepening twilight. "We paid for what we didn't do — oh, how we suffered for pleasures we'd really not enjoyed, you know. Now we take what we've paid for anyway . . ."

"This way we'll have done our penance in advance," I said, hanging my trousers over the back of a chair.

I did not forget my mother in the jasper dusk. As I climbed into bed I remembered having promised her I wouldn't do this sort of thing. My religious training passed before me. I recalled a line from the Bible, "Thy belly is an heap of wheat." By pretending a fit of passion I managed to smother a nervous laugh in my pillow. I felt sorry for that. I quickened the play of my hands and panted deceptively. "Oh, Mrs. Thicknesse."

But she was not fooled.

"These things are always psychological," I said at last, falling away.

"I suppose," said Mrs. Thicknesse hopelessly.

We lay in a truce for a time. Then out of her own gathering tensions she took over prosecuting the hour herself. "What ails thee, knight at arms?"

This was the wrong approach to take with me. All her efforts only multiplied the torpor in which I lay disabled; which in turn drove her to redoubled efforts. "You're hurting me," I said at last, trying to free an arm pinioned in her embrace.

She lay over with her head on her own pillow and brushed a ringlet of hair back from her brow. "Go light the fire. It will give you something to do. Relax you . . ." I thought

that she had never seemed more royal than now in aban-
don, and I wanted very much to let her know I felt this.

"My own queen," I said, and backed out of bed.

I set briskly to work at the hearth. No fire, but my joints
crackled merrily as I stooped to prod it into being. "Damp,"
I said. I sat for a time on the floor, dueling the inanimate
wood with a black poker. I thought I heard a low grumble
and looked to the darkened window beyond which the
storm might be brewing. I remembered reading somewhere
that the signs of middle age begin to set in at twenty-six.

Between the sheets again I was at least as hot from my
exertions as the fire would have made me had it caught.
Mrs. Thicknesse had devised in my absence a new stratagem. She now cultivated the fiction that it was I who was
the impetuous one, the principle being presumably that of
suggestion, which obtains results by pretending that they are
under way. Taking my hand in hers, she conducted it on a
tour of her divinity.

"No," she said at length, as though I required bridling.

"Yes," I said, falling in with the plan.

Here another damnable association befell. I remembered
a man who boasted of having "rutted and roostered his way
across the eastern seaboard" once describing the three stages
of love making as those of golf: namely the drive, the approach, and the putt. I wondered at which of the stages I
was, and became self-conscious. However, Mrs. Thicknesse
noted nothing this time.

"You like this sort of thing?" she whispered.

"Very much indeed."

A corner of the fire caught. It illumined the room momentarily, fluttering wild shadows on the ceiling. Then it
died away and the room became dark. "What was that
noise?" I said, sitting up. "I thought I heard something."

182

"Come, come," she said, drawing me back. "Don't start imagining things. Lie still, palely loitering one, think of nothing . . ."

There was a blinding flash in the room. We both sat up.

"Lightning?" I said.

"But no thunder."

"Are all the windows closed?"

"Yes . . . Lie down. It will be wonderful in bed with a storm."

We had been lying down about two or three minutes when there was another flash of light. This time it stayed on, and a middle-aged man in well-cut tweeds turned from the wall switch and began to set up photographic equipment at the foot of the bed.

"Bennett, what is the meaning of this?"

"Suppose you tell me."

Mrs. Thicknesse sat against the headboard with the sheet drawn up to her chin, an arrangement which covered me completely and for which I was grateful; in fact I ducked even farther under the covers as the colloquy overhead went forward.

"Bennett, aren't you being ludicrous?"

"Not I, my dear."

The voice was rather pleasant, in a nasal way. Its possessor was outwardly pleasing too, from the brief look I'd had at him. A handsome man of medium height, in his fifties I should have judged, with a sickle nose and one eye a bit higher than the other. He looked like a seasoned character actor.

"What do you want?" Mrs. Thicknesse asked, threshing in such a fury that I clutched at the covers to keep them around my head.

"Just one or two more. The one I got looked good, but you can never tell. If the young man will oblige."

"Never!" I called through the bedclothes. "And that's final."

"I can wait."

"Oh!" Mrs. Thicknesse gasped, and flung round and buried her face in her pillow. Lying over on my side, rolled up into a tight foetal ball, I did some clear, hard thinking.

No picture not discernibly containing both of us would cut any ice in litigation. I knew without being told that that was what Thicknesse wanted the photographs for. Mrs. Thicknesse had once hinted that he wanted a divorce, and more than hinted that she would not give it to him. "I have it on good authority he's keeping a young chit in an apartment in Buenos Aires. A café society girl, you've probably seen her picture in the supplements, those horrible brown things that come on Sunday. He wants to marry her. Well, I'll not be treated in any such fashion." All this went through my mind now as Thicknesse adjusted his tripod or inserted flashlights or whatever he was doing out there. There was a long pause broken only by those sounds; then even they stopped; we had reached an impasse. Since a likeness of either of us would be useless without the other, I reasoned forward, it would be safe for one of us to emerge and try a little persuasion. So after whispering to the overturned Mrs. Thicknesse, "Don't show yourself till I get back," I lowered the sheet cautiously till only my eyes were visible above it and raised myself on one elbow.

"I'd like to propose a meeting of minds," I said.

Thicknesse cleared his throat and took in what he could of me, which wasn't much more than you can of a face wearing a yashmak. I appraised him more fully in turn, and found my original fleeting impression confirmed in detail,

184

except for a small trim mustache not then noted. I said at last: "I understand you're quite a camera fiend."

"This will be the first time I've shot a man in bed."

I dropped the sheet to my shoulders and sat up against the pillow. I watched him tilt the camera down a bit on the tripod, at an angle more accurately in relation to the occupants of the bed. "I hope you don't think I'm a sexual bolshevik," I said after a moment.

"Not at all. You're probably a nice enough sort, and I'm sorry about this for your sake. But there are quite sound reasons for my — for this."

"Rake!" came muffledly from the rigid Mrs. Thicknesse. I reached a hand to make sure she had not uncovered herself in the flounce which accompanied the exclamation, and also to tell her to let me handle this. Her hand groped out and drew my pillow over her too, so that her head lay between two. I returned my attention to Thicknesse.

"I suppose this is nothing by your standards, breaking in like this. Sex isn't sacred at all to you, just a farce. To be indulged in according to one's whims too, I have no doubt. A mere bagatelle. Well, let me tell you something, sir — "

"I'm not the judge," he replied dryly.

I paused and watched him again as he made cryptic minor adjustments in his gear. I must take another line; gain his confidence and friendship.

"I take terrible pictures," I said. "I mean the ones I take of other people. A poor subject, too, for that matter. What do you think people will think when they see a picture of this scene?"

"I don't think they'll think it's a mere bagatelle."

"In that case I bagatelle out of here," I said, and smiled shyly at him to see if I hadn't a certain saving humor. "I guess I lack the bump of sense."

"You may get one."

No need to worry about the unction with which this was going forward. I could only be grateful to him for the support he gave me in handling the contretemps with at least a bit of dash, style. This was a duel of wits. Very well then. I glanced covertly at the chair with my clothes on it, then quickly in another direction so as not to give my game away. I mentally plotted my dash for freedom as I continued to engage him in diverting conversation.

"I understand you've been in South America."

"Yes. I returned unexpectedly, as of course you know. But then I often do. Affairs have a way of winding themselves up without warning."

"That is very true," I agreed.

"Although that was my longest stay yet."

"You're in soft drinks I believe? One of the better Colas Mrs. Thicknesse tells me."

"And a number of other things."

"Oh, really?" I said. "Tell me, do you know Elizabeth and Neil Gumm? They live in South America."

"I can't say I've ever met them."

"Down around Bogotá way I believe. What are you thinking as you stand there? What a fool to get caught like this?"

"Not at all. Just rotten luck. You're probably a finished Casanova."

"Would you give me a cigarette? There's a pack on the dresser." I pointed in a direction away from where the chair was. A naked leap, a moment of anthropoid comedy, and the thing would be over.

"Try one of mine," he said, extending a pack to me. Turning back after I'd taken one, he drew the impeding chair away toward the window, quite out of reach. Asphyxiating that hope.

Of course I could have leaped out of bed, grappled with the sonofabitch, smashed his camera to bits or at least overturned it, but I didn't. It was never a question of a scuffle. Instinct, breeding, call it what you will, precluded any such squalid messings about. We were two men of the world who could certainly resolve this in a manner consonant with that plane.

But try as I might to put my brain to work at the problem, all I could do was barrenly revolve the thesis that this was a day I should have stood in bed.

"I pictured you as different somehow," I said, judging him sorely over a width of upheld bed-linen. "Not someone who'd do a thing like this. I thought of you as more . . . more . . ." The fact was I hadn't thought of him as anything but cuckolded, and very little of that. "What's so damnably unfair about it all is that it's not in the least the way it looks. We haven't actually . . ." A smothered sound came from the pillow sandwich as of woman wailing for her demon lover to *do* something. "When two essentially decent people get together like this, morality, the higher things or whatever you want to call them, intervene, so that one is unable to consummate . . . is up against . . ."

"Pricks of conscience?" he said, sighting me experimentally through the finder of his camera.

"You could call them that."

"Well, you can always pride yourself on having been good in bed."

He prolonged squinting at me, then turned his camera a hair's-breadth.

"We'll die if anything comes of this," I said. "We'll absolutely die of . . ."

"Exposure? Oh, I'm sorry. You want a light."

"No, I don't!" I hurled the cigarette into a corner. The man's *sang-froid* made my blood boil. Indignation now seized and shook me like a reed. I plowed the bedclothes with my legs and said, "Maybe you're the wicked one. Wanting in the capacity to appreciate the kind of thing we had between us. An intellectual union — oh, yes, it was! — of the sort Voltaire and Madame du Châtelet had. Not that I'm comparing myself to Voltaire, that's not the point. But the point is that *her* husband under*stood*. Voltaire and his wife, du Châtelet's that is, had many pursuits and interests in common. They shared books, listened to music. They conducted scientific experiments together. Together, they tried to weigh fire."

"Did they ever play with it?"

I turned with a disgusted expression to Mrs. Thicknesse and said, "Suppose you talk to him."

I had meant that she spell me while I went back under the covers and tried to work out a plan there. Instead, in a burst of anger ten times more vehement than my own she suddenly hurled about and said, "Bennett, you can go to Halifax! I will not stand for this! All right, *have* your divorce and your golddigger!" — into a burst of light that seemed to fuse with the blaze of her own wrath. He had his picture before I could get under the covers again.

So now he had two. Enough for a divorce on the grounds he wanted — adultery. Guaranteeing the settlement he wanted too, not merely what Mrs. Thicknesse would voluntarily have agreed to. All these speculations went, quite accurately it turned out, through my mind as I dressed in silence presently, after Thicknesse had gathered up his truck and gone. "I'll have a drink ready for you downstairs if you want one," he told us as he made off with the tripod over

188

his shoulder, for all the world no more as if a ruckus had been concluded than if he'd been an itinerant photographer snapping kiddies in a donkey cart in their back yard.

So that was the way it was, I reflected. Instead of committing what we'd paid for in advance, we were to be hanged for what we had not done at all. I saw the scene in court clearly. The *Pick* would have no reporter there but the *Herald* was a flourishing new morning paper, addicted to scandal and with a keen sense of rivalry. *Lamplighter to take stand today . . . Co-respondent confronted with pictures . . .* No, damn it, no! There must be some way out. Something at least easier than those photographs.

My eye fell on the white envelopes on the dresser where they'd been dropped in our merrymaking. The letters . . . I picked them up, put them in my pocket and went downstairs.

Thicknesse was sitting in the living room stroking the stem of a Martini glass between his fingers. He got to his feet and asked, "What would you like?"

"The same," I said. "Very dry, if you don't mind."

I looked up the staircase down which faint sounds of lamentation came. Mrs. Thicknesse had remained in bed. "I shall never rise again," she'd exclaimed as I'd left the bedroom. The last sight I had of her was lying with her hair streaming out over the edge of the bed, like a smoking torch. "I shall never, never rise again. I shall see no one, I shall take no nourishment . . . " There was certainly no point in expecting her for cocktails, whatever portion of her vows she kept.

"I'm sorry about all this," Thicknesse said as he handed me the drink which had been prepared with pharmaceutical care, "but if you knew the whole story I think you'd feel less bitterly than perhaps you do. I'd got wind of your little business here, it makes no difference how, and it seemed absurd to pass up a chance for which I have really every justification. Clara's a splendid as well as attractive woman, but it just didn't wash, with us. Yet she's refused to give me a divorce. That strange pride women have about a thing like that." Something occurred to him and he asked, "Are you married?"

"Yes, I am," I said.

"Oh. I was just thinking if you two hit it off — "

"Look, those pictures," I cut in. "You can't put me through that. I've got some letters here that would be equally, well, convincing, but not as rough on a man, if you know what I mean. I'm willing to trade them for the negatives. Oh, you needn't worry, they're authentic," I said as he eyed me skeptically over his Martini. "Here. Sit down and read them."

He took them and did, after another dubious glance at me. His face was expressionless as he turned the pages. Then his eyebrows lifted. I was glad now for Lammermoor's emendations, which gave the letters at least the force of the photographs, which they might have lacked in their unbutchered state.

"You'd have me dead to rights," I said, pressing my advantage. "Nothing could stand up any better in court than those. They'd suit your purpose admirably while being from my point of view a little more . . ."

"O.K." He stuffed the letters in his pocket and rose, setting his drink down on a table. "The negatives are upstairs. I'll get them. Call it a fair exchange." He paused at the foot of the stairs. "You might write something on a slip of paper, so I'll be sure these are your handwriting. Just an extra precaution."

"Of course."

When he returned I had the handwriting sample ready, and he compared it with the script in the letters to his satisfaction. Then he gave me the negatives, which I promptly destroyed. As I did so I reflected that the substitute evidence would be infinitely better for Mrs. Thicknesse too, as documentary matter in which she was verbally extolled rather than caught *flagrante delicto*.

"No hard feelings I hope?" Thicknesse said.

"No," I answered in a tone as dry as the Martini. "We'll drink to it."

"We'll do better than that." Bennett Thicknesse came forward with his hand extended. "Shake."

I was.

Fifteen

Troubles are like hills. They look impossibly steep from a distance but as we approach them they seem to flatten out before us," I wrote. I applied the maxim to the necessity of telling my wife about Mrs. Thicknesse, with no cardinal reduction in the size of the incline stretching before me. Two weeks had passed and I knew nothing more. No one answered the telephone at the Thicknesse place.

It was hot again and I was working home in the silo (as we still always called the library), where it was a little cooler than the *Pick* office, but only a little. I paced the floor naked except for an eyeshade, and the clouds from chain-smoked cigarettes which enveloped me. The need to break the news of my affair to Crystal became momently more urgent as that hour drew near in which the expected summons from Thicknesse would be served. Some preparation must be made for its arrival. But instead of getting the matter out in the domestic open, I had been spending my spare time repeating words until they became meaningless. I had the day before seen a book of songs on the piano, opened to its index, and my eye had lit on an entry reading "Camptown Races, De." This monstrosity resulting from the simple convention of putting the article in a title last had been enough to keep me awake half the night. *Camptown Races, De . . . Camptown Races, De . . .* went maniacally through my head. Now in the silo something else got its hooks into me. Among the overflow from the living room was a beer mug from Germanic Milwaukee which bore in Gothic letters the inscription *Gott Mit Uns*. It stood on a shelf in my line of vision, and I must ceaselessly revolve this legend as a declaration that one had gloves. *Gott Mit Uns*, I read, *Gott Mit Uns* . . . Was I going mad? No such luck.

But I was not without means of soliciting leniency. I had just come from my dentist where I had taken leave of a corrupt incisor, and my jaw was so swollen that everybody felt sorry for me. Surely enough sympathy could be extracted from my wife to at least blunt the edge of the scene we were about to go through.

The door opened and she brought in my third egg-malted for that day.

"I think something's bothering you," she said as I sucked at the straw, fixing her with eyes that mooched pity.

"Why?" I said, exaggerating the difficulty I had in talking, and giving her telling glimpses of the bloody gap in my face. I belched dismally and said, "Why do you say that?"

"All this food! You've put away enough for an army the last week. Gluttony is an emotional escape, a sign something is eating us. Why do you laugh? You said so yourself in your column."

"You put things so much better than I," I said, catching sight of my ruined grin in a wall mirror.

"You've got suitcases under your eyes."

That reminded me of her "overnight bag" crack at Mrs. Thicknesse, in the repartee I fabricated for her and thanks to which she was now the rage of the international set. Ready to throw me over, everybody said. "What does she see in him?" I heard them all ask. Her latest went like this.

Someone at Cannes had commented, "Clara Thicknesse makes friends easily." Crystal had retorted, "And they make her easily." How I writhed under that one, perhaps her best. I never begrudged her the time and effort that went into confecting rejoinders of which I was the butt, never complained or whined about the mental labor — often very great and undertaken to the now almost total neglect of my own fantasies — which was earmarked for her idealization. But the idealization had become so vivid to me that I was sometimes startled by the real-life dissimilarity to it. Once, for example, she had jarred me out of an intense concentration, during which I was trying to get her entrance right, at a party at Maugham's at Cap Ferrat, by suddenly asking, "Where are you going all duked up?" I had replied, "Not to see anyone who says 'all duked up' and 'my main meal.'" The wear and tear of all this had many angles and ramifications. I answered now about the suitcases under my eyes: "I work hard. I have four mouths to feed."

"Four?" she said, mentally tallying the members of the family. "How do you make four? Whose is the fourth?"

"My own!"

I gave the visor a tug and drank some more malted milk, cross with myself for letting myself get cross. Suddenly I had to have the whole business over with.

"Won't you sit down?" I said. What an idiotic opening to one's wife. "I mean stay awhile. It's a little cooler in here and I like to have you around," I added, drawing on shorts. "You don't even bother me when I'm working. Get your fingernail stuff or whatever you were doing and stay in here with me. Mother can keep the kids awhile. Listen to them thudding about overhead."

"I'm through with my nails — that country-club dance tonight, don't forget — but I'll sit down." She did so with the kind of prim expectancy of women in plays who are about to get acquainted with a man. Which was probably about the size of it here!

I sat down at my desk and began shuffling through some papers in elucidation of a man who can work with his wife around. The wooden chair was clammy against my skin. I gave the eyeshade another tug and sighed efficiently. "Now let me see. Where was I?" I faked some jottings, then I turned a little and said over my shoulder, "I saw Syd Phaneuf the other day."

This was a carefully planned opening. The program I had roughly devised was, first to speak in general terms about extramarital affairs, laying the groundwork for a tolerant viewpoint which would be highlighted by a display of that virtue in my own attitude toward human frailty. Then, having laid this groundwork, to disclose my own tangent. I chose Syd Phaneuf to tee off with because his own marriage had been rocked by adultery but was now again on an even keel.

"Syd Phaneuf, really? How is he?"

"Oh, fine. Grace too. I've heard that from other sources, that everything is dandy between them after Syd's little peccadillo. In fact they seem to be hitting it off *better* now than they did before he got mixed up with that Akron woman. Sometimes a thing like that is good for a relationship."

"How do you figure that?"

"Plows it over. Opens two people's eyes to what they've got, by putting it momentarily in jeopardy. Brings them together with a richer, deeper understanding."

I paused to let this sink in, more particularly to watch her in the wall glass in which she was visible if I raised myself in my chair a little. I could see her select a nut from a dish at her elbow and chew it. She swallowed and said, "There must be easier ways to find happiness."

"There are, but it isn't the same thing. Happiness comes hard," I said, writing. "You have to work for it, deserve it. Its price is eternal understanding, just as that of liberty is eternal vigilance."

I peeked in the mirror again to see how this line of thinking was going down. She selected and munched another nut.

"Does Syd still make that funny noise out of the side of his teeth? That hotcha noise? *Tsck, tsck.*"

"I don't know. We only talked a few minutes on the street. I can find out."

"I don't know why he makes that noise. He's been through college."

"No he hasn't. He's only had two years."

"Of course I haven't seen either of the Phaneufs in over a year, but at parties he was always kissing somebody's wife behind a door. Such shenanigans."

"I agree with you. You mean if two people are going to have an affair, for heaven's sake go ahead and have it."

"Certainly not! I think it's disgusting."

"What would you do if you were the wife in a case like that?"

She drew a finger across her throat and made a tearing noise, a good deal like the one she had just imitated of Syd Phaneuf's, as a matter of fact. The gesture left a vivid red smear under her chin, indicating that her nails hadn't fully dried, but the gesture itself was ambiguous. My next question was aimed at clearing up a point.

"Whose throat would you cut, your own or your husband's?" I asked, hoping for the best.

"My husband's."

196

I turned back to my desk and focused on the more general aspects of the subject. Evidently a little more groundwork had to be laid.

"I was reading an article the other day by a noted anthropologist who claims that man is not instinctively monogamous. His name is Schnewind. For that reason, tensions are built up in civilized man, and digressions are the rule rather than the exception, notably among the more evolved levels," I said. If this seems a little polished for domestic conversation it's because I was reading it from some notes I had prepared for the occasion and which lay in a drawer which I had furtively slid open a crack. I had my back to her of course. "The very generalness of the defections proves that a more resilient attitude is imperative, Schnewind says."

"Cut open Schnewind's head, and inside will be found a large helping of fried noodles."

I cleared my throat and continued: "Think of Warren Gamaliel Harding, said to have had a mistress while occupying the high office of . . . "

I was reading the wrong card. I had jumped way ahead in my remarks, like a lecturer perceiving in panic that he has got his notes mixed. This was from a section about Noted Men Who Have Had Affairs, which was to have been led up to by a series of lesser examples shading modestly upward from Syd Phaneuf.

"You think statisticians exaggerate?" I said, not having mentioned any statistics yet. "But if you stop to think, you realize that almost every couple we know has had something of the sort, provided they've been married long enough. There's the Phaneufs, Ned and Phoebe Shields, that blowup the Hushneckers had — " I could have bit my tongue off, too late.

"Blowup is right. I don't blame Frieda for sticking him for every n i c k e l he's got."

I wheeled about in my chair. "They've been divorced?"

"Where have you *been?*"

I turned around and went back to my column copy.

"What brings all this on?" I heard behind me, presently.

My plan was like a road map in that it was hard to unfold in part. One premature word, an overemphasis, and she would see male trade-unionism coming at her. Maybe I had already given the game away.

"Oh, we were talking about Syd, and then we got on this," I said. "But the thing is, statistics show that the average mature American married male has a point-seven affair."

"A *what* affair?"

"Seven-tenths of an affair. In other words, among ten married men, seven will have had complete extraconnubial relations. And this article says — and it was the point I was trying to make about Syd and Grace — that most marriages survive them. In the vast majority of cases the men remain model husbands after their misstep." I rose and stood facing her with a tremulous smile. "I've got mine out of the way."

She had picked up another nut, which never reached her lips.

"What are you talking about?"

"My seven-tenths of an affair. I'm that all-American, typical, average man. My digression is out of the way and we're statistically secure. For the rest of our lives." My smile broadened as it became more tremulous. "Aren't you glad?"

She said in a lowered, altered tone: "You've been seeing another woman?"

"We were fools. Caught in something that — I wrote some foolish letters which unfortunately fell into the hands of her husband, who's going to name me in an adultery charge, but don't you believe for one minute that — "

"*Ohh!*" she gasped, and turned away. "Do anything but don't stand there and try to justify yourself."

"Now don't call me a liar before I've started. Wait till I've finished."

"You're finished as far as I'm concerned."

"Don't go. We've got to talk about this."

She went to the door where she stood rigidly as though ill. "Put some more things on," she said, turning her head away.

I hurried into the rest of my clothes, which lay scattered about.

"Do you think I don't know how you feel? The man you've lived with all these years turning out to have feet of clay . . ."

"Feet! It's your head that's clay! Getting into a muddle like this."

"I know I've got it coming, but damn it, for a man who himself has always been broad-minded — "

"*Broad*-minded is right. Where did you pick this one up? What's her name?"

A funny thing was happening: she began to approximate the apotheosis.

It goes without saying that I was grateful to her for flaring up instead of bursting into tears. But she is one of those people whom anger makes articulate, and I was subjected to a rain of barbs at least as keen as those I had fashioned for discharge at Mrs. Thicknesse, in my penitential dreams. I was a Pygmalion whose statue had come to life, but to express enmity rather than love. That was

199

still not the core of the irony. She had always lacked, to me, a certain sophistication, worldliness, call it what you will; she was too innocent of mind for me to feel us completely compatible. I had fixed all that. No sentimental, gullible girl stood here dishing out what-for. The woman of the world I had for years tried in vain to make her into was crystallizing magically before my eyes in a matter of minutes. Disillusionment with her husband did the trick.

"The lady's name," I said, "is Mrs. Thicknesse."

She paced away from me.

"It's not as bad as you think, and that other developments will make you think. It was only an intellectual friendship. She just appealed to a certain side of me. You must believe this. There was that facet of me wanting expression. I saw the opportunity and embraced it."

"I can see you."

"The real villain is her husband, a smooth rogue who has got hold of these letters, doctored ones, I'll explain that later, and when they're read in court — "

"Court!"

"I'm afraid so. He's going to sue her for adultery which we have not committed and I'm to be named co-respondent."

She turned in a complete circle, plowing her hair upward.

"The way I feel . . . A man couldn't ask for a better wife."

"Please omit the flowers. Go on. Where does Mrs. Sickness live?"

"Thicknesse. In a house out on Bulfinch Highway. It's an old place but nice, on beautiful grounds. They were formal once but have been let go, and the result is really quite picturesque. Really lovely grounds. Why, it's just past that long curve where the new motels are. Have you seen them?"

"Not inside anyway."

"Let's see. Where were we?"

"Grounds. Probably for divorce."

"Wonderful. You can make a sordid thing sound like a brilliant drawing-room comedy. Probably a fear we have of facing up to the real issues. Could you say we were guilty of Noel Cowardice?" I picked up a cigarette and threw it down. "Oh, damn! This is a muddle I'm a victim of as well as you. If I could only make you skip everything up to now, the way I feel in relation to you, what it's made of me. It's not only that I'm going to wend my maze. Mend my ways. Please believe that the husband you see," I went on, rather inappropriately as she had put her hands to her face to blot out the sight of me, "is ten times more loyal, more sure he wants you than when he walked into it." Here I remembered something from the notes. "Our morals, like our bodies, are better for a little relaxing." I realized as I uttered it that this couldn't possibly be taken seriously and quickly added, "You don't like my little joke?"

"Joke! Don't make me laugh."

"Wow."

This time she opened the door and marched out. And as I dogtrotted beside her from room to room, crying "Touché!" and reiterating that I had been faithless in my fashion, I could feel the gap closing between us. We were now compatible. Completely. And as she threw a suitcase on the bed and began flinging things into it with the declaration that she was leaving me and never wanted to see me again as long as she lived, then ordered me out and slammed the door after me, I knew, as I had never known before, that she was the woman for me.

Sixteen

She decided, on second thought, in order to give the children as little sense of ruction as possible, to stay but to banish me to the spare room. This was my old room, the one to which I had been sent for paradoxes in the long ago. The dear dead days beyond recall. I remembered as I moved out of ours a pleasanter migration in which we had jocularly swapped sides of the bed, because we "both needed a change." The switching of bedside truck such as reading matter and pet ashtrays and lamps, over the cords of which we hilariously tripped, had been only last month, yet it, too, was another time, and involved two other people.

Crystal had lost interest in the dance. I went, because anything was better than staying home, where in addition to everything else there was my mother, ever telepathically alert for trouble to get her teeth into. Besides, I wanted to at least look at the Thicknesse place which was on the way to the country club. I was to tell anybody who asked that Crystal wasn't feeling well, as I had told my mother in explaining her absence from the dinner table. Dinner consisted of an incinerated rack of lamb fixed by myself, equally burnt potatoes, and popsicles. My mother, though outwardly hale on arrival at table, pleaded indisposition in the early stages of the meal and betook herself to her rooms.

Hanging over the table chin in hand, I watched Mike and Fillmore lap their sweets. These popsicles were blue, a color certainly absent from the gamut of latter-day ices as I knew them.

"What on earth flavor is that?" I asked Mike.

"Blue."

"What *flavor?*"

"*Blue.*"

After a few more contented licks, each preceded by an anticipatory glance at his target, Mike asked:

"Does God go to church?"

"No."

"What's wholesale?"

"Lots and lots."

"Why can't you tickle yourself?" I had noticed him earlier in the day, rummaging in his ribs in a baffled attempt to provoke mirth.

"I don't know," I said, and rose to gather up the dishes. "The maid left because she was dissatisfied with her quarters. Should have paid her in half dollars, eh, Mike? Eh, Fillmore?"

The Thicknesse house was dark. The shutters were closed, the doors locked — as one knew without trying them. I got out of the car and peered in a garage window. The garage too was empty. Where had they gone? Thicknesse to gird himself for litigation, Mrs. Thicknesse — God only knew. Perhaps she had gone mad, deflecting the course of things . . . I stood bare-headed in the moonlit driveway and listened. The garden among whose byways we had ambled in another year whispered behind me, its trees rustling in a wind which had sprung off the Sound, setting astir within one-self, as it were, a whole foliage of associations one wished he might shed as simply as the trees did theirs, when the time of tempests came. I climbed back into the car and sped for the country club.

Here all was light and revelry. The nearest place I could find to park seemed half a mile away.

I locked the car and started toward the clubhouse across the golf links.

"That's illegal you know," said a familiar voice. Nickie drifted out of the shadows, hand resting on sheathed baton, into the moonlight.

"Are you on duty here tonight?" I asked, taking in his uniform. "I thought you were at the summer theater." These were both nuisance chores at which local cops took their turns. Nickie had been assigned to the traffic-directing stint at the theater for the night, because they were doing *Lady Windermere's Fan.*

"Took care of the arrival jam. Have to be back at eleven for the leaving. Dundee's sick and I'm filling in here too as long as I'm out."

"I'm sorry to hear about Dundee. Chris is sick too."

"Oh? I'm sorry to hear about that."

We strolled toward the swimming pool where Lila had by prearrangement grabbed a table for four of us. She was alone at it, behind a highball, chin in hand, in the fashion favored by all of us that summer. We joined her and I explained Crystal's absence again. Nickie relaxed and talked for all the world as though he were in summer linens like the rest of the men and not sitting there in a cop's habit — for he had learned the frustrate's trick of inverting a disadvantage, the shock value of being a flatfoot who talked about the Pre-Raphaelite movement. As he began to now in a loud voice. People at nearby tables turned and looked, but none came over. Friends who might once have stopped by now waved and hurried past in consternation. A waiter bending over him with some muttered challenge was sent packing by a membership card which Nickie whisked from his wallet.

Lila looked into her drink. Nickie addressed his remarks on Dante Gabriel Rossetti to me, ignoring her tolerantly, as a man who has simply married beneath his intellectual level. A delicate Swiss watch who must make the best of a union with a dollar Ingersoll.

"How about the Van Allstyne jewel robbery?" I asked in a pause. "Do you think it was Cheshire?"

Nickie had no doubt about it. Cheshire had been run in again for questioning but had wriggled out of things, as related to me at dinner with Lammermoor. Nickie fell to the discussion with zest, for he had been putting his mind zealously and painstakingly on that crucial case.

"Cheshire could actually have looked into Mrs. Van Allstyne's bedroom from that scaffold where I determined he'd been painting at the time. With a good pair of binoculars I mean," he said. "But again the son of a gun's alibi is watertight."

"What is it?" Lila asked, looking up with the first show of interest in the conversation. I remember her glance, as I do every detail of these next few moments, because it was only about two minutes later that disaster struck.

"Well," said Nickie, leaning back in his chair and crossing his legs, "the time of the burglary has been fixed at one twenty-five in the afternoon, from an electric clock which was stopped at that time. It had been standing on her dressing table and was knocked to the floor and unplugged in the course of the thief's ransacking drawers for the jewel box. I ought to say that another link in the chain of evidence against him is Mrs. Van Allstyne's testimony that she had discussed her jewels and where she kept them with a woman she'd been lunching with at the Jolly Fisherman when Cheshire was waiting on tables there."

"Good. Everything fits so far," I said.

"Well now." Nickie uncrossed his legs and leaned toward us, warming to the subject. I noticed that in spite of his confident manner his face was drawn and his color poor. He had been thinking of little else for days. All his eggs were in this basket. "With those binoculars I know he owns because he goes to the races, Cheshire could have seen Mrs. Van Allstyne leave the house with her maid and drive off to do the marketing, as she did that day. She's a widow, and since the maid is the only servant, that would leave the house empty. Pete saw his chance, stole into the back yard from the alleyway that runs behind the restaurant too, and shinnied up the rainpipe that goes along the bedroom window. It's been established that he wasn't on the scaffold painting at the time, but he has an airtight alibi. He had finished painting the white part of the building and had to go to the hardware store for paint to fill in the letters and the lobsters, which were only done in outline. They were to be filled in in red paint, which he hadn't bought yet. His story's been checked and he *did* go to the hardware store. I've retraced his walk from the job to the store and back, and allowing for five minutes in the store and another five he spent dropping in for a Coke somewhere, it accounts for forty minutes of his absence from the scaffold. But the testimony of others proves that he was gone for a full hour at least. Problem: how to account for the remaining twenty minutes?"

"How do you?" I asked. I recall noting again that Lila was watching Nickie and listening closely.

"Cheshire's story is that he had been given a paint chart with two shades of red marked by the proprietor. Either would be O.K., whichever he could get. But Cheshire claims that he had begun to take pride in the job and wanted to get the exact shade of a lobster. So — this is his story — he walked around by way of Captain Ambrose's waterfront market to have a look at the lobsters and match the color."

"Why couldn't he do it in the restaurant?" I asked. "They serve them there."

"It didn't occur to him to do this until he was on the way, he says. By that time it was easier to drop by the market than go back. He only stopped at Captain Ambrose's to see which of the marked shades of red was truer to life, and went on, but it *could* account for the other twenty minutes. The alibi has a flimsy sound, but how can you break it down?"

"Easy," said Lila.

"How?" Nickie asked, smiling tolerantly.

"Because only cooked lobsters are red. Live ones are brown."

Now his own color was better, Nickie's; lobster-red, you might say. But only for a moment. Then it drained out of his face leaving a pallor which was conspicuous even under the dim, mottling lights of the Japanese lanterns.

"So he couldn't have been doing any matching at any fish market. The whole story is ridiculous."

I said, "Most fish markets sell both kinds."

"Not Captain Ambrose. You ought to know that. You've been there often enough."

"But surely Cheshire wouldn't make a mistake like that. He must have seen both kinds every day at the restaurant," I said, my voice shrill with fear.

Nickie was lowering his drink to the table. "Not necessarily," he said in a tone that was odd and dry despite his just having copiously wet his whistle. "You see, as a waiter his sight of lobsters was preponderantly of the cooked ones, and could very well have blotted out his impression of the live ones — if he ever did see them. At any rate he forgot about the difference in the heat of hammering out his alibi."

"It could have slipped anybody's mind," I said. "*It was too obvious not to be overlooked by the active intelligence.*"

Nickie wet his lips with his tongue. We all three looked thoughtfully into our glasses and then raised them simultaneously, so that someone glancing over might have thought we were drinking to something. Which could scarcely have been less the case.

Nickie rose and shoved his chair in under the table.

"I really must get over to the theater," he said, consulting his wrist watch. "It'll be out in fifteen or twenty minutes, and it's a nightmare when there's nobody on traffic."

"Sure," I said.

He seemed to hesitate, and we, motionless in our chairs, with him, as though jammed in some horrible traffic of the nerves which was beyond any hope of organizing. Lila impulsively put out a hand to him, and out of her woman's depth of compassion said — and no one will ever know whether it was the right thing or the wrong: "I'm such a buttinsky. Always finishing people's stories for them."

"Always, Sis," I said, my feet dancing under the table in rage and pain. "I remember one time, I mean the way she seems to know what's on the tip of people's tongue . . ."

"We won't tell anyone. No one need ever know . . ."

Nickie drained his glass standing up and said, "You two have a good time. I'll be back in about an hour."

I watched him shoulder his way through the crowd past the far edge of the swimming pool and out across the golf course, its groomed grass silver in the streaming moonlight.

The last thing I saw was his broad back vanishing into the shadows of a cypress grove which skirted the final hole.

I looked at Lila. She was sitting with her hands in her lap, her head bent. At last, darting me a glance, she picked up her glass and quickly emptied it.

"I suppose you realize," I said, "that you've just destroyed your marriage."

Seventeen

THE REST of that night remains a jumbled but nonetheless dramatic blur of recollections, like the climaxes of a pageant witnessed while one is intoxicated. Which as a matter of fact I soon was. I'm not sure of the precise order of events but I remember at one point a woman imploring her wet-blanket husband to stay. "The night is still young," she said. "Yes, but you're not," answered he. That must have been relatively far along in what I do remember — after I caught my last sight of Lila waltzing lethargically in the arms of a bond salesman named Nat Williams, as I made my way out of the dance floor out onto the lawn where stood the chance booths, and specifically toward a pair of rangy girls who were standing together somewhat off from the crowd.

The woman in charge of arrangements for the affair, a benefit, was an industrial psychological consultant who was currently being retained by a corporation with feelings of anxiety. She was one for turning every opportunity to therapeutic account, and at her suggestion the jobs of hostesses had been given these two gawky girls on the ground that they above all needed the experience of greeting people, to build up their poise. The oncoming crowds had instead shattered what little self-confidence they might have had, and as a consequence they spent most of the evening cowering in corners together. I made it my job to try to put them at their ease.

"Why does a shaggy dog cross the road?" I asked, walking up to them.

They giggled and looked at one another. The taller mortifiedly fingered a badge pinned to her dress which read "Hospitality Committee."

I drank from the double Scotch I was carrying and said:

"It is possible to administer a bromide without inducing a headache."

They tittered, exchanging glances again, and shrank farther back into the shadows. I pitched a cigarette into the shrubbery and went back toward the clubhouse. On the way I stopped at a fountain. Brooding there, I thought I had more tears to shed than it, could they but be unstopped. I hurled my glass into it. It shattered on a stone dolphin. The fountain plashed serenely on. I got a fresh highball at the bar and then I was sitting with it on one of the many folding chairs arranged along one wall, watching the dancers. They seemed, in my haze, to have a busy and yet at the same time dreamy quality, like speeded up slow motion. I turned to look at the woman sitting on my left and the profile seemed familiar. It was Mrs. Gutman, to put it crudely. My old first-grade teacher. She recognized me and was off.

This person was a deluge of words and a drizzle of thought. And I imagined as she talked how that fluency ought to be channeled over her chin and down along a spillway for conversion into cheap power. She breathed through a gherkin in the middle of her face, audibly over some of the softer orchestral strains. Her hair was an arrangement of plaited bowels, and her face was a spiral nebula of freckles. It merged into other Milky Ways running along her neck and shoulders, which were lost in turn in further super-galactic systems at which the imagination reeled . . .

"What is the matter with you, Charles? Are you ill?"

"Not yet. Go on. You were saying?"

Because I wanted to sit glazed in stupefaction and listen to Mrs. Gutman. I wanted to be bored to death, as good a way to go as any. I wanted to lie down in boredom as in drifted snow, numbed to rest. The liquor was warming me for that farewell, and I sank in grateful somnolence as the flakes everywhere dreamily descended. She spoke of her garden and what seemed a way of broiling roses. That couldn't be right, any more than the floors of pork on which she next seemed to be discoursing. Cork? No, leave it pork. Pork floors. Go out on that note.

Where was Lila? What was Crystal doing? Mrs. Thicknesse? Nickie? Would he come back later after seeing Oscar Wilde suitably adjourned?

" . . . Need good eyes for driving. Since I learned to — "

"Driving, my dear Mrs. Gutman, has become pedestrian. Jay-walking is the last adventure open to man." A final twitch of assertion, a hand raised feebly in the falling snow . . .

Later beneficent hands, very possibly Mrs. Gutman's, laid a plate of foodstuffs in my lap. Tilting to the left, I watched beet juice trickle off the scalloped edge of the paper plate and stain the knee of my trousers, and laughed weakly. Because I hated me so. Was it a character in Millay's *Aria Da Capo* who loved humanity but hated people?

The industrial consultant hung over me.

"Look, the hospitality committee feel left out of things. Could you dance with them?"

"One at a time?"

"They're over there."

"I'll be glad to," I said, already weaving a little as though in preparation as I rose. She took my plate.

"It would help make them feel at home." She was a thin, frail bulldozer of a woman who was bent on seeing her stratagem through, even if it meant nervous breakdowns for the beneficiaries. The hostesses had been cajoled, threatened and possibly dragged indoors by sheer physical force, and now stood quaking in a corner of the dance floor as the woman led me toward them. She towed me along by the hand, like a boy at his first function.

But not for long. I broke free of her grasp and capered on across the floor in a pantomime of already holding someone in my arms, in a general invitation to hilarity. Without missing a step I caught up the taller of the hostesses and plucked her away into the swirl. "When will the dancers leave her alone?" I quoted prettily in her ear. I had been wrong about mankind. We were O.K. We were all right in there. "And I said to the rose, 'The brief night goes in babble and revel and wine.'" Next I would snatch up her friend, and after that the psychological consultant and even Mrs. Gutman herself, with whom, a broiled rose at her waist, we would glide till dawn across floors of pork.

"Santayana has called skepticism the chastity of the intellect," I panted. "Just so might we call chastity the skepticism of the flesh."

We bore through the traffic toward a palm, also potted. Another couple bumped us, and I paused to jot an imaginary license number, amusing all. Then off and away again. The band paused between songs and we stood a moment. I put the flat of my hand against the trunk of the palm and leaned against it with one foot crossed over the other. I drew a long breath. "Chesticism —"

I went over in a wealth of foliage.

"Officer! Officer!"

"Where's that cop?"

"Here he comes. Officer!"

Then unseen arms were bearing me up, and I was going away in a chair of hands like Sewell Avery from Montgomery Ward. Only we swam drowsily through enlarging seas, lost latitudes from which in youth we'd heard the names of ports like summoning bells. A surf of voices beat about my ears. Did I wake or sleep? The mad bronze of moonlit waters stretched a path to islands held to be blessed. But the waters darkened subtly; and at nightfall, plunging downward to their velvet depths, we sank to rest among the stars we had not touched.

I came to in my living room with Nickie bending over me. When he saw I was all right he sat down in an over-stuffed chair and returned to a cup of coffee he'd had on a table. His coat was off and his tie loose.

I sat up slowly. He looked over without getting up. "I took you home. It's only a quarter to one. Lila's still there. It'll probably last till dawn."

"More than I will," I said flopping back and putting my hand to my head. "Where's Chris?"

"Went to the dance after all. Jumped out of bed and off in a taxi. We probably passed her coming home. I took you in your car. It's in the garage. Your mother told me about Chris. She helped me drag you in."

I rolled an eye apprehensively around. "Where is my mother?"

"I made her go back to bed. She wasn't well. Something she ate, apparently." Nickie sipped coffee again.

"Could I have some of that?"

He got me some from the kitchen, strong and black. After that and a raw egg in cold tomato juice, drunk in the kitchen, I felt better. But when I wandered back to the living room I saw something that stopped me short.

Nickie was sitting in the chair with his police special pistol in his hand. I watched him raise it in an arc till the muzzle came to rest against his temple.

"Stop that," I said, these words tasting like tinfoil in my mouth.

"Don't worry," he said, taking another drink from the coffee cup which he held in the other hand. "Just getting the feel of it. When I do I won't take any chances." He shoved the pistol back into its holster. "What I'll do is drive out to the Bulfinch Bridge. I'll tie a rope around my neck and the other to the parapet. Then I'm going to drink a bottle of poison, slash my wrists, put a bullet through my head and jump into the river."

What a death was that for a man pledged to understatement? Besides, it was derived from Mencken. I remembered Mencken's description of just such a suicide in one of his reminiscences.

I sat down on the sofa again, slinging my legs out on a chair.

"I'm considered a marriage counselor too, you know," I said. "I've got an idea."

"That's what I was afraid of."

"The idea that for you to go down to headquarters and wrap the case up for yourself and family will take more plain heroism than either of us is likely to see again in a lifetime. I don't know whether you've got it in you. Maybe you have. My one regret is that no one will ever know about it, except two other people. Not even my wife. Now what do you say? I'm very tired. I've been through a lot and have

215

more to face tomorrow. I'm going to be named in a divorce action for adultery."

He looked down at me, for he had gotten to his feet and was putting his coat on. "Sweet jumping Jesus. Who's the woman? You never told me."

"Do you remember Mrs. Thicknesse? You drove her out of the bookstore."

"Yes. Hm . . . I thought her quite attractive. In fact I was trying to impress her."

"Would to God you had!" I groaned, turning my face to the wall — for I myself had lain down again. "Now I don't want to talk about it tonight. But let's keep in touch. We've got to help one another — because that's all each of us has got now."

"You can count on me. But won't it be a little like the two bums in the loan office offering to co-sign for each other?"

"Something like that. I'll see you tomorrow."

He hadn't been gone five minutes when the phone made me jump off the sofa. I answered it before it could ring a second time.

"Hello." It was Mrs. Thicknesse. Her voice was like something puncturing my middle, out of which my insides seemed to be running like sawdust out of a rag doll. "Is it all right to call you? I thought I would because it's good news."

"What is it? Where have you been? I've been trying to find out what's going on."

"Everything is all right."

"All *right*," I exclaimed, incensed. "All *right*. What the devil —"

"Bennett got a crushing wire from his girl saying she'd

married someone else. A younger man. He was in Sheol for two days —"

"Where is that?"

"Hell. The Old Testament. But slowly came out of it. We went to Lake George for a week, a sort of second honeymoon. The rebound, I believe they call it. I was in such a dither I forgot to phone you then. Of course there'll be no action, since we've patched it up. . . . "

I didn't hear the rest. After hanging up I sat, walked, lay in a daze. I was free! Free! I don't know how much time passed. I listened in a heavenly fog for the front door to open. At last it did, and Crystal entered. She started right on upstairs.

I followed slowly, after turning the lights off and locking up the house. I took my time, holding in the good news for a bit, savoring the very agony as one with a glass of cold water in his hands savors a moment his thirst.

"Did you have a good time, darling?" I asked from the bedroom door, through which I could see her undressing.

"Who gave you permission to come into this room?"

"I've just talked to Mrs. Thicknesse. Everything is all right. There'll be no suit."

She answered from inside the closet: "Don't be too sure."

I came into the room a step.

"What do you mean?"

"I'm going to sue."

"Who?"

"Her. For a start."

"Her?" The word came out in a falsetto of extraordinary purity. "What for?"

"Alienation of affections."

"Oh, no. Can't you see it along the lines I said this afternoon? A little affair like this is a slight form of the real disease against which, as a result, lifelong immunity may in most cases be expected."

I watched her timorously through a crack in the door as she pulled her dress over her head and hung it up.

"How much are you going to sue her for?"

"Sixty-five dollars."

"Sixty-five! Is that all?"

"I don't want to overcharge her."

"But my God! You'll make me a laughingstock."

"Then you'll know how it feels."

"But I'm trying to tell you you *won't* be. Everything's blown over."

"That's what you think."

She came out of the closet and went into the bathroom to take a shower. I was waiting for her when she came out, in her nightgown.

"Can't you up that figure a little? Make it ten thousand. That's the least you can sue for and still leave a man with a grain of self-respect. To broadcast to the world that sixty-five dollars is all you value his feelings at — You must be mad."

"Plenty!" she said, getting into bed. She hurled my pillow at me.

"It'll go out on the AP wire and everything," I said, catching it. "Why, hell, that's probably no more than a man is worth chemically these days."

She snapped the light out from a switch accessible from the bed, leaving me in darkness.

"It's an outrage," I went on, finding my voice. "You've been drinking. That's it. You don't know what you're doing. How can a man handle anything as unreasonable as this? What am I to do?"

The last was an apostrophe, not uttered for an answer. But I was given one anyway.

"Why don't you write Norman Vincent Peale?" came ironically from the darkened bed. "He's that man who helps people in trouble."

Eighteen

THE DEFLATION of the lobster ruse brought the first break in Cheshire's composure and in the Van Allstyne case. After two hours of hammering interrogation he admitted the jewel theft, or rather took credit for it. He denied authorship of the other jobs at first; but when the flashbulbs began to explode and the prospect of his picture in the paper to materialize, he suddenly blurted out that he was the Smoothie. The photograph that greeted me on the front page of the *Herald* the next morning showed him declaring as much with a smug grin, under a caption reading "Local Raffles." Next to him, grasping him firmly by the arm in the established tradition, was the rather sheepish "officer whose brilliant sleuthing cracked the case."

So Nickie was man enough to put Cheshire away on the strength of his wife's wits. But that was all he would do. I mean he wouldn't take the promotion offered him in his now skyrocketing prestige, not even with the promise of an opening on the detective bureau in two months. He did what he had to do, to keep the wheels of justice turning, but he couldn't build his career on it. That much pride he couldn't swallow.

He quit the department and got a job driving a truck for a diaper wash. I could see his own private wheels turning. Working in an office, or at any white-collar job that made some kind of sense, he would be just another chap who hadn't lived up to his promise. Driving a laundry truck was an indictment of society. Also, he knew now the pleasure of talking Shakespeare and Kierkegaard while incongruously clothed; for he wore a uniform now too, a gray one across the back of whose jacket was written in crimson script, *The Tidy Didy*.

So I would trail him furtively again in my car and watch him rub it into society. He would twirl the pick-up bags on their necks to knot the tops, fling the bags into the back of the truck, slam the doors shut and clap the locking hasp to, as if in sardonic suggestion that anyone would want to steal the contents, get behind the wheel and drive off with one foot hitched up on the dash and a pencil sticking out from under the side of his cap and that cap at a heedless angle, in abnegation of all vainglory. I would shake my head as I was supposed to and as any who saw him were supposed to, in witness of the ever-rolling mockeries of Time, the hustling and no longer even protested vanities of sentient dust. I used to think that he must have some almost mystical bond with mischance; that he was *geared* for it, simply put together wrong, like the differential installed backwards by the Canadian car owner, so that the car had one speed forward and four in reverse. Not that the comparison is anything but metaphorical. As a matter of kinetic fact, Nickie went like hell behind the Tidy Didy wheel, rocketing like a madman through traffic and taking corners on two wheels, as though still experimenting with that recipe for self-destruction.

Lila didn't understand it. Or she understood it but couldn't have any patience with it. Or wouldn't. She stormed out of the house one night after a particularly vehement quarrel about it, taking the now two children with her, and moved in with us. She made it plain that she wasn't "leaving" him, merely using the move as a lever to make him come to his senses and go back to his old job. She wouldn't go back to him till he went there.

I was content thus to let our two domestic situations hang fire for a bit, since my own work was taking my full time and mental energy. My mail was by this time itself almost exclusively psychological. Waves of this or that theme appeared in it. For instance, there was a rash of letters from wives complaining that their husbands "stuck up" for meddling mothers when it came to. that. I struck out sharply at the apron-string male in a series of articles which I ran under the title "Oedipus Wrecks." I went into the whole Mom thing, equally rebuking husbands who didn't realize where their responsibilities began and mothers who didn't see where their rights ended. Sometimes I scolded the complaining wife for detectable impatience itself neurotic. "The bonds of matrimony," I wrote in a concluding Pepigram, "are like any other bonds — they mature slowly."

I had heard mumblings and mutterings from psychiatrists before, about newspaper counselors muscling in on their profession, but this time there were shrieks and howls even from plain psychologists and case workers telling me to get out of a field for which I had no training. I replied quietly that I was simply doing my best to help the overflow which was mysteriously piling up in the face of all the sterling healers that were around. This "stink correspondence," as Clammidge relishingly called it, added to my swelling chores — which included more and more people coming to my office to see me personally for help. One of these was the expected friend of Lammermoor's.

Sherry Budd arrived one warm afternoon toward the end of summer. She was a small sumptuosity in a dress of blue silk which wasn't so much dress as another layer of epithelium. Its neckline, nowhere near her neck, was secured by a drawstring which ill contained the tender chucks within. What struck the nervous system was a plectrum so crude as scarcely to constitute temptation. I laughed at the transparency of Lammermoor's gambit. What kind of fool did he take me for? Sending this creature to lure me no doubt to a worse vulnerability than that from which I had just climbed free, with correspondingly higher profits to himself. That was why he had solicited my confidence by so freely releasing the letters. "Confidence" was the right word for this game. Well, let him fancy himself another Yellow Kid, but get himself another mark!

I began by not shutting the door, then or during subsequent interviews (for I would discharge my side of the bargain, and besides I was curious). Sherry made for the sofa I had in my office to take naps on, curling up on it rather too felinely for neural excavation, but anyhow. She started to talk about her childhood. She had a habit of shifting about on the couch, so that I was always presented with a decolletage or its thermal equivalent. So as not to be accused of aerial reconnaissance, I paced at the other end of the room or sat listening in the club chair, with her behind me. I would sit there tasting my own worthiness and smiling secretly at what she must think of the Jesuitical back offered to her.

"When I was a little girl," she related in a high yet somehow throaty voice, "we lived in a rambling house on the outskirts of Bridgeport, and blee-me, it was no fun. It was old and drafty. My father had a greenhouse behind it. He grew flowers for commercial use. The greenhouse was really his sole love. Until one day."

I waited in my chair, notebook in lap and pencil poised.

"The greenhouse was pretty big and so was his business. He had to have a helper, he said. Of all the applicants who answered his want ad, the best one he said was a woman who lived near there. He hired her. He said she had experience. She did, all right. I used to take coffee out to him in the middle of the morning, but now he told me that wasn't necessary any more. But one day I went out there anyway with some. He and the woman were on a pile of peat moss over which they had thrown a blanket. I was shocked. I didn't know what to do. For days I thought to myself, Shy tell Mother? Shy?"

"And did you?"

"No. So hence it's been bottled up inside of me all these years. Mixing up my whole viewpoint and coloring my whole attitude toward men."

I made a notation, then asked: "What are your current connections, if any?"

Here she described being "interested" in somebody who answered to Lammermoor's description without a doubt.

"The thing is that I cling to him, but emotionally, not letting it get physical. I suppose I'm looking for a father image and that's why I can't cross the line and become physical with any man."

Now I thought I understood the nature of Lammermoor's agony all right; involved with a girl who held him at arm's length at the same time she dressed, sprayed and deported herself as aphrodisiacally as the law allowed. Poor Lammermoor. I drew myself back to the subject at hand.

"The thing you have never been able to do is forgive your father," I said, rising and walking about the room. "You extend your animosity to every man you meet. What we must do is make you forgive him. When you've done

224

that, you'll be able to judge every male on his own merits. That will be the object of our treatment."

"That makes a lot of sense. How can you make me do that?"

It was a problem. Her father sounded like a shabby sonofabitch indeed. Still he was gone now, and what difference did it make how we silvered him o'er, if it meant easing the burdens of someone yet alive? At last I had an answer worked out.

"The temperature in a hothouse is high," I said, leaning back against a window sill and looking over at her. "The air is close, heavy, exactly like that in the tropics. Don't you think that being thrown together under these circumstances must be as demoralizing as it is in the jungle countries? It's been proved that that kind of heat has a pathological sexual effect, especially in combination with the suggestive vegetative lushness that goes with it and that went with it in the case of your father's day-to-day environment."

I watched her as she nodded thoughtfully. She was sitting up on the sofa now, lengthwise, with her hand on the back.

"Suppose your father had been an official in the British Colonial service, assigned, say, to Tanganyika. And suppose rumors reached you that he was conducting himself in a manner like that you've described. Wouldn't you have the same tolerance we customarily show toward men who have gone native, as the saying is?"

Again she nodded. I drove my point home.

"Crossing the few hundred feet between your kitchen and that greenhouse every morning, your father crossed the five thousand miles of ocean that separate us from the steaming countries of the south. He became a primitive. He went native. Think of your father, out there on that blanket

225

over the peat moss, as having gone to pieces in the tropics," I finished, "and I think you'll find it in your heart to forgive him."

She lowered her head and looked into her lap.

"How much is that?" she said. "How much is all this brilliant advice costing me? I never thought I'd find anybody this keen, and this understanding, What you say is absolutely right. I must learn to forgive him, starting today."

Feeling this was the right note on which to close the interview, I set my notebook down on the desk and said, "That will be all for today."

"I can't thank you enough," she said, rising. She hesitated with her bag open. "I don't know how much you charge. By the interview or send a bill for the whole — ?"

"No charge," I said, waving the query off. "Any help I can be is reward enough."

She came the next week, by appointment, and the one after that, and the one after that. She declared that I was helping her a great deal, in fact that she looked forward to our visits intensely.

"I suppose I'm clinging to you," she said at last, looking at the floor.

I got behind my desk.

"This must be what they call transference," I said in an unsteady tone, casting an anxious eye at the open door. "It's a stage a patient goes through, and our object will be to get you through it as fast as possible. What's the matter with Lammermoor? I thought you were clinging to him."

"It's not the same thing."

"What did you dream about last night?"

"You."

"We can't go on meeting like this," I told her the next

time. The week after that I was my brisk, efficient self again. Folding my hands on the desk I asked:

"Now then, what did you dream last night?"

"I didn't sleep. I felt I had to see you. I was going to call you at home."

"No."

"Hypmatize me."

"I will not."

"So I can at least get some rest. Go on — hypmatize me."

"Never."

"I love you."

I stepped over and closed the door.

"This is crazy," I said.

"I know. It's just the way it is."

"What about your father?"

"I've forgiven him."

I stood over her, holding my eyeglasses firmly by the braces.

"Now, look. This has gone far enough," I said. "And you can go tell Lammermoor for me — "

She flew to her feet.

"That's all finished. Haven't you got eyes in your head? Oh, everything you suspected about us is true — that he put me up to this and all. But I'm through with him. It's you I love. I love you, love you, *love you!*" she repeated with grueling zest.

"*Shh!* Someone might hear you," I said. "Now sit down there calmly and listen to what I'm going to tell you. Because I'm only going to say it once."

I got out the bottle of whisky and poured her a drink. I had one myself. I got down to brass tacks. I told her we were through. I made it plain that she was never to set foot in here again, and certainly never to phone my home under pain of death. She protested at first, but finally gave in. She said in a low, quite controlled tone: "Then I want to pay you what I owe you."

"I don't want anything. I've told you that."

"But don't you see, it'll help me realize this was a purely professional relationship, as you say. Get the other nonsense out of my head. It's the best beginning I can make toward that and besides, it's something I want very much to do. For my own self-respect if nothing else. I don't care what you do with the check. Give it to your favorite charity, eat it. The important thing is the act of my giving it to you." She had produced a pen and checkbook and was already writing on the arm of the sofa.

Since I had no intention of doing anything with it but tear it up, I saw no harm in letting her draft the check and drop it on my desk. She suggested a hundred dollars and I said that was all right with me. I just wanted to get her out of there as fast as I could. Before going, she asked me to recommend a sedative. I told her only a physician could do that, but did give her the name of a new pill, Easerol, for which no prescription was required. She asked me to jot it on a slip of paper in case she should forget.

After bundling her out the door, I poured myself another stiff one. Sipping it gratefully, I congratulated myself on having wound up the nuisance and extricated myself from it as adroitly as I had. I was free, free! My eye fell on the check, lying between my two feet which I had hoisted up on the desk. I reached for it and was about to tear it up when something made me pause. Instead of destroying it, I put it in my wallet, tucking it well down in a secret compartment. I couldn't have said then just why I did that. But I wasn't long in finding out.

We say that nothing succeeds like success, and so, I suppose, nothing deteriorates like deterioration. Lila held fast to her ultimatum, but not to the exclusion of running over to the apartment now and then to try a little verbal persuasion on the hermit. One night she phoned me ten minutes after she'd left our house on one of these often impromptu descents.

"Can you come right over?" she said. "He doesn't know me."

"Who doesn't?"

"Nickie."

"What do you mean?"

"Just what I'm saying. He was sitting in the armchair with the glazed expression when I walked in, and said, 'Who are you?' Then he asked me what I wanted. He doesn't recognize me."

"Great Scott, he's denying you."

"Can you come right over?"

I did, and what she'd reported was true. But he did know me. In fact he greeted me with every indication of being delighted to see me, if not of having been expecting me. He rose and got into a tweed jacket.

"Shall we go have some of the Greek's alleged coffee?" he proposed with the airy unconcern of ten years back. A delicate chill went up my spine.

Lila now insisted on going back to him, but I talked her out of it. It seemed to me precisely the wrong thing to do. She could do him no good, and the sight of her might make him worse. "Who'll look after him?" she asked.

"I will," I said. "You stay at the house. I'll move in with him." I went on to explain that I was in the doghouse anyway and would be killing two birds with one stone by moving into a house where I was needed as well as out of one where I wasn't wanted. Besides, I had a plan for straightening him out.

Nickie had made reality livable by editing from it what was insupportable. So far so good. But why banish the *person* responsible for the incident that was repugnant to him? Why couldn't merely purging the incident itself from his memory be enough? My aim was to manipulate the factors in the case in such a way that he could take his wife back into his cognition while the episode for which he could not forgive her remained excised. It would be a delicate operation, to be performed slowly and subtly through the day-to-day contacts which living with him would afford me, and without his realizing what was going on. The important thing was to keep him out of the hands of some quack who might botch the job and leave him off somewhere in the backside of beyond.

So I moved in and we batched together. I kept his environment reduced to as narrow a compass as possible. I made no reference to my own marriage, at first. He thought he was around eighteen or nineteen again, and I too, and that our favorite haunt was still the Samothrace. His kids slipped his mind, along with his wife, as was to be expected. In fact, he expunged from his ken everything that had happened since the old days. He wrote plays again, also a little verse. Correspondence with the dreadful Al Roquefort was revived, experiments in half-assonance resumed. He knew he worked for the Tidy Didy, which job he regarded as a stopgap until his plays were produced or his poetry published. He became a *boulevardier* again, strolling with the renewed ease of one who has got out from behind a perambulator. Alone of all of us, he seemed in excellent spirits.

He spoke once of sinking into eternal darkness but nothing ever came of it.

"Let's go to the Greek's tonight," he suggested at breakfast one morning. "I don't know why you keep resisting the idea. He has liquor now, you know. Since Labor Day."

"How's he doing?" I coughed and scuffled my feet about so I wouldn't hear Nickie's answer.

The thing was, I knew very well the Greek had acted on my advice, from the brewery name in red neon letters now over his door, but, afraid to learn how things were going, I had postponed dropping in to see him. I knew that if they were going poorly he would give me a bad time. That was why I preferred facing him alone first. So I pulled myself together and dropped in that afternoon.

The Curator looked as though he had been waiting for me.

"Well, well," he said, raising his head from a newspaper he was reading at the cash register. "Look who's here."

"Hello, hello, hello!" I advanced to the counter with a pantomime of soaping my hands. Beverage glasses were geometrically ranged among the ice-cream ware, and two shiny new draft taps flanked the soda-water spigots. Whisky bottles with pouring spouts also stood ranked along the base of the back mirror, and among these gleaming props a second pair of moose eyes, the brother-in-law's, quietly awaited me. The scene had the expectant gravity of a tribunal. I saw that I had my choice of stools.

"I haven't seen you lately," Nachtgeborn said, coming down behind the combination bar and soda fountain. "You weren't here for the Grand Opening. There was room."

"I happened to be out of town at the time on business."

"Some firm that you're in the advisory capacity of?" The

Greek brushed a shred of tobacco from the otherwise immaculate counter with his little finger.

"I should have sent you a congratulatory wire, I know." I put myself astride a stool and rubbed my hands some more. "Well, so! How's business?"

"Russian."

"Russian by the door," the brother-in-law put in. They operated like a vaudeville team.

"Let me see," I said. "I think I'll have a — Tom Collins! The days are drawing in again."

"Yeah, they're drawing in."

"Is nothing changed then?"

"Oh, I wouldn't say nothing is. Some of the teen-agers we used to get for Cokes, their parents won't let them come in now that hard liquor is being served here."

I saw that I was not to be let off lightly. Nachtgeborn donned his spectacles, which he had just removed, and began to thumb through a liquor recipe book, looking for the one for Tom Collins. The brother-in-law hung over his shoulder.

"Oh, give me a glass of beer," I said. Pasted to the mirror I saw a homemade sign which read: WET YOUR APPETITE WITH ONE OF OUR TASTY COCKTAILS. I bowed my head in misery. Nachtgeborn drew the beer, with every indication of its being an operation not frequently required, trimmed the collar and set it before me. I drank to their health and said "Ahh!" with false gusto. I watched the Greek swab the counter with a fixed gaze, as though something in the act mesmerized me. Pausing to scratch at a blemish with his thumbnail, the Greek said, "Any more ideas?"

I swung around on the stool and looked down the street.

"All right, now let's see. Four taverns in one block," I said analytically.

232

"This neighborhood is going to pot."

"Yours is the only place with any character, Nacht-geborn." I glanced over at the nickelodeon. "Let's have a tune!" I said, making for it.

"How about 'Ida, sweet as apple cider?' " said the Greek, whose gift for irony was apparently infinite. "You haven't brought the family in for chicken and pilaf lately." He drifted over.

"Like I used to?" I put a nickel in the piano slot.

"Mrs. Sleet was in last week," he said, referring to my high school English teacher. "With her nephew."

"He sells clever remarks," the brother-in-law said. He held aloft a sign reading, WE CAN'T ADMIT YOU TO THE BAR UNLESS YOU'RE OF LEGAL AGE. I opened my mouth to comment but was cut off by the nickelodeon starting up. I waved a finger rhythmically in the air and rocked my head with a smile. However, the piano stopped almost imme-diately with a strangled groan and some of its giblets were heard to clatter to the tile floor. I wished we were all dead and in hell. But I ordered a hamburger, which I didn't want any more than I did the beer, and gnawed it moodily while the Curator hinted that the drinking trade I had so recklessly foretold was sitting this very minute in the new Roof Garden at the Windsor, three blocks away.

"Roof Garden! On top of a three-story hotel!" I said, inviting them to laugh with me at this uproarious thing. Revived, I drew a distinction between culture and mere swank, looking the Greek straight in the eye as I stated that all that was good in our civilization we owed to the golden Athenian age.

"We're morally bankrupt," I finished.

"We're a damn sight worse than that. We're bankrupt."

Having again drawn off the Greek's accumulated venom

for the time being, I felt easier about going back there in the company of my cloven friend. Needless to say, visiting the Samothrace with him was the least of the hazards in the obstacle course over whose hurdles we fraternally flew. The mechanics of living with him were too involved to recapitulate in full here: how, if he was single, we were to explain the arrival of mail for a woman with his name, the presence of her and the children's effects, and so on and so on. I let *him* try to account for it, as the best way of driving home that something was wrong. He felt that we were renting a furnished place sublet us by a relative. But each explanation bred a new discrepancy, and finally I told him frankly what was what. I said he was married and had suffered a blow on the head. Which was after all pretty much the case. I filled him in slowly, clarifying as fast as I thought he could take. I took Crystal to see him and he recognized her. (She had had to be let in on everything, of course). Had he got worse I should naturally have called in help; but he got, as I am implying, better. He recalled what he damn well wanted to, and taking his own sweet time. Perhaps he knew more than he let on, even to himself. For the game was being played out within himself. The fabulous fish we hunted, the Ego, sported at depths impenetrable to himself, and in those dim, washed solitudes where even the ships of memory sink. One of the authorities over whom I now continually pored in my spare time put it this way. He said that, rather than plunge after that fish and lash up a great froth and maybe scare it to the bottom for good, you try to coax it to the surface. That was why I stressed one thing every chance I got: namely, Nickie's brilliant deductive powers, which remained unimpaired throughout.

One night, for example, he came home from a walk and

asked suspiciously, "Who called while I was out?"

"How did you know anyone called?" I asked.

He pointed to the phone. "It's been put back from the right, which is the ear you listen with. I listen with my left and set it down that way. That's how it was when I went out because I'd just phoned the drugstore. It's the other way now, so you've been talking."

"Nickie, you ought to be a private eye."

Which put us back where we started, you think? Maybe so, but with one important difference. I had the case with which Nickie could reclaim his ego, and be taller than she was. I would be his first free-lance client.

Lammermoor was an adversary made to order for him — if only I could draw his fire. At the same time, a fresh turn in my own affairs might resolve my domestic woes, provided it was for the worse. My reasoning was as follows. Crystal eventually dropped the threat of the heart-balm suit, if she had ever seriously meant it. But while that had blown over, she still wouldn't let me come near her. The only solution was to make her come to me. I felt that I would have her at my side fast enough if I could only manage to get myself unjustly accused. Admiration would follow on sympathy when it was learned that I had deliberately put my neck in a noose in order to give my friend a second chance. I thought it over from every conceivable angle without seeing how I could lose by acquiring a martyr's status. Only it would have to be a clean-cut martyrdom, not inconclusive and half-baked like the other two times. Of course Nickie might muff the rescue and it would be bye-bye baby for both of us, but it was a risk that had to be taken. I had nothing to lose but my head and he didn't even have that, as it were.

But how to make Lammermoor show his hand? Should I get involved with his decoy again? I was flogging my brain over the problem when the solution came to me, suddenly, one afternoon in a diner.

I was alone, lunching on what the management represented to be macaroni. It was an off-white matter made of dried toothpaste, eraser crumbs and old regrets. The counterman stood by and watched with pity and loathing as I ate it. I wished now that I had gone to the restaurant across the street where the food had at least the merit of being tasteless.

I chewed a mental cud as my earthly jaws wagged, reflecting on how true it was that experience kept a dear school but fools would learn at no other. A parody favored by my older son went through my head:

> Ho, hi-ho,
> It's off to school we go;
> In mi-ser-y
> From nine to three,
> Hi-ho, hi-ho.

Bad as the macaroni was, it was the coffee that separated the men from the boys. It was from the Mississippi River where she churns away between Missouri and Illinois, along about in there, and from well down in the bottom after the spring rains have roiled her rich brown depths. I drank about half of this fluvial guck and turned to see how the only other customer in the place, on the third stool over, was making out. It was a thickset, very sunburned woman with fingers indistinguishable from the French fries she was eating with them. She seemed to be enjoying herself. Maybe I was getting spoiled and fussy.

> Ho, hi-ho,
> It's off to school we go;
> We eat some junk
> And then we flunk,
> Hi-ho, hi-ho.

236

When I opened my wallet to pay, I saw no money in it.
"I'm sorry," I said to the counterman. "I'll just have to leave a check."

He was quite grumpy about that. Then I remembered the secret compartment, in which I usually had a ten-dollar bill stashed away for just such an emergency. The bill was there — and so was the check from Sherry Budd. I had completely forgotten about it.

I paid the counterman, who now groused about the size of the denominations which had been given him all day. As I stood at the cash register waiting for change, something nagged the back of my mind. That check — was it the answer? Then I realized in a flash what Lammermoor had been waiting for.

I endorsed the check. I put it in an envelope and addressed it to the local Red Cross. Then, crossing my fingers, I dropped it into the nearest mailbox.

Nineteen

I'm in help. I need trouble."

With these words I dropped on the dining room table at which Nickie sat poring over a chess problem a document that had been handed me earlier in the day by a deputy sheriff. He picked it up and read it.

It was a summons for me to appear in the Bridgeport superior court and answer to a charge of having emotionally impaired one Miss Sherry Budd through the illegal practice of psychiatry. It had been issued from the office of an attorney named Bruno Bloodstein and was most admirably worded. No state has a law forbidding the unlicensed practice of psychiatry as such, but the situation is covered by the law regulating that of medicine, and since a psychiatrist is expected to have a medical diploma (I found out now) it comes to the same thing. The complaint which the summons went on to set forth included allegations like "did willfully and irresponsibly practice hypnosis," "did deliberately abort her emotional relations with a man whom she had expectations of marrying," and so on. Damages in the amount of fifty thousand dollars were asked. I liked that, and I also liked the juxtaposition of "abort" and "illegal," in what I had no trouble foreseeing in headlines as the Svengali Case. I was already mentally at work on a series of disguises; had, indeed, begun to prepare for the day when feeling would be running high, by slipping across town that afternoon in sneakers and dark glasses.

"Is there any beer in the icebox?" I asked Nickie when he had finished his study of the greetings, conducted with ill-veiled fascination.

"Let's see."

I followed him into the kitchen.

"They can't pin anything on me," I boasted in an old man's voice. "I never practiced any psychiatry. Just human relations."

"That's not the line to take. What you'll do is not deny it but say it was psychoanalysis. It's another breed of dog, and while the regulations are just as strict if not stricter for a full-fledged psychoanalyst, there's no law against its practice in a lay form. I understand that's the loophole all quacks and impostors use."

If this was my defense talking I couldn't wait to hear the opposition.

Watching him dig in the icebox with the old omniscience, knowing where everything was — cold beer, legal wrinkles — I felt better. Or at least that my sacrifice would not be in vain. In my first horror on reading the complaint I had thought of pleading insanity, but that probably wouldn't look good for an analyst. I didn't want to give the profession a black eye.

We sat in shirt sleeves at the kitchen table, drinking beer and hammering out a plan of action. I told him everything about Lammermoor and Sherry Budd from their roots in the Mrs. Thicknesse business, and why the charges were, perforce, hogwash. Lammermoor's plot was now at least clear, and no man could have asked for hotter water. The fox had probably read an article somewhere about the ambiguity concerning the law and psychiatry, the desire for a test case, etc., and had dreamed up this gimmick, which he figured was better than blackmail since it might drag in the newspaper.

"That's it!" Nickie brought his fist down on the table. "He's banking on the *Pick's* eagerness to settle out of court and hush it up. The paper's liable, since you acted as their employee."

"And Bloodstain, I mean Bloodstein, fully expects us to dicker on that basis."

"Right. It's just a bluff. He takes for granted the paper'll settle for you, just to avoid a stink." Nickie paused in the act of puncturing a fresh can of beer. "Didn't Clammidge put pressure on you to dabble in this stuff?"

"The *Pick* is to be kept out of this, anyhow by name," I said.

This was absolutely essential to my plan to become a scapegoat. Nothing less would fetch my wife around. I had to be a solitary figure, deserted by all — at first anyway. Later I saw people as rushing to my aid in great numbers, creating a suction against which even an outraged wife would be powerless. But for the time being, all I wanted was to be treated shabbily.

I added to Nickie on a note of quiet integrity: "You see, I'm going it alone."

There was a pause long enough for him to express admiration in. He licked his lips, after a copious swig of the beer, and lowered his glass to the table.

"What I shall want is a private eye," I went on. "I hereby retain you in that capacity, Nickie. To dig up what you can about this girl's connection with Lammermoor, maybe some facts proving collusion, proving she isn't emotionally ruined — anything. But no pulling a rabbit out of the logical

240

silk hat. *Dig*. Meanwhile I suppose I ought to get a lawyer."

"Fifty grand is no geezer."

Well! Was he talking like a private eye already? Coming down out of the ivory tower to walk the earth at last? Or was it just your intellectual's oral slumming? Much remained to be seen. Could he do this job at all? Or was I sending the China pitcher to the well again, putting tobacco in that bubble pipe again?

"Yes, I'll take a crack at it," he said. "And do have a lawyer get in touch with Bloodstain — damn it, you've got me doing it now — with Bloodstein, and feel him out." He drank off his beer after a few minutes and rose. "Now let's get a good night's sleep. We're going to have to be on our toes."

I stood up.

"Freud," I said, detaining him, "would have no patience with what he called *schlammerei*." It means sloppiness but I wasn't going to tell Nickie that. Let him sweat it out. I could tell from his expression that I had him at last. This was for all that Rilke he had belched at me. "I have always tried to avoid *schlammerei* in my work and I'm sure you have in yours."

He nodded and started away.

"*Schlammerei*," I speared him back, drunk with power, "is the enemy of everything. What undoes the diplomat? What trips up the criminal?"

He picked up his glass and tilted the last few drops of beer into his mouth.

"It should be abhorred equally by him tracing the fruits of human evil and him searching out its even more treacherous roots in the dark loam of the mind. Let's always be on guard against the foe — *schlammerei, schlammerei,*

241

schlammerei!" I swayed against a chair, signifying that the interview was over. "Good night."

Lying in the bed I occupied in that apartment, I could hear him snoring away in the next room ten minutes after his head hit the pillow. I had been glad to see him acting with the old peerlessness, and not the newfound *pathétique*, but the least he could do was have a *little* trouble getting to sleep. My hands under my head, I stared up at the dark ceiling and got in some more rehearsal. . . .

The plan was to seize the Lamplighter in his bed, those to whom the plot was entrusted little dreaming that it would also be the King's. For the same savoir-faire *that excited interest among the natives made every woman singly met a Trilby to his will, and he mounted from princesses toward queens, to his final doom.*

That one Sheba lured him to her chamber with the assurance that the monarch was on a hunting expedition, as indeed she believed herself. In his arms, she unburdened herself of her cross. The King was impotent.

"He's a terribly mixed-up person," she murmured in perfect English. "It all goes away back. He has a complex mother."

"And vice versa."

"Not so loud. Tee-hee. The walls have ears, and he is furious enough at the laughingstock your quips have made of him. In fact, what is that noise?"

The door came down and eunuchs with drawn sabers poured across the parquet floor. Arms bound, the two were jostled side by side to prison. The doors clanged open and they were flung into separate dungeons.

He was tried on some trumped-up political charge, but everyone knew the real source of the King's jealousy — he himself was genitally defunct. The Queen had been released when it was learned that she was to bear him an heir, rather a farce under the circumstances. "He has no issue so he picks one with me," the Lamplighter chaffered through prison bars. The guards loved him and secretly sent all his wisecracks out into the world, laughing like anything as they did. The King was always afterward to be known by the nickname the Lamplighter gave him: Barren von Munchausen.

The trial was a mockery. The Lamplighter was denied counsel and sentenced to death by firing squad. He was executed bright and early and spirited away for secret burial, so there would be no remains for the populace to sanctify. That evening some travelers from a far country arrived, bent on seeking out the sage of whom they had heard so much, to ask him certain questions of philosophy which had baffled their own wise men. But it was too late. He was dead.

While Nickie got to work on his front, I hustled around on mine. First I went to Clammidge's office and rubbed his nose in the summons. I stood watching him as he read it in his desk chair. For some minutes the only reaction was a change of complexion. Then he cleared his throat. Ladies and gentlemen, our sponsor.

"How could you—"

"Please don't reproach yourself."

"What?"

"Because if you hadn't told me to take this tack I wouldn't have been put in a position where I could become a victim of such perjury—is that what you're thinking? Forget it!" I laughed generously. "I'll see to it that the name of the paper is kept out of it."

"Paper." He plowed his hair and writhed a little. "Drag us into it. Scandal," he continued in a kind of hysterical shorthand. His eyes faltered like dying bugs down to the summons again. "Some of these *charges*. I always thought you — "

"Of course there's nothing to them." I sketched in something of the nature of the scheme behind them. "Absolutely nothing to the whole thing."

He looked at me askance. "Are you sure?"

I got a job as a dock walloper and trundled him, boxed and gagged, on a handcart to the edge of the wharf, where I nudged him over into the water without being seen. I took a course in airplane writing and wrote obscenities on the sky. I befouled a summer's day from horizon to horizon before I was caught — brought down by a pursuit plane over the Brooklyn Navy Yard.

Slipping down in his leather chair, Clammidge dropped his hands on top of his head, let them flop there like exhausted birds onto a nest, and said, "Just when the missus and I were planning a Caribbean cruise."

"You will be on that boat. I shall never involve the good name of this paper. Do you think that I would even mention that memo from you calling for the change in the column, and also urging me to see readers in person who wanted that, come to think of it — a directive, as I suppose it would be called in court. Do you think I would breathe a word about that, which I've still got somewhere in my files?"

"You need an ocean voyage yourself," he bleated. "Have you ever been abroad?"

"All expenses paid, is that what you're insinuating? Why not, when this is over. Blackmail is a tough thing to have to go through, and I'll need that vacation I've been putting off. My missus will too."

His palms slid down along the sides of his face like gastropods from a rock to which they no longer have the strength to cling. "All right."

"Not that I wouldn't keep on working. As a matter of fact I could send my stuff from Europe."

"Europe!" He got a grip on himself and straightened in the chair. "Little vignettes about life there? How human nature is the same all over? Well, it might make a series. If you don't end up in jail."

"We must avoid that at all costs. Do you suppose you should call Sipperly for me?" I asked, referring to the attorney the *Pick* retained.

"Yes. As your lawyer — not ours." He darted me a last panicky look and reached for the phone.

And so to Sipperly, who laughed when he read the complaint. He got Bloodstein on the wire and the two chatted like old friends — about how the families were, and so on. After conferring about the matter on hand, Sipperly, a thin bent man who resembled a wilted reed, was able to assure me that settling out of court was what the other side took for granted, and for a lot less than the sum named, or even a lot less than half of that. "It's simply a question of how high the paper is willing to go to get a rather routine legal burr out of its hair," he said.

"I don't want to settle," I said, seeing my predicament being pulled out from under me before I had made the hay I intended. People were rushing to my aid too fast. "It's our duty to fight these rascals. You can tell Bloodstein to go to — No, don't tell him that, but what kind of *case* does he think they've got? What evidence?"

"I'll find that out next time. I'm having drinks with him Sunday. Justice moves with dignity, you know."

On Monday, I learned that the major evidence was the check I had accepted as payment for services (and deliberately endorsed, of course); the slip of paper with the name of the drug written on it; and something I hadn't, certainly, suspected existed. It was a diary of Sherry's, in which was presumably recorded from day to day the agonies she had undergone in the course of my thrall.

"It's not much to stand on, as Bruno knows," Sipperly said. "I think we can wind this up without any trouble in a week or two. Oh, and Mr. Clammidge phoned this morning. He said to bill the paper for my fee. So there's nothing for you to worry about." And with a smile, he clapped a hand on my shoulder.

It was now high time to tell my wife what was going on. I had meant to reveal it when my danger was at its peak, but the gravity was draining so rapidly from my plight that the minimum which could alarm her on my behalf might already have been passed. I therefore made all haste in getting over to the house, stopping off only at a drugstore which carried Schrafft's candies.

The house seemed empty. Lila I knew to be shopping in town. Her oldest child and ours would be in nursery school, the rest napping or upstairs with my mother, who took the children over part of every day. That left only my wife to be accounted for. I found her at last on the back porch. She was sitting on the glider in a halo of gnats — which had been given a new lease on life in the late Indian Summer we were having — and sewing the cuff on a boy's pants.

I set down a wrapped box of peppermint sprills beside her

246

on the glider, and said directly, "I'm in trouble again."

She drew the length of thread through the cloth and pulled it tight, the needle aloft. Then she thrust the needle back down for another stitch.

"Don't say anything till I'm through," I said into the stony silence. "At an earlier stage in the Mrs. Thicknesse business, now so happily concluded, the letters fell into the hands of a guy who gave them back to me on a promise that I would psychoanalyze his girl, for free. I did, knowing he was trying to lure me into some kind of a mess with her. We'll see in a moment why I finally walked into the trap. But first, a word about my initial reactions."

I unwrapped the peppermint sprills and offered her one. She shook her head without taking her eyes from the sewing. I ate one, walking slowly around the porch. I stopped and shook my head in amused recall.

"Picture the scene if you will. This ravishing creature stretched out on the couch in my office, all there for the taking for your obedient servant. Well," I related, strolling, "I was glad for the temptation. I welcomed it. Why? It would be a test of my immunity to that disease against which my previous bout had presumably left me with sufficient antibodies — to revert to the figure you'll remember I used to explain the other. You know how the writers for the *Reader's Digest* entitle pieces 'Thank God for My Ulcers' and so on. Just so I said, 'Thank God for my previous affair.' For a stumble may prevent a fall, and we are indeed strongest where broken."

"Have you been drinking?"

"What?"

"Have you been drinking?"

I drew in a breath which drained the porch of gnats. Which lungful I immediately coughed back, as being a man and not a nightjar which subsisted on such fare. I paused long enough to scribble a supplication on the roof of my mouth with my tongue — hastily — there was so little time. Then I went on:

"Strongest where broken, but even then it is best to be safe. So you'll be glad to hear I took precautions."

She put the sewing down.

"Yes, I'm glad you did that," she said stiffly, and rose and walked into the house.

I stood looking after her open-mouthed. Open-mouthed I heard her march upstairs. This was the end! I was about to spring up the stairs after her and straighten out the muddle, explain what kind of precautions I had meant, when I said to myself, Wait. Now you have the grievance you want and from an unexpected quarter. What I had been playing for was to bring her to my side when others wronged me. Now she was chief among those who were wronging me. What luck! Work this right and I would have balanced the moral ledger by evening: she would be owing *me* an apology rather than I her. The longer I permitted the misunderstanding to continue, the more time she would have to look back on as having caused me suffering in.

So I stayed out on the porch awhile, eating peppermint sprills and imagining to myself the scene that would follow. I would go to the bedroom where she undoubtedly was, and, taking it from where I was open-mouthed, say, "Oh, *I* see what you mean. Oh, how could you! I only meant so and so." Then after I had straightened that part of it out, I would reveal the deed of moral worth, rare in our time, that was behind it all. "Oh, darling, how can you ever forgive me," she would say, and I would answer something like, "No, it's all my fault. I should have made myself clearer.

There, there, now let's forget it all, shall we? We've got a bit of a row to hoe — together."

Five minutes passed, ten. I paced on the porch in a kind of nervous ecstasy, hoping I wasn't letting the fires of confusion burn *too* long. This had to be seized at the psychological moment, for the reconciliation to follow right. I flung away a cigarette I was smoking and hurried up the stairs two at a time.

Standing at the closed bedroom door, I could hear indeterminate noises inside. Rustlings, a slid-out drawer. I turned the knob expecting to find the door locked. It wasn't.

"What do you want?" Crystal said from over an open dresser drawer.

"Oh, I see what you mean. Oh, my God." I stumbled blindly to the bed with my face in my hands. "How could you know me so little?" I sat on the bed rocking from side to side, watching her through my fingers. The scene suddenly had such reality that tears came to my eyes. "All I mean was that I took safeguards against even suspicion of anything — kept the door open every interview, and so on. Do you think I could want a little package of sachet like that? Even if I hadn't known her game? Well, anyhow," I continued, able to walk about again, "the long and short of it is that I thought there'd be a case in it for Nickie. One last chance for him to rehabilitate himself. And he's got it. He's out every spare minute investigating this chit and her friend. If he muffs it, good-by. If he comes through, everything may be all right. I feel the risk was worth taking to save a life. Did you think I was thinking of myself?"

She sat down on a bench before the dresser.

"But how can Nickie do anything for you? I don't understand what you mean."

"Read this." I drew the summons from my pocket and handed it to her.

Her face darkened as she took in its substance. When she reached the end of it, she put an elbow on the dresser and leaned her head in her hand.

"Please don't reproach yourself," I said.

She lifted her head "What in the name . . . ?"

"Just because you put pressure on me to play ball with the office? Do what Clammidge wanted, get mixed up in this kind of thing to where I could get maneuvered into such a box — is that what you're thinking? Forget it, darling. It's no more than any loyal husband and father would do — what he has to, to keep his job. So forget it. I won't let you say what you're thinking, about this or that other little misunderstanding a minute ago."

"Have you called a lawyer about this?"

"Clammidge did. *He* feels guilty. The whole thing is trumped up, *except* for the practicing psychiatry without a license. That's a very grave charge. But I do wish you'd all stop crucifying yourselves on my account. Clammidge embarrassed me with his attitude; gratitude for being man enough to go it alone. Practically saving the paper to hear him tell it. So let's not hear any more about it, or that other either."

"What other?" her blank expression asked.

"That one who sailed through bloody seas, who put his hand in the flame for his friend. Courage? A touch of moral grandeur maybe? Cut it out!"

"Fifty thousand dollars!" she said, reading the summons again. "It'll ruin us."

I felt justified in concealing the true size of our danger until some acknowledgment had been made of my valor.

I therefore turned and walked to the window, where I stood gazing out.

"So they're hanging me in the morning." I shrugged. "It was something I had to do. Because there are still standards. So let's not hear any more about it. About that high fealty to firm and family, not to mention friendship which if it be truly that —"

"The *Pick* will bail you out financially, at least behind the scenes, won't they?"

I shrugged again.

"They'd better! They got you into this and they're going to get you out, if I have to go down there and beat it out of them with my own two hands."

Good. I turned, to welcome whatever other words might fly, like birds, across the gulf between us. But she seemed to bridle as she said:

"Oh, Chick, how could you be so foolish as to stick your neck out this far?"

I played my last card — my trump.

"I don't think your father would have said that to me, Chris," I answered softly.

She jerked her head away and stared at the dresser-top.

"That's the final reason why I wanted to do this thing. I've always felt — how shall I put it? — not big enough for the mantle I inherited. Walking around in shoes not my size at all. I wanted to do something that would bring me more nearly shoulder-to-shoulder with the man from whom I got my job."

I was standing behind her now, a little to the left, to avoid any reflections in the mirror. I saw one shoulder twitch and the fair head drop.

"I don't know how this will turn out, but at least I'll

251

have done one decent thing. I don't suppose he thought much of me in life. Maybe I can fix that yet."

Her eyes were institutions of mercy which must decide in their own good time when to stop dunning me for payment and start binding up my wounds. Her hands lay on the dresser-top like pale, malingering starfish. I wanted to reach down and take them in mine, but I knew better than to press this moment. I had gained enough for now. Beneath the frostline lay the eternal feminine warmth. Wait.

"Now how about something to eat," I said, "maybe after I run up and see the kids and Mother. I'm starved."

"Starved." She threw up her hands. "Other people *can't* eat when they're in trouble. Come on, I'll fix you something. . . . Anyhow, that'll be something in your favor. No jury could picture you a Lothario very easily. With that pot you're getting."

While Sipperly concerned himself with negotiations, and Nickie scrounged around on his side of the street, I prepared for the eventuality of a court appearance by trying to take off a little weight. To that end I permitted myself to be methodically flailed by a giant Swede in a gymnasium which I joined for the purpose. I lost no weight, but the violence of the Swede's exertions suggested it might be otherwise with him. I walked both to work and on brisk hikes into the nearby countryside, armed with a stick to fend off the numerous regional dogs in whom apparently boiled an accumulated resentment toward a man remembered as someone barreling down the road in an Oldsmobile to their constant peril. I got more exercise out of swinging the cane than out of walking, but in any case my exertions were as fruitless as the Swede's. I did extract from these all-weather rambles a certain lyric sustenance; I had a sense that, for housewives glancing from their cottage windows and for passing motorists, I pulled the whole scene together by offering to the eye that solitary figure for which all landscapes cry; of representing, as I strode cross-lots or climbed a stile, abiding values. I walked everywhere I had to go, determined on the satisfaction of at least looking like the part of which I was being falsely accused. I wanted an acquittal, but not one which I would have to be ashamed of myself about. I walked to Sipperly's. What he had to report was that he was making an "interlocutory motion" before the court for the right to examine the documents on which the plaintiff was basing her case. I had asked what the chances were of getting our hands particularly on that diary, which I wanted Nickie to see as possible grist for his genius, and Sipperly had offered to make a stab at it. The motion would be entered on what he called "short calendar," evidently a term used for the court's availability, every Friday, to hear preliminary motions and other incidental business connected with cases due to come up.

"It'll be next Friday or the one after," he assured me.

"Can we all go? This friend I was telling you about too?"

Sipperly shrugged his shoulders, a gesture almost imperceptible in his case, they were so thin. "Why not?"

I walked home and when I got there I weighed myself, gingerly boarding the bathroom scale. There was some change but not much; I had gained four pounds.

The reason was not hard to find. I returned from my excursions ravenous, and as a result (taking the fueling of a furnace as the metaphor for caloric consumption) I had been shoveling it in as fast as I was burning it up — faster. At about this time there fell into my hands a document containing some computations made by a Dr. L. H. Newburgh of the medical school of the University of Michigan, who had done work in the metabolism of obesity. A man weighing two hundred and fifty pounds, he wrote, "will have to climb twenty flights of stairs to rid himself of the energy contained in one slice of bread." A horizontal walk of a mile will reduce the man's weight "only 12½ grams (less than one-half ounce). He must walk thirty-six miles to rid himself of one pound of adipose tissue — how disappointing!"

On the basis of Dr. Newburgh's findings, I figured that the only way for me to make appreciable inroads on myself on foot would be to walk across the United States, like Bernarr MacFadden, a discipline almost certain to be neutralized by Gargantuan snacks at Altoona, Chicago, Salt Lake City, and so on, along the way. The inevitable remained.

There are of course numerous diets always being recommended, published and discussed. One is the familiar "du Pont's executives' diet," which I tried first. Its motif is meat. For lunch the first day I had a pair of lamb chops with accessories too dismal to mention. For dinner I had a planked steak. Steaks and chops two or three times a day are, in addition to an ideal way of sustaining the high protein intake required, a neat formula for bankruptcy, unless you happen to be a du Pont executive. I realized, as the long, carnivorous days went by, that I was eating myself into destitution, and switched to another feeding plan — hastily, as the hour of my initial court appearance was drawing on.

This one permitted me, implacably, for breakfast half a grapefruit, one boiled egg, black coffee. To eat that at seven A.M. and nothing till lunch at one o'clock is to engage in what theologians call mortification of the flesh. Noon, in fact, often found me close to that crystalline fatigue in which the early Christian anchorites are said to have had their visions. I carried a check-list of low-calorie foods with which to assuage the worst pangs of hunger. One was tangerines. I once ate seven of these blameless things at a sitting, pips and all. Another was cottage cheese, of which I sometimes devoured an entire container. One Saturday Nickie came home to find me hunched over an eighteen-ounce jar of it, a flying spoon in my hand.

"What are you gorging yourself for?" he asked.

"I'm on a diet. You know that. Have you found anything out?"

"She's been seeing Lammermoor regularly, and if he's the matrimonial prospect you sabotaged — *well*. I got a snapshot of them mushing about on a park bench," he said, setting down the tiny camera which he carried concealed on his person. "I hope Sipperly's arranged for the motion next Friday. I'm dying to get my hands on that diary."

I began a third diet without wholly abandoning the other, then still another while retaining features of its predecessors. Soon I had three or four going simultaneously, and grew bewildered and discouraged. Nickie observed, "Getting a bit thick in the flitch, aren't you?" My excess weight was now one of the very troubles from which I sought emotional escape in food. What a vicious circle! I once heard of a man who hit the bottle because of a number of harsh realities, not the least of which was the realization of the wasted, bibulous years behind him. Hence he had reached a point where it was in large measure liquor that was driving him to drink, just as the melancholy of expanding girth was driving me to the pleasures of the table. I must stop all this nonsense and forget about it if, when the flashbulbs started to explode in the courtroom, I was not, rather than having mortified my flesh, to be mortified by it.

Sipperly alerted us for an appearance the following Friday. I was still staying with Nickie, and Lila still keeping away from him. I felt that to be wisest, till we saw what we saw. My mother had had to be given some explanation of the arrangement but it had only been a partial one. I decided to disclose the legal involvements to her the Monday evening before the court appearance, when I had a chance to talk to her while driving her to the doctor's to have a blistered foot attended to.

"I'll be all right, Moms," I said as she kneaded my hand. "Don't worry."

"But I do. All those lawyers and things. Is Nickie handling this all right?"

"It's the chance he needs. That's all I know."

When we stopped for a traffic light, a cop sauntered over.

"No one-arm driving in this town, Mac," he said, his head at the window.

"This is my mother."

"Oh."

I shifted gears and started away.

"The problem is to make people grow up," I resumed. "Some live in a dream world till some rude awakening brings them down to earth. I think things will work out all right, so let's talk about something else. I've been on a diet, Moms. Several in fact. Do I look thinner?"

She inspected me dubiously.

"No," she said at last, with a shake of her head. "The only thing about you that's getting any thinner is your hair."

The barber saw that he hadn't tightened the gown around my neck quite enough, so he unpinned it again and gave it an extra hitch, till my eyes were bulging nicely and my face was the color of eggplant. A newspaper ad had led me to this shop, which was one of those where they claim to check molting. Glancing furtively about at the owners of shrinking oases in adjoining chairs, I said in a low voice, "Give me the treatment that you say saves hair."

After covering my head with oil and kneading it to a muck, the barber applied to my skull one of those machines with which paved streets are torn up. When I had been sufficiently clobbered, I was led blind and groping in my toga toward a milking stool, onto which I was pushed and my head flung into a bowl. A stream of water was trained on it, and when I opened my eyes and got a glimpse of the inside of the washbasin, I thought I pretty well understood how these places stopped falling hair.

What they do is systematically and vehemently loosen a year's supply in advance. You go home and weeks pass, months, and it seems to you your hair is no longer falling out; and it isn't, all the weak soldiers have been washed out for the nonce. Then it starts falling again — time to go back to that wonderful place where they stopped it for a while. You go back because you hadn't chanced to glance into the basin the last time. Then they uproot another year's loss, and so on.

To postpone going back into the outside world for a bit, I let this man shave and then massage me. I brooded under a succession of scalding towels. No use trying to cut a figure in time for the trial. Fat, balding, with a missing tooth the press of events had prevented replacing, I would resemble no rogue of parts at all, but only what in fact I was: a cracker-barrel philosopher.

On a mumbled complaint from me about the temperature of the towels, the barber snapped his fingers and a manicurist grasped one of my hands and immersed it in a solution; a shoeshine boy followed. I had somebody hanging on every member, and half expected a psychoanalyst to stop by and give me half a buck's worth of brain picking.

Having received a bill for nine dollars and twenty cents, I distributed tips with a malevolent grin and made for the exit, where another coin netted me my coat and hat. I paid the bill and the door was opened for me by a man who seemed the proprietor.

"Come again," he said, "and tell your friends about us."

"I will," I said. "I know some masochists."

"Thank you."

"Not at all."

"Good-by."

"Good-by."

Our short-calendar appearance was on the twenty-fifth of November. I selected a jacket of barleycorn tweed, a canary-colored suede vest, white shirt and plain knit olive tie. Mrs. Lamplighter drove the tumbril. I insisted she come along, so she could report Nickie's success, if any, to Lila, who we thought had best stay home, in case the rocket didn't go off. The nonpareil himself sat in the back seat, mostly quiet. We hoped our hearing would come up before noon, so he could get back to at least some of his laundry rounds.

As we wound our way toward Bridgeport, twenty miles away, I looked out at the familiar fields and woods, dearer now in the bright vestments of autumn.

"I wonder if I'll ever come this way again," I said.

Crystal cleared her throat and shifted up on the seat. She was silent most of the trip too. I smiled with Christianity out of one side of my face while witn the other I expressed outrage. I saw her in the near future, my body claimed and the insurance collected, going about in widow's tweeds (*sic*), and fetching at last a new and no doubt worthier father for her young. I turned to see what she had on now. She was wearing a belted beige cashmere coat, and a bright print dress covered with vegetables of colors not corresponding to those in nature.

"There's the courthouse," I said. "You can start looking for a parking place any time now."

Twenty

THE JUDGE's name was Merle Walnut. I don't know what he may have thought of that in more formative years, but as for now he breathed an air of comprehensive ennui; as though life had done its worst and never touched him, its best and left him unamused. He suggested vaguely a background of independent wealth, and of good living though not of *joie de vivre* — of enjoying himself. He was not that hale archetype who keeps the economy sound by splashing about in the advertisements with wife and child and exclaiming, "We never dreamed a Carey pool was within our means!" He owned such a pool but never used it. He presented, rather, a look of *Weltschmerz*, which gave you pause as to the rightness of that attribute on the bench. My lord had sideburns which stopped just short of being axhelves, eyebrows dense as mustaches, and a mustache trimmed to such a fine line that from a distance it appeared first to be a scratch across his upper lip. I thought that if you took one of the eyebrows and put it under his nose — now get this, because I'm only going to say it once — if you made a mustache of one of the eyebrows, separated the two parts of the already neatly segmented mustache and put half over each eye, shaved the sideburns and threw away the other eyebrow, you would have a pretty good-looking man.

Of about fifty-five. He had a habit of scratching the backs of his hands and yawning unobtrusively.

Appraising him from the first of two rows of benches and chairs that ran across the rear of the courtroom for spectators, and where my wife and Nickie and I sat while Sipperly wedged his way into the bedlam that boiled about his throne, I thought with a flicker of pleasure that I saw a kindred spirit: an ember of that continentalism which was my sometime daemon. It dwelt in the expression with which he heard arguments for and against motions of piddling moment for cases of no interest; in the gestures with which he granted or denied them; in the tone of voice, dry, pointed, with which he interrupted comments or injected them himself. We would surely understand each other when the instant came: when I would have but to rise and, a thumb hooked negligently into a pocket of my canary-yellow vest, murmur, "Man is conceived and bored in sin," to resolve the whole *brouhaha* and send us home to our several concerns.

Yes, there was a place for *Weltschmerz* on the bench.

Except that something was funny here. The eyes beneath the shaggy brows lifted to follow, along with scores of other pairs, the figure of Sherry Budd entering from the door at the right rear. A long-headed man who appeared to be part schnauzer pattered in her wake, clutching a decayed briefcase. Bloodstein.

"That's her," I whispered to my wife.

She was wearing a pale blue suit, a white blouse of the kind that I believe is called waffle piqué, and a hat of pillbox persuasion matching the yellow bag she carried. Sherry had lost her excess weight, and beneath her eyes were shadows, skillfully applied. The din of voices dwindled to a hum, and that to near-silence as what was, after all, some pumpkins made its way into the other end of our row. She saw me and averted her face, abruptly sitting down. She lowered her eyes and drew the skirt of her suit demurely down over her knees. I crossed my legs and glanced at the carafe of drinking water at the judge's elbow. The only other person in the bleachers was a fat woman in a pepper-green dress who was leaning forward and eating her beads.

A day of short calendar consists in the judge's reading off the cases listed for that term and of lending an ear to any interlocutory motions either side might care to make: requests for postponement, say, for physical examinations of principals, for time to locate a witness, for disclosures. Ours was to be a motion for disclosure — of evidence the other side planned to use against us. Many of the cases met with no such impediments at all and few took over a minute. It was shortly before noon, when the courtroom was almost cleared of lawyers, who had left one by one as their business was transacted to dash off elsewhere, that I heard the judge drone, *"Budd versus Swallow."*

Sipperly, who had come back to join us after one or two skirmishes at the front on other cases he had coming up, sprang to his feet and called, "Your Honor: As counsel for the defense, I should like to move for disclosure of evidence. Opposing counsel plans to feature a diary purporting to detail the stresses undergone by his client at the hands of mine, over the period of time concerned. Permission is respectfully requested to examine and copy the contents."

Bloodstein had by now joined him, and the two were standing shoulder to shoulder before the bar as the former countered:

"Your Honor: May I protest this motion. The contents

are of too personal a nature to justify such free exchange preliminary to trial, and I also submit it would set an unfortunate precedent to make general the circulation of courtroom evidence at a period prior to the trial itself." Bloodstein possessed to an evidently full-blown degree the lawyer's knack of amplifying his effect by saying the same thing two ways.

Walnut was reading the complaint. A copy had been handed him by a clerk seated on his left, who put things in and out of a file in front of him. Without looking up Walnut murmured, "It is rather late in jurisprudence to hope for precedent coming out of Bridgeport."

I laughed. I was on his side. A sheriff dozing on a nearby dais twitched erect like a puppet and slammed a gavel down. "Order in the courtroom!"

Sipperly pitched into the argument again.

"I submit, your Honor, that since this document will no doubt be central to the plaintiff's case, it must also perforce figure in the defense's. It may spare a good deal of the court's trial time if the defense will have an opportunity to peruse its contents beforehand."

"The feelings of my client," Bloodstein came in, gesturing with tender concern in her direction, "are already such that riding roughshod over them by such a demand would be highly inadvisable at this time. She is in a critical emotional state."

"But able to attend short calendar, an ordeal which most counsels spare even their sturdy clients."

"I see yours is here."

"He has no reason to be shaken."

Judge Walnut laughed through his nose with no expression of mirth on his face as he took us in, back there. "This is certainly getting to be a full-dress affair, for short calendar," he said. I drafted a violent oath on the court-room floor with the toe of my shoe. Walnut let the complaint fall from his fingers as a thought occurred to him. "Perhaps I might have a look at this diary first."

Bloodstein swept an arm at his client.

"She has it, Your Honor."

Then with what cheesy dramatics didn't he walk over, lay a deacon's hand on her shoulder and whisper something in her ear. Sherry lowered her head and nodded. She opened her bag and produced a book bound in red leather and fastened with a gilt clasp. Then she gave to Blood-stein a small key. He unlocked the book, returned the key to her, and carried the book up and laid it before the judge. I sighed sharply around, as if to ask didn't we all think they might have cut *that* out in New Haven. All eyes, however, were fixed upon Walnut's hands as, *Weltschmerz* all forgot, he reached to take the diary from Bloodstein.

The judge read the book, which the gilt clasp made vaguely ecclesiastical in appearance, with his head leaning slightly into a propped-up hand, in that attitude favored in portraits of bibliophiles. He turned the pages slowly. Once his eyes lifted and sought me out. I tugged the vest down over a bulge where my shirt may have gaped between it and my trousers. Walnut must have been three or four minutes poring over the exhibit. Which at last he closed and said: "I think the defense's request to examine and copy is a reasonable one."

Sipperly took it from him and carried it over to a council table. Nickie and I popped to our feet and joined him there. As we sat huddled over the diary, Sipperly was called back to the proceedings when Bloodstein moved for a delay in order that his client might have time for the thorough physical checkup she needed. This was granted (I learned later), but then Sipperly moved for disclosure of the canceled check, adding jocosely that he only wanted to see it long enough to make sure the Red Cross, to whom it had been sent on endorsement by the payee, had endorsed it in turn.

"Look, this duel of wits is wasted," Walnut drawled sardonically. "I'm not conducting the trial yet, appearances to the contrary. If you men are using the occasion to show respective strengths for bargaining advantages in settling out of court, I must remind you —"

He was interrupted by Nickie's voice, clear, firm, amused, and out of order.

"This whole thing is so absurd it's hard to know where to begin," he said. "It's obviously a fake."

Well, distraction was by now the better part of valor, and so, stark, staring mad, I heard myself say, "How do you figure that, Mr. Sherman?"

"Who is *that?*" This from Walnut.

"Mr. Sherman is assisting in my defense, Your Honor," I said. "I'm the accused, and allowed to speak in my own defense, am I not? I'd be most grateful should it please the Court to hear him out, if he should have something to say on my behalf." Aimed at a formally respectful tone, my words sounded curiously like Yiddish dialect. Turning to Nickie before Walnut — quite cured of *Weltschmerz* now — could answer, I asked, stooging amazement for what must be absolutely the last time, "How on earth could you tell the diary was a fake?"

"Internal evidence. I'm sure His Honor knows the trust which can be put in handwriting as an index of the emotional state. It is a cardiogram of the nervous system, in

265

which the least sign of agitation is reflected. But if ever I saw evidence of a tranquil spirit, this is it."

"I object!" Bloodstein huffed.

"So do I," said the judge. "But this is no proper trial, and I should think plaintiff would welcome a dress rehearsal by the defense in order better to prepare its rebuttal when the time comes. Nor does anything but custom circumscribe the bench's interest at short calendar." He was itching with curiosity. "Counsel for the defense may at any rate complete the point on which it has launched," he said, scratching his hands.

He thought Nickie was another of my lawyers! So we had a man accused of masquerading as a psychiatrist being defended by someone impersonating a member of the bar. Sipperly made a spastic motion of panic but I pulled him back by the coattail.

"Thank you, Your Honor." Nickie went on practicing law without a license. "You will no doubt have noticed the even line of the script, which never thickens and then thins again to show that the pencil used was ever sharpened, or had to be. But it is in pencil, and my suspicion is that it's the new liquid lead. That's only just on the market and was not, I believe, generally available at the time the first of these entries were supposed to have been made."

"Could have been an Eversharp. Makes an even line too," said the judge, holding up his own.

"Perhaps," said Nickie, who was of course feeling around experimentally. "But continuing the point His Honor has instructed me to develop, may I refer the court's attention to a passage in the diary dated August 19. I quote: 'Today he hypmatized me for the first time. Oh, diary, I'm weak, like putty in his hands. He called me the apple of his eye.' "

"But you turned out to be a little tart," I evolved as a

266

rejoinder three days later. Now I muttered under my breath, "Apple of my eye my eye."

" 'He leaves me so shaken with his ardor,' " Nickie read on, " 'that he seems to draw my very soul out of me whenever he takes me in his — ' "

I laid my head back and howled like a dog, mentally. A man is made of chalkstone — don't take him for granite. No amount of incantatory scrawls could relieve the pressure building up inside me now. I was glad to hear Walnut himself interrupt at this juncture.

"The details are perhaps not germane to your point. Which is?"

"Simply that this diary is not bona fide, not in good faith. It wasn't kept from day to day at all but dashed off at the last minute when the plan to milk my poor friend there — "

Here both lawyers *and* Walnut broke in, the latter no doubt anticipating Bloodstein's objection to the broad irregularities on which matters were proceeding. "Counsel for the defense has no right to make lurid claims of this sort without corroborating evidence."

"Right. What proof do you have?" Walnut demanded of Nickie.

"That's not what I — " Bloodstein began.

"What I'm trying to say is that this particular entry is fraudulent even to the most superficial eye," Nickie said. "The writer goes on to state that she was so shaken by the accused's impetuosities that she had to have a drink when she left his office. 'So I stopped and had a glass of whisky at the Samothrace. Two, diary. Where will it all end?' Well, that's very interesting in view of the fact that the Samothrace did not install hard liquor until sometime early in September. On August 19 it was dispensing nothing stronger than ice-cream sodas."

As one, we turned to see what Sherry Budd had to say about that. She was looking into her lap, her hands gripping her bag.

"This diary is obviously not in good faith. It was hastily thrown together when the plaintiff, or possibly some master mind in whose power she really is, suddenly figured the case needed a little more pizazz," Nickie went on. "Perhaps Miss Budd will exp — "

"I object!" Bloodstein barked, looking more than ever like a schnauzer. Smiling gently, the judge was jotting something on the back of an unexpectedly long envelope drawn from the judicial bosom.

" — will explain the discrepancy. And also if the entire diary isn't made out of whole cloth, and while she is at it, if the accused sabotaged her love life, how it is that she was sitting at the Samothrace with her fiancé as late as last week, happily drinking the highballs now available there, as these snapshots I happen to have here will — "

The seat Miss Budd had occupied was empty. The swinging door at the rear flapped back and forth. Bloodstein rose and hurried through it in excited pursuit.

I got to my feet, clapped my hands and shouted, "Bravo!"

Some seconds went by without my being joined.

"Bravo," I continued. "Bravo."

Tipped slightly back in his chair, the sheriff looked sideways at me without expression, as though we were involved in some dreamy inexactitude of procedure about which nothing could be done but which would right itself momentarily. "Bravo. Bravissimo," I persisted. Years passed; faces changed, became those around my father and me in an auditorium two decades ago when he had leapt to his feet following the convulsive close of a sonata rendered by a visiting pianist. Finally a man in a black coat had got up several rows ahead of us, then someone else to the right, and so on, till my father had the whole resentful and by now rather hangdog audience standing in a "spontaneous ovation" which had, however, taken an eternity to generate.

"Look at my client," said Nickie when my unilateral applause had died down. "Could anyone think him capable of philandering?" I buttoned my jacket and looked non-chalantly away. "*Him?*"

"What made me suspect the thing," Walnut contributed, "speaking openly of a case we can be reasonably sure will not come to trial now, what indicated to me that the diary was hogwash was the brand of ministration laid to the accused's door. Would you just let me have a look at that again?"

"Certainly," said Nickie, handing up the diary.

Walnut looked for a passage. "Oh, yes, here it is. It has to do with an early memory of the writer involving some misconduct of her father in a greenhouse with a woman assistant. She states that the accused analyzed this as equivalent to her father's having gone to pieces in the tropics."

A round of laughter went up around the room, as Walnut himself smiled.

"That *must* have been made up out of whole cloth because not even the most amateurish quack could think up anything so idiotic."

I spread my arms in a shrug and smiled charitably, as if to say, "We-ell, the poor girl, after all . . ."

"Going to pieces in the tropics. Really!" Walnut put the diary down and his face became sober. He regarded Nickie with an odd, intent expression. It was that with which an ornithologist might contemplate a bird he had never seen before and hadn't expected to. "I haven't seen you in court before, to the best of my recollection, and I don't know what you expect the future to hold for you. You're young, and that future will be long. But I would be derelict not to warn you that life will not oblige you by imitating art to this extent, as a general rule."

"Thank you," said Nickie. "But all the same, let's not sell reality too short. Everything is, really, its own open book. I can relate Your Honor's entire life from just this brief but happy association with him."

I tried to catch his eye but he sailed ahead. And Walnut grumbled, "Go on."

"I would say that your background is Middle Western but your training has taken place in Eastern schools. The Seaboard diction superimposed on the tight vowels characteristic of northern Michigan and Wisconsin, such as 'meek' for 'make' — that's important."

The judge was swinging from side to side in his high-backed leather chair, and his face was expressionless. His eyes were normally colorless like mica, except when some inner or outer light drew out hazel values, as now. I knew damn well that Nickie had looked him up in *Who's Who*, dug him out of feature articles in the files of Bridgeport papers and what not, in preparation for this encounter. What judge will sit on a case can of course be found out in advance, and he may even have tailed Walnut for all I can say.

"Isn't cooking one of Your Honor's hobbies?"

"How do you know that?" the other inquired with some reluctance.

"That rash on your hands which you keep scratching — I believe it's 'baker's fungus.' It comes from kneading dough a great deal, I understand, which would argue that your specialty is pastries. And perhaps selected breads. . . ."

270

Here I began to tear hair which I could ill spare. I sat with my head down through most of the rest, and was glad to hear the gavel and the sheriff's voice booming, into some laughter provoked at a reference I didn't get because now I had my fingers in my ears, "Order! Order in the court!"

"The court will now adjourn for lunch," said Judge Walnut, at this point, and rose.

The rest of the morning passed without incident except for a brief episode outside the courthouse. Leaving Sipperly to fly off in a shaken state to other business, Crystal, Nickie and I went out chattering happily. As we descended the stairs to the street, I caught sight of Bloodstein on the bottom step, talking excitedly to someone on the sidewalk. A yellow hat was visible just above his left shoulder.

". . . realize I could be cited for malpractice, entering evidence like that? Do you know that? A forgery — "

He heard us behind him and turned. We all stood stockstill a moment. I was too elated about the outcome to feel any ill toward anybody, but I couldn't resist a stiff word to Sherry Budd.

"Do you know what I ought to do to you?" I said. "I ought to take you over my knee and give you a good spanking — you little brat!"

"Oh, shut your ignorant mouth," she answered, turning her head away.

It was here that the moment for which I had all along been toiling and struggling materialized. My wife came over to me. She not only stood at my side, but she took my arm in hers, and in a firm, clear voice for all to hear, said:

"He doesn't have to."

Twenty-One

I SAT in the deck chair and listened to the sheared water frothing away behind us. We were on a French liner bound for LeHavre, the four of us: Crystal and I, Nickie and Lila. It was the following summer. The children were all at the old house with my mother and a nurse hired for the six weeks of our holiday. Two days more at sea, and then a month in Europe before returning on the *Queen Mary*.

My eyes closed. My three traveling companions were swimming in the ship's pool and I was alone for an hour, and, alone, I dreamed. Everything was going beautifully. Aboard ship I was known as Beau Jest, at least to my own satisfaction, and my conversation had been tailored to that supposition. I reviewed my arrival in the bar the second day out, when I had joined a group of seasoned wanderers fingering stemware about a cocktail table — a parched company whom zephyrs of my wit revived.

The member of the circle for whom I had conceived a special inclination was a passenger named Beryl Hoyt. Middle-aged, handsome, she represented a class distinct in our culture: women who get about. Without being millionaires they have money, which they have but to marry to appear to have had it all their lives. They are between marriages or married, and are often encountered without their husbands, a factor that never in itself gives them an air of being between divorces. They have two children or none, and they can talk about the best schools as well as they can about the best watering places. They have nephews of marriageable age who rise up on the balls of their feet when they walk, and they can shop for men as unerringly as they do for themselves. Beryl Hoyt was known as Googoo to her friends, of whom one or two were on hand to indicate this. She had been telling about a young cousin studying at Boston University, and as the waiter brought my drink I heard her say, "He's writing his doctor's thesis."

"Why can't his doctor write his own thesis?" I said.

Here some slight movement about the table afforded the first sign that the group were stirring from their slump. Mrs. Hoyt continued her story, which next touched on the cousin's father, a broker who found that he had so completely devoted his life to giving his children everything that he had nothing for himself, not even, now at the age of sixty, enough cash on hand to swing that trip around the world he had always promised himself.

"What does he do but up and borrow enough on the first thing he lays his hands on," she related. "Some debentures or something."

"Debentures?" I said. "He must have wanted to go pretty bad to hock his teeth for it."

The grim faces which greeted this reply told me how badly the comedy relief was needed here, and I redoubled my efforts.

"No more than boarded ship yesterday," I related, crossing my legs, "when a total stranger came up to me. Well, he was al*most* total. He had three fingers missing on one hand and a cropped left ear. Anyway, I was sitting at the bar — that stool right 'there, as a matter of fact — and after a few drinks he began spilling his troubles. He was worried because his daughter had just left her husband of a month. I cheered him up by promising him they'd be back together again before he knew it. Because before marriage a girl makes up and kisses, but after marriage, you know, it's generally the other way around."

By now my hearers were so far delivered from the palsy in which I had found them as to be able to rise and make off for other parts of the ship, some quite briskly. I waved farewell as they took their leave, with every assurance that we would meet again.

Left behind with only the cherishable Googoo Hoyt, at last, I was pleased with how things were going. I had hacked out a conversational compromise which utilized, quite successfully in the main, the very materials of my workaday and of necessity less rarified side — as my last remark had exemplified. Yes, it could be done. For as the delicate crouton is made from stale bread, the humble potato transmuted into Vichyssoise, so even the lowliest Pepigram could be elevated into dialogue of considerably greater merit than might at first have been supposed possible.

At last even the gregarious Googoo excused herself with the reminder of imminent dinner, and departed for her stateroom, leaving me to muse pleasantly on how matters were turning out — as I was doing now, again, on the deck chair.

My wife has blossomed into quite a woman of the world herself. Her belief in my pat moralities has all but vanished, thanks to the private example I set, and a markedly more cosmopolitan outlook has supplanted it. I am to that extent a much less severely divided man. She gets off more and more bright asperities of her own, too. Her remark that you need two years of medical school to be a

274

patient these days had vastly amused the tweeded youths seen tramping about deck with her. My own comparison of an affair to a cup of Turkish coffee — "The trick is to stop before you reach the grounds" — had met with studious frowns, due no doubt to the unexpected weight of truth in the statement. Another gauge of her progress into a more companionable modernity lies in her use, now, of the word "wonderful," for something quaint appreciated on another level. This means we have come full-circle from the days of our first acquaintance when I had thought her father wonderful but had not dared to say so, or at least to explain how I meant it. Not that Crystal Chickering would have understood, back then in that far-off time.

Nickie bloomed under his success in Bridgeport, when he showed what a fine lawyer he would have made. News of it had been telephoned home, and he perfectly recognized, on his return to the apartment, the flattering, fluttering wife who was waiting for him there. He remembers everything again, or almost everything. Lila's share in the conversation that night at the country-club dance still seems rather a blur in his mind. He took his old job back again with every implied hope of going on from there. He got the "scholarship" to the Police Academy run by the F.B.I. in Washington, and had the six weeks' special training course they give promising police there. He elected detective work, of the several categories offered. It's hard to say how he'll end up, though we know he wants to practice privately. I suppose a free-lance status is the one in which he could best pursue that dream of princely skill in which, for him, the ideal resides. That is the yeast that worked in all three of us; him, Cheshire, myself; the link we had in common. You could call it the romantic ideal, the idea that life can have style. Nickie will lack no challenge for his wits, even in Decency, for Cheshire will certainly try to add new laurels to the nickname he's earned for himself, when he gets out of jail two years from now. I can't wait for that day. For each of them is useless without the other, like halves of a pair of cymbals. I hope Nickie goes on to more definitive glory than he won in my cause. As for me, that his friend will find the Golden Fleece is all that can be hoped by a man who must, himself, milk what éclat he can from being Lamplighter.

Once in a while, when some chance sight or random notion rends me with a memory of Great Expectations, I have a wild dream of being sacked for paradox and starting fresh. But where would I come out anyway, other than where I already am? There is a bird we've all heard singing but none has ever seen; not even the completest apparent success fulfills the visions entertained for it. We return from journeys on which we have set out hunting unicorns, glad to have bagged a boar. I fold my hands and rest, content to let the dream dwindle away like my poor hair, now a countable residue which I valiantly organize into a herringbone down the middle of my head. So, enjoying ourselves as best we can — which is often enough quite considerably, if we would be honest about it — we spend what time we have of Time, that river down whose chuckling waters we are carried to the sea.

The Greek awaits deliverance yet. But his hour will come, I know. A figurine factory is going up two blocks from the Samothrace, and I tell him to hold on till that begins to send its hundreds into the streets at lunchtime, and by his door twice else during the day. Of course the factory will spoil the neighborhood, but that is a consideration into which I cannot again be drawn. Mrs. Thicknesse I never see. I had cast about for some note on which to close the books on that account, and at last found one. Speaking of another woman altogether, I had assured Crystal that she was "all wool and a yard wide." To which Crystal made unhesitating reply, "I don't know about the all wool part of it, but she's certainly a yard wide." It was no trouble to graft this onto a continuity involving Mrs. Thicknesse as the butt, the curtain came down, and I could rest my mental bones.

I have no idea even of Lammermoor's whereabouts. Neither does Pete Cheshire, who writes me occasionally from prison and whom I answer not only with letters but with gifts of money, cigars and, of course, advice. His letters indicate a growing willingness to open a diner when he is released, but a diner of the better sort, to be known as a flyer. Of course it will only be a front for other things. I don't know what's become of Sherry Budd either. Maybe she and Lammermoor have settled down together in some other city. I think of them all now with affection: Bloodstein and Sipperly, too, the mildewed magistrate — all of them.

Their faces mingled drowsily in my thoughts as I lay back, eyes closed, in the deck chair. I was utterly at peace. The voyage was a balm as well as an intoxicant. The faint unending swish of water seemed the peacefullest I had ever heard. That the sun in whose warmth I basked was a ball of deliriously exploding gases was mildly interesting. As I sat there, I became aware of someone settling into the chair next mine. I knew who it was without opening my eyes. A thin, memorable musk had marked my hour with Googoo Hoyt at cocktails, and it was that perfume which unmistakably reached my nostrils now. I could hear her idly turning the pages of a magazine, and then that stopped. I smiled and prepared a few oral savories. She was going for a long stay in England, under whose disreputable skies we went for long walks in the bracken, and our lips soon met . . .

I opened my eyes to find Mrs. Hoyt leaning forward in her chair in order to scrutinize my bosom. I was wearing a stiff white collar of the detachable kind coming back into vogue again, at least according to advices in a magazine advertisement I had read. The specimen around my neck had rounded points, and I had put it on with a shirt of thick blue stripes, another period revival stressed in my source as the mark of a well-dressed man. In the advertisement, both of these had been modeled in a picture of a young executive having his shoes shined while standing at his desk with a letter in his hand. That I had seen neither on another living soul meant that I was well in the van of fashion, unless the refreshed observer thought me to be that much in arrears of it.

Mrs. Hoyt sat back.

"Hello," she said, smiling.

"Oh, hello there," I answered. "It's you. Isn't this a beautiful day?"

"Magnificent. I have a special reason to be grateful, because do you know what I was just reminded of? It's my birthday."

"No!"

"Clean forgot it."

"Well, happy birthday! We must have a little celebration."

"Oh, no, please. Thank you though. But do you know how I found out? A present from my husband a while ago. He'd got it aboard before I sailed, with instructions to the

steward to deliver it today. This ring — do you like it?"
She extended a hand on which a fire opal burned.

"It's beautiful," I said, taking her fingers to inspect it.
"It's just exquisite. I love fire opals. I gave my wife one
once."

"Did you really? How nice. I'm glad." She folded her
hands on her lap and closed her own eyes, sighing pleasur-
ably. After a moment she said, "My husband always gives
me something to wear but not anything I *need*. That's
important. Never give your wife anything she needs."

"Oh, indeed not. I never do that."

"Last year he gave me a belt."

"I hope you hit him back on his."

She threw her head back and laughed. "A gold leaf
business that I'd admired in a shop window on Fifth Avenue. I love it so much I buy gowns to go with it."

We were hitting it off like this when a third presence
materialized. Nickie sauntered into view from round a
nearby funnel. He was dressed in tweeds up to and including his head, and swinging the blackthorn.

"Ah, greetings, greetings," he said, stopping by.

I began the long process of climbing to my feet.

"Through swimming?" I asked.

"Yes. Lila thought she'd take a nap before dinner and
Chris is in your stateroom too. She said to tell you she'd be
there, in case I ran into you. I think she wants to have
drinks with Chiffon Smith and those two boys from
Waltham. Don't get up."

"No, I must be getting along." Pique at the intrusion
was at least balanced by the wish to take care of something
that could only be attended to in my stateroom. "Please
take my chair," I said.

"Thank you," Nickie said, easing himself into it.

I said good-by and strolled away. The collar and shirt were now within five minutes of being removed and shoved through a porthole into the sea; but before that I had something else I wanted to do.

I ambled in a leisurely fashion till I was sure I was out of sight. Then I broke into a trot and ran clear around the ship till I had fetched up again behind the funnel near which the two sat. I flattened my back against the funnel and edged my head over their way as far as I dared, after twisting my tweed cap to one side so the peak wouldn't show. In this position I strained to catch what they were saying to one another.

Mrs. Hoyt was talking. At first her words were an indistinguishable murmur. Then there was a pause, after which I heard her say more clearly:

"Your friend. Have you known him long?"

"All my life, practically. Yes, we're old friends," Nickie answered. Another pause, and then he asked: "What do you think of him?"

"I like him fine," said Googoo Hoyt. "He's wonderful."

I tried not to let it spoil my trip.